WIDOWS WAIVE THE RULES

JULIA JARMAN

B
Boldwood

First published in Great Britain in 2025 by Boldwood Books Ltd.

Copyright © Julia Jarman, 2025

Cover Design by Alice Moore Design

Cover Images: Shutterstock and iStock

The moral right of Julia Jarman to be identified as the author of this work has been asserted in accordance with the Copyright, Designs and Patents Act 1988.

All rights reserved. No part of this book may be reproduced in any form or by any electronic or mechanical means, including information storage and retrieval systems, without written permission from the author, except for the use of brief quotations in a book review. This book is a work of fiction and, except in the case of historical fact, any resemblance to actual persons, living or dead, is purely coincidental.

Every effort has been made to obtain the necessary permissions with reference to copyright material, both illustrative and quoted. We apologise for any omissions in this respect and will be pleased to make the appropriate acknowledgements in any future edition.

A CIP catalogue record for this book is available from the British Library.

Paperback ISBN 978-1-78513-049-6

Large Print ISBN 978-1-78513-050-2

Hardback ISBN 978-1-78513-048-9

Ebook ISBN 978-1-78513-051-9

Kindle ISBN 978-1-78513-052-6

Audio CD ISBN 978-1-78513-043-4

MP3 CD ISBN 978-1-78513-044-1

Digital audio download ISBN 978-1-78513-046-5

This book is printed on certified sustainable paper. Boldwood Books is dedicated to putting sustainability at the heart of our business. For more information please visit https://www.boldwoodbooks.com/about-us/sustainability/

Boldwood Books Ltd, 23 Bowerdean Street, London, SW6 3TN

www.boldwoodbooks.com

1

ZELDA

August 2015

A luxury cruise – is that the answer?

Zelda was on Libby's patio, feet up on a sunbed, looking at her phone as she waited for her friend to bring out a bottle of fizz. She'd been invited round to celebrate something or other, Wednesday perhaps, or Thursday, or the cat's birthday. That was the great thing about Libby, she could always find something to celebrate. Her zest for life was why The Muscateers, aka The Widows' Wine Club, had welcomed her to their merry throng.

Flipping adverts. Zelda deleted another screenful. How had she got onto so many mailing lists? Delete. Delete. Delete. All these should have gone into spam, but perhaps not this one? She read it again.

> Enjoy a luxury cruise on *Queen Mary 2* at unbelievable prices. Seven nights aboard Cunard's number one ocean liner, a night in New York and return flight, for only...

'Make way! Move your bag!' Libby landed the tray on the table between the sunbeds without spilling a drop, though she'd already filled the glasses. 'I left the bottle in the fridge as it's still warm out here.' She sat down and raised her glass of afrothi, Greek fizz, supplied no doubt by Nikos, the new man in her life.

'Yamas, Zelda!' Libby looked great, her blonde hair recently re-styled at Zelda's salon. The girls had done a good job. The short bob suited her, but then anything did.

'Cheers!' Zelda raised her glass.

What luck that Libby was a neighbour as well as a friend, living only three doors up, so impromptu meetings like this were frequent. Not so often in the garden though, but now the weather was perfect for al fresco. Summer had arrived at last. It was a balmy evening with a couple of swallows wheeling around the cloudless blue sky. Bees were buzzing in the colourful borders and red admirals fluttered round the buddleia. Cornflake, Libby's cat, milky white with ginger splodges, was stretched out on the warm tiles.

'Wish my garden was as nice as yours.' Zelda breathed in the scent of lavender, growing in a pot beside her.

'It would be if you weeded and watered the pots.'

'Now you're sounding like Viv.' Zelda changed the subject. 'Listen to this.' She read out the advert for the *Queen Mary 2* cruise. 'Isn't that exactly what we'll need in December when the days are cold and grey, the nights long and dark? The Muscateers, I mean, the four of us, especially Janet.'

They had been looking for a way of raising Janet's spirits ever since Alan, the love of her life, had died back in February, shocking them all and devastating Janet. She'd been low ever since. No one understood better than The Widows' Wine Club how harrowing losing your mate was. They'd all been through it, more than once in her case and Janet's, and it got worse each time. Grief doesn't make you immune to grief. It piles it on, so you start to think life isn't worth living. Alan's death was so unexpected. He'd been a fit man, happy and healthy they thought, till he'd had a massive heart attack while walking his dog. It was so unfair. Janet had been married for forty years to stingy, two-timing, demeaning first husband Malcolm. Then only four to the new man in her life, the loving super-practical Alan, who'd helped her in every way he could, appreciating her quirky, sometimes spiky personality, adding to her joie de vivre, boosting her morale. You don't bounce back after a blow like that. Janet was hurting...

'...but her life isn't over even if she thinks it is or more accurately *feels*.' Libby voiced Zelda's thoughts. 'She's stopped enjoying the simple things, this for instance.' She waved her arm, encompassing the garden, the sunny weather, the delicious fizz and their friendship. 'But is a cruise the answer? It's hard to get her out of the house these days. I asked her round tonight by the way.'

'A change is as good as a rest?' Zelda googled to find out more.

The advertised holiday was for one specific week – there was no choice – the week before Christmas, departing Southampton on 16 December, arriving in New York seven days later, early in the morning of 23 December. That night would be spent in a four- or five-star hotel, giving them time to enjoy nearly two days of sightseeing in New York, including all the Christmas decorations, before getting a cab to John F. Kennedy airport on Christmas Eve evening and flying back to Heathrow, arriving on Christmas morning.

'All for less than the cost of a return flight from Heathrow to New York.' Zelda could still hardly believe it. 'What's not to like?'

'The timing? Who wants to be away from home the week before Christmas?' Libby was unusually downbeat. 'It sounds too good to be true, and you know what they say. Could it be a scam?'

Zelda did more googling and found a plausible explanation for the next-to-nothing price. It was a once-in-a-year 'repositioning voyage', a travel guru said. *Queen Mary 2* was at this moment cruising in the Mediterranean and Near East with passengers paying the full whack. But in December it – or she? – would return to Southampton to refurbish before sailing across the Atlantic to pick up more full-price passengers in New York. The full-price passengers boarded there for Caribbean cruises over Christmas and the New Year.

'So they need passengers to fill the gap, any passengers, including ones like us who haven't got a lot of cash but fancy a bit of luxury. The journey is just to offset costs, so they're not sailing across the Atlantic completely empty, with all the expense and no income. And they'll be hoping we get a taste for cruising so we book more holidays at full price.' Zelda was becoming more enthusiastic by the minute, as she'd thought of another important very personal plus. The dates were perfect for her. She was planning to spend Christmas with her dad and the newly discovered Afro-American side of her family in North Carolina. What a way to get there! The *QM2* was a floating five-star hotel, but she would save money even if she flew on to North Carolina from New York, and then back to the UK in January at her own expense. It was a bargain, a no-brainer. 'And,' she thought of another reason why the holiday was cheap, 'they need us as ballast.'

'Now you *have* lost me.' Libby shook her head.

'Ballast, the heavy stuff they put in the hold to keep the ship steady. They need us to stop the boat keeling over, so eating too much and putting on weight will be compulsory. Take a look at these menus.'

Zelda was only half tongue-in-cheek. She'd remembered that Janet was losing weight because she wasn't eating or sleeping much according to Viv, who lived near her in the same village. The delicious food on board could whet her appetite. Libby agreed that might be true, but said she'd checked her diary when she was inside and the dates didn't work for her. 'I'll be in Athens with Nikos.'

'Poor you, ha ha. It will have to be Viv and me then, but that could work.'

Libby looked doubtful.

'What is it now?' But Zelda guessed even before Libby spoke. 'Viv?'

Libby nodded. 'Can't see her on a cruise somehow, the captain's table and all that. Dressing for dinner. Are denims allowed on the *QM2*?' Libby was scrolling. 'Everyone looks very glamorous to me, especially in the evenings. I see ball gowns and tuxedos and quite a lot of sequins but no fleeces and denims.'

This was a snag.

Zelda loved dressing up, but Viv didn't. She liked her jeans. But if Viv wouldn't go, she couldn't go. She needed Viv to share costs. The bargain offer was based on two people sharing a cabin, one of the cheaper inside cabins. Janet, she knew, wouldn't share a room with anyone, but could afford a double room for herself. That's what she always did when they stayed in hotels. Zelda looked up the *QM2* dress code, but Libby had got there first. '*Queen Mary* allows non-ripped denims in most areas.'

Phew! But would that be enough to get Viv aboard?

2

ZELDA

In fact, persuading Viv wasn't as difficult as they feared. A phone call from Zelda was all it took. It was just what Janet needed, she agreed.

'If I have to endure a week of cordon bleu cookery and fine wines so she will come too, well, I'm prepared to take one for the team.'

The timing worked for her, she said. The week before Christmas was ideal. She could take a break from her gardening job – not much doing in December – and leave Patrick to get everything ready for Christmas Day. His son and partner were coming to stay so they could help. Arriving home on Christmas Day when all the work was done would be perfect. She had already extracted a promise from Janet that she would come for Christmas Day lunch. Janet's only son lived in New Zealand, so otherwise she'd be on her own and there was no way Viv would let that happen. Now they could be sure of a superb lunch without either of them lifting a finger.

Libby's offer to lend Viv evening clothes cleared away any last doubts. Viv didn't mind investing in a new pair of jeans, she said, and maybe a shirt or two – smart casual she did – but she hadn't got the cash or the inclination to buy a lot of fancy clothes she'd never wear again. Luckily she and Libby were roughly the same size. When Libby took a few dresses round to Viv's for a try-on, she also pointed out that the décor on *QM2* was art deco, inspired by the first *Queen Mary* built in the thirties. 'So, you'll feel at home, Viv.'

'It's okay, Libby, you've sold it to me.' Viv lived in an art deco house that she and her first husband had lovingly restored, and she adored that period, even the glitzy bits. She was looking forward to stepping back in time and enjoying the splendour of *QM2*.

Persuading Janet was the hard bit.

She was slumped on the sofa in front of daytime TV on Wednesday afternoon when the three of them called, not like Janet at all. They had invited themselves because she'd declined Viv's invitation to come round to hers for a coffee, though she only lived round the corner. She rarely went out these days. If it weren't for having to walk Kenny Dog Leash, Alan's bereaved spaniel, twice a day, she wouldn't go out at all. Kenny was the first reason she gave for turning them down. She couldn't leave the dog and she didn't want to. Her feelings were the second. She didn't feel like going on holiday, least of all a cruise. She'd been on several and knew the form. You met new people and she didn't feel like meeting new people. You had to be sociable and she didn't feel like being sociable. You had to dress up and she couldn't be bothered.

Zelda wished she'd brought her hair-dressing scissors with her. Janet's usually short white hair needed a trim, another sign she was letting herself go. The old Janet was stylish, very Judi Dench, but she'd stopped coming into Sophisticutts, Zelda's salon, to have her hair done once a month, and the baggy beige trousers she was wearing didn't go with the faded cotton top.

Libby, keen to persuade Janet, though she wasn't going herself, tried appealing to Janet's do-good side. Eleanor, her daughter, would love to have Kenny to stay she said, because she wanted to try out having a dog in the house. Ellie-Jo, Libby's granddaughter, who adored dogs, was nagging her mum to get one, but Eleanor wasn't sure. The week before Christmas would be perfect as Eleanor, a head teacher, would be at home and so would Ellie-Jo. Kenny would be very well looked after, in fact spoiled rotten.

Janet said she didn't want Kenny spoilt rotten.

Zelda kept her mouth shut and didn't point out that the large black-

and-white cocker spaniel, lolling on the sofa beside Janet, had put on weight and was obviously having more Waggie Treats than were good for him. She was wondering what she could say to change Janet's mind, and cut through all the negativity, when Viv, quicker off the mark, tried another tack.

'It's on Zelda's wish-list, you know.'

'What is?' Janet snapped.

'Crossing the Atlantic on the *Queen Mary*.'

This was news to Zelda. She wanted to go on this trip but it wasn't something she'd been longing to do, well, not before Wednesday. It wasn't on her wish-list. She hadn't got a wish-list. But if Viv needed her to have one to twist Janet's arm that was fine by her.

'I thought we helped each other realise our dreams,' Viv went on. 'All for one and one for all. Isn't that what we're about?'

Zelda saw Janet register this with a frown. Viv had pressed a button. Putting others first was Janet's default position and she'd taken longer than the others to accept the idea that being good to yourself was also important. Strictly brought up, she was more duty-driven than any of them. The Muscateers had brought the pleasure principle into her life. If you haven't got a partner to be kind to you, you have to be kind to yourself, Viv had explained early on. You had to be at least as nice to yourself as you were to others. It had taken all of them an effort not to feel guilty when they'd started enjoying life after their partners died, but they'd worked at it, Janet harder than any of them. Recently though, she'd reverted to being the self-denying, rule-driven, rather disapproving person she'd been when they first met her.

Viv started collecting the empty cups. 'We'll be off then.'

Libby picked up the cafetière, as if she'd given up on trying to persuade Janet.

'Hold on. Let me think.' Janet stroked Kenny's head. 'I would have to be completely sure that Kenny was happy with Eleanor and Ellie-Jo.'

Zelda held her breath, as Libby said she could arrange a visit so Janet could meet Eleanor and Ellie-Jo and check out Kenny's possible living quarters.

'And I won't share a cabin, if I go that is, you know that, because I need to get up in the night.'

'Fine,' said Viv, coming back from the kitchen and sitting down. 'Zelda and I will share.' They'd discussed this already. 'You can have a cabin to yourself.' Luckily, Malcolm, Janet's first husband, had left her a fortune, so she could afford it.

'And we all go Grill Class,' Janet added, 'at my expense, because I'm the one insisting. I need to be on an upper deck so I have a room with a porthole at least, maybe a balcony. I get claustrophobic if I'm too far below. They're called staterooms, by the way, not cabins.'

'Grill Class, what's that?'

Zelda was glad Viv asked. She didn't understand either. But as Janet explained that Grill Class was modern parlance for First Class, she wished she hadn't. Viv's face fell as Janet said that Grill Class passengers had bigger rooms, a whole suite of rooms in fact, including a kitchen and lounge, and they could eat in the more exclusive restaurants like Queen's Grill and the Princess Grill, as well as all the other restaurants on board.

'Sorry.' Viv got to her feet. 'But you've just put me right off. I realise now why I've never done this before. First Class. Second Class. Them and us. I like 1930s design, well, some of it, but I don't like its class structure.'

'Oh, Viv, it's not like that, not in practice.' Janet moved Kenny's head from her knee.

'How do you know if you've never been?'

'Because I've been on other cruises.'

Zelda googled frantically. She liked a bit of glamour but she didn't like snobbery either. What did other people say about it? She got onto Tripadvisor as Janet carried on trying to convince Viv that it wasn't really elitist. 'You won't know who's who, Viv. Some people pay for bigger rooms, that's all, like they do in hotels – or on trains.'

Janet was well-heeled and often forgot how the lack of cash restricted other people's choices. She was sounding much more like the old Janet though, the old *new* Janet that is, the one who'd begun to enjoy the good things in life when she'd discovered how much her stingy first husband had been stashing away.

Zelda started to feel hopeful. Janet was looking almost enthusiastic.

But Viv was looking as if she'd like to sink the ship. 'Getting dressed up is one thing...' She was putting on her Barbour.

'It's not as bad as you think, Viv.' Zelda found something useful on a feedback website. 'Anyone can pay to eat in the Queen's and Princess Grills, if they want to pay through the nose, but you don't need to. There are lots of other restaurants to choose from, where the excellent food is part of the deal.'

Viv still didn't look convinced.

There was only one way forward, Viv must be hoist with her own fibbing petard. Zelda made her lip tremble. *'I'll* be upset if we don't go, Viv. As you said to Janet, it's been on my wish-list for some time, and this is the only way I'll ever be able to afford it.'

Viv had the grace to laugh. 'You win, Zelda.'

'No.' Janet was on her feet. 'We all win. I'm coming too. I need to get a grip.' Moving faster than Zelda had seen her for months, she headed for her kitchen. and came back with a bottle of prosecco and three glasses. Glasses filled, she raised hers. 'All for one and one for all! Widows rule the waves!'

3

JANET

What have I done?

Janet had second thoughts as soon as her friends had gone. She had been uplifted by their company, as she had the first time they'd met. She'd been buoyed up by their enthusiasm, but now she was sinking. Fortunately this trip was months away – she counted on her fingers, four – because she needed more time to recover some of her joie de vivre, to make her presence tolerable to other people. She was not good to be with at the moment. She still cried a lot when she least expected to. Not just on birthdays or anniversaries, but at odd inconsequential times. When she glanced out of the window and was about to say that it was a lovely sunny day for instance, and there was no one to say it to. Except Kenny, but the dog, deaf now, wasn't responsive to remarks about the weather unless she had a lead in her hand. Still lying beside her on the sofa, snoring, she did wonder how much Kenny missed Alan, or if he missed him at all. Was he longing for walks with his master when he whimpered in his sleep, as she did sometimes, reaching for the man beside her and waking to find he wasn't there? Kenny seemed content as long as she remembered to feed him and take him out. If Libby's daughter and granddaughter attended to his basic needs, she was sure he would be fine without her. But would she be fine without him? His heavy warmth beside her was a comfort, she had to admit, which was why – she could hardly believe this – he now slept at the end of her bed.

'I might be a wet blanket, Kenny. No one likes a wet blanket.'

Kenny certainly didn't. He liked his warm and dry. If she shed a few tears it wouldn't throw Viv or Zelda, she knew that, but it was several years since their husbands had died and they had both moved on in their different ways. The Muscateers believed in moving on. Zelda, resolutely single, was pursuing all sorts of interests. Viv, still working as a garden designer, had found a new partner. The Muscateers believed in enjoying the years you had left.

But I'm not sure if I can.

Oh dear. Sorry-for-herself she must not do. It was the slippery slope. 'Sorry, Kenny.' She lifted his head from her knee. 'I've got to move. I'm going to get my laptop.'

Half an hour later, back on the sofa with Kenny, she was feeling brighter. How lucky she was to be able to do this. She was taking a virtual tour of *QM2* which was even more impressive than she'd imagined. She had been on other cruises and enjoyed them. The ships had all had excellent facilities, smart décor and delicious food, but this was something else. Sumptuous was the word she kept coming back to, opulent, palatial even. She was reminded of a trip to Buckingham Palace as she virtually stepped into the ship's Grand Lobby with its curving staircases, rich red carpets and classical columns. Those wide staircases were made for stunning entrances in regal robes, the balconies for royal waves or romantic liaisons.

QM2 was a floating palace.

'What's not to like, Kenny? Oh, this!'

She'd zoomed into the acclaimed Britannia restaurant, and something she definitely did not like caught her eye. Luxurious it certainly was, the décor to die for if you were Viv with her love of art deco, but the round tables covered with white tablecloths were all laid for four, six or eight persons. She looked closely. There were some square tables laid for two, but none for three. Life aboard *QM2* was geared to couples it seemed, and sociable couples at that, just like it was seven years ago when she'd first become a widow. Singles should stay at home and cry. Tables for two had to be booked in advance, she read. Tables for one or three didn't get a mention, but she had to have a table for three, for Viv, Zelda and herself. She wouldn't go if this couldn't be arranged. She didn't want to have to make small talk with strangers for the hour or more it took to consume a five-course meal each night. She knew how it worked. You breakfasted and lunched wherever you liked each day, and so met a variety of people, or none if you didn't want to. But you ate dinner at the same table each night, with the same people, those you'd sat down with on the first night.

She got on the phone to Zelda, who said she was sure she could sort it. She'd talk to the captain himself if she had to, the admiral of the fleet if necessary. She said she was glad Janet had rung because there was something else she wanted to say.

'Viv and I are sharing as you know, and we've agreed to an upgrade as you suggest, and we'll let you pay the difference, so we can be nearer to you, but we don't want a suite to ourselves. We don't need a kitchen, and don't want one. We'll be happy to slum it in a Britannia Balcony stateroom on Deck 12 so we have a bit more room and a sea view. You can have a suite as big and swanky as you like.' Zelda said she'd found one on Deck 11 that looked perfect. The Queen's Grill suite on the portside was 2,249 square foot in area not counting the balcony, with kitchen, spacious living area, double bedroom with king-size bed, dressing room and bathroom with separate shower and whirlpool bath. 'And, oh yes, optional use of a personal butler serving pre-dinner canapés.'

'No need to go that far, Zelda. You're sounding like a travel agent.'

'That's because I'm reading from the *QM2* website, and I'm trying to sell it to you.'

'Sold,' Janet found herself saying, 'as long as you make sure we have a table for just the three of us every evening. You may have to speak to the purser.'

'Will do, and if I succeed, can I go ahead and make the booking?'

'Y-yes.'

'Sure? Because I'll be putting down my own money as a deposit – it will go on my credit card – and then there'll be no going back.'

Janet took a deep breath. 'I'm sure.'

4

VIV

Wednesday, 16 December

It was a grey and drizzly day, already quite dark, though only three o'clock in the afternoon, when they arrived at the massive Southampton terminal. Patrick had just dropped the three of them off, after leaving their luggage at a collecting point earlier, as instructed by the company, and Viv was feeling apprehensive. She'd have liked a reassuring hug from Patrick, and some encouraging words, but there hadn't been time for that and non-passengers weren't allowed any further. It had felt oddly upsetting leaving him and their luggage behind, as if she might never see him or their cases again. What if she hadn't labelled hers properly with the right cabin number? Stateroom number – she corrected herself – not cabin. And they were about to aboard a ship, not a boat. Ships had boats, but boats didn't have ships, someone, probably Janet, had said. Lifeboats, Viv couldn't help thinking, trying not to picture the *Titanic*. *Queen Mary 2* was, to be precise, an ocean liner, uniquely so, the company claimed, so they were not going on a cruise, they were crossing the Atlantic like people did before air travel.

Viv thought of refugees clutching their bundles and told herself she was supposed to be enjoying herself.

There was a very long queue for the check-in desk. It was good to be inside out of the rain, but the processing was slow, though they had priority boarding and had done all the bits they could the day before online to speed things up. Zelda had checked them all in the previous day, and printed their boarding passes for them. Perhaps the people in front hadn't got a Zelda to organise them. The trip had been her idea so she felt responsible, and looked anxious, her shoulders hunched, but Zelda wasn't responsible for everyone's happiness.

Viv tapped her on the shoulder of her glamorous faux Astrakhan coat. 'All for one, remember. We all agreed to do this.'

Zelda hadn't just made the booking, Viv remembered gratefully, she'd done most of the boring paperwork and reminded them both to do the bits she couldn't do for them, like getting their ESTA cards and surrendering their credit card details for spending aboard ship. Giving her credit card details had made Viv uneasy. Handing over her details to people unknown always made her uneasy, and she was worried how much extra she'd need to spend. Not a lot, she hoped. But the other passengers looked very well-heeled and well-hatted and -coated. There was a lot of fur, she hoped faux, and expensive bags.

Patrick's hurried words were in her ear. 'Enjoy yourself, darling. Have fun. Don't worry about a thing. Guy and I have Christmas covered, including getting your mum down from Newcastle. I've put a bottle of fizz in your bag.'

Passengers could bring one bottle aboard. But only one. Crikey! Were bags being searched for bootleg liquor? Was that what was causing the delay? Viv had done her research. Fortunately, all their food was included in the deal, more than they needed probably, but they had to buy wine, and not at Aldi prices. Fine wines, spirits and cocktails were the order of the day. She might have to cut down a bit she feared, and wondered exactly how enjoyable this trip was going to be. Zelda still looked anxious. Janet, staring ahead, looked sad.

'It's okay.' Janet had caught sight of Viv looking at her. 'Sorry. I'll admit to a negative thought but that's the last for a week. Promise. Listen to that band.'

A brass band was playing Christmas carols. They could just see the top of their peaked hats at the end of the room where 'O Come, All Ye Faithful!' rang out. The queue started to move faster as the band struck up 'God Rest Ye Merry Gentlemen'.

'God rest merry gentlewomen too.' Zelda turned to chivvy them, smiling, Viv was relieved to see. 'Passports and boarding passes ready? We're nearly at check-in now.'

They held them up, dutifully. 'Exciting, isn't it?' Zelda looked more cheerful now, as if she really was about to realise one of her dreams. 'Can't wait to get aboard.' Janet looked happier too and Viv felt herself smiling.

'Look at that!' Zelda pointed to a window, and they got their first sight of *Queen Mary 2* in all her majesty, all eighteen decks of her, a floating palace. 'There's our luxury home for the next seven days, ladies. Can we handle it?'

They hugged in solidarity.

'We will handle it. All for one and one for all!'

5
ZELDA

'Wow!' Viv opened the door of their cabin. 'And there are our cases! Phew!'

Zelda shared Viv's delight and relief as they were reunited with their luggage. So far, so brill. Ocean View, their room was called and although they couldn't yet see the ocean, as they were still docked, they would when the ship set sail. Not long now! Zelda felt herself unwinding, helped by the glass or two of champagne already consumed. Things were going very much as she'd hoped and planned. She so wanted everything to be right for Janet, who they'd just left in her luxurious suite on Deck 11. She was thrilled with everything too and had insisted on opening the complimentary bottle of champagne right away. There was a bottle in their fridge too – Zelda checked – but, she closed the door firmly, they'd have that one later.

'This is great!' Viv pulled off her boots and collapsed on a bed. 'Okay if I have this one?'

It was the bed nearest the window.

'Fine by me.' Zelda collapsed too, on the one beside her, pleased to see that there were twin beds, just as she'd ordered. She'd spent the best part of an hour, back in August, specifying that this was what they wanted, along with the table for three in the dining room. She loved Viv dearly but didn't want to sleep with her.

'Dare we close our eyes?' Viv's were already closed. 'I feel an old-lady nap coming on.'

'Don't think we dare.' Zelda longed to close her eyes too, but reached for the Daily Programme on the bedside table. The steward who'd handed it to her had mentioned a mandatory emergency drill before embarkation. 'No, we definitely dare not,' she said, after checking the time on her phone. 'It's four o'clock already and we are supposed to be in the Kings Court Buffet on Deck 7 learning what to do if the ship hits an iceberg. Viv, move!' Zelda shook her arm. 'There's an emergency drill before the Sail Away party on Deck 12! We've got to go! Now!'

Janet was there already, of course, wearing a bright red and blue lifejacket. It took more than a couple of glasses of fizz to stop her from doing her duty.

'Where are yours? You should have brought them with you. They're in the wardrobe of your stateroom. No matter. I anticipated that you would forget.'

Two spare lifejackets were on a chair beside her, and she told them how to put them on.

They apologised for being late but she said it didn't matter too much as she'd been in time for the demonstration. 'I know what to do and will tell you later. It was all women and children first, of course, if we have to get in the lifeboats, but I told them to make sure young women got on first.'

'Thank you, Janet. Thoughtful.' Viv was sarky. 'I hope there is enough room for all of us.' Viv was still in the fleece and denims she'd travelled in – but Janet had already changed for dinner. She seemed revitalised. Being away from home was doing her a power of good. She was wearing a stylish tunic and velvet pants, her favoured Judi Dench style. 'Now what time is it? Time to go upstairs to Deck 12 for "Sail Away with Vibz".' She had the Daily Programme in her hand, but quickly tucked it into her bag and put on a black velvet cape, which had been draped over a chair. 'It will be a bit breezy up there, don't you think. Now, take those lifejackets off and put them on that pile, then we can go and wave goodbye to good old England, before we set sail for the Big Apple.'

'Lift or stairs?' Viv asked.

'Lift this once,' said Janet briskly. 'Because we're late, and because it looks amazing. We'll get fit tomorrow.'

The Perspex lift gave them dramatic views of the ship as it slowly ascended from Deck 7 up to 12, including a close-up of the star on top of the gigantic Christmas tree, standing in the lobby far below. A band was playing as they stepped out of the lift onto the open deck. Was this the same band they'd heard in the terminal? Zelda wasn't sure, but these players wore smart tuxedos, not uniforms with peaked caps, and they'd moved on from carols to 'We Are Sailing, We Are Sailing'. They looked like a dance band and some people were already dancing while other passengers were singing along and swaying to the music. The ship must have left her berth some time ago, Zelda deduced, glancing over the rail and seeing water. There was quite a lot between them and land already and the twinkling lights of Southampton were fast receding. They were sailing!

'Champagne, madam?' A white-coated steward at her side held a tray. 'There's Veuve Clicquot Brut or Rosé, or a Lanson if you prefer.'

Zelda took a glass of pink fizz.

'Madam?' The steward turned to Viv, who took one too, as did Janet.

'Cheers!' They all clinked glasses. 'All for one!' What the hell if they were already a bit tiddly. Free fizz was not to be shunned!

But it wasn't free! Oh dear! Here was another steward with bills to sign and the price for one glass was more than for a whole bottle of prosecco back home.

As Viv near-choked and Zelda reached for her credit card, Janet whipped out hers, waving away their protests. 'Now remind me where we're having dinner, Zelda. You did put us down for the early sitting, didn't you?'

Zelda said yes, she had booked a table for three in the Britannia restaurant as instructed, and they ought to get moving as soon as they'd finished their fizz. The restaurant was down on Deck 2 and the early sitting was at six o'clock. The early sitting seemed to be popular as a lot of people left when they did, and the area round the lift doors was crowded. As they stepped back to let one packed lift go and wait for another, a woman greeted them.

'What a jolly trio you are!' Blonde and dressed in black, except for a white pussycat bow at her neck, she was about their age, Zelda thought.

'Oh, you're from Edinburgh!' said Janet, presumably recognising the woman's accent.

'I am. Are you?'

'I am,' replied Janet with more enthusiasm than Zelda expected. 'And I miss it sometimes, do you?'

'Oh, I'm still there. Never moved away.'

They enthused about the delights of Edinburgh till a younger woman tapped the blonde woman on the shoulder, and she stepped aside to talk to her, after a 'See you all later, perhaps?'

'What a friendly lady,' said Janet as the lift arrived and they piled in.

6

VIV

'Wow!'

Viv was aware she was wowing rather a lot, but this was art deco on steroids. The Britannia restaurant they'd just stepped into was like nothing she'd seen before. They'd come in at Deck 2 level, but the gilded ceiling she was staring at, her head stretched so far back it hurt, was above Deck 3 where there was a mezzanine floor to the restaurant. The golden ceiling glowed.

'Ladies,' said a white-gloved waiter, 'may I show you to your table? Name, please?'

Zelda gave hers and the three of them followed him, weaving their way past maybe forty or fifty white-clothed tables, most of them already full, to the far end of the room.

'Wow!' Viv couldn't help it. Their table was directly beneath a gigantic tapestry of QM2 which filled the entire wall, towering over them, giving the impression it was sailing into the room.

'But I booked a table for three.'

Viv, mesmerised by the splendour, took a few seconds to realise that Zelda was complaining to the waiter, and that the table was set for four.

'Sorry, madam, I'll remove a setting immediately.' The man took a step forward.

'Er... perhaps I can save you the bother?' Ms Pussycat bow from the lift had re-appeared. 'It's just that,' she smiled apologetically, 'as a solo passenger I have to admit to envying you all your camaraderie.'

Viv wondered how to say piss off politely.

Zelda was quicker off the mark. 'Sorry, but we *need* a table for three.'

But it was as if she hadn't spoken. 'Would you mind awfully if I joined you?' The pushy cow addressed Janet, who replied, 'No, of course not.'

'Sorry,' Zelda persisted. Viv could only admire. 'I'm very sorry but we would mind. Please don't take it personally, but our friend is recently bereaved...'

'But so am I.' She touched her cheek with a finger.

'Honestly, Zelda, it's all right.' Janet sat down. 'Please join us, er...?'

'Primrose,' said the interloper, sitting next to her, 'but only if you're sure I'm not intruding...'

Zelda sat down, though clearly furious, so Viv sat too and they eyerolled each other across the table, while Janet and Primrose returned to Edinburgh.

Viv shared Zelda's fury 100 per cent. Zelda had gone to a lot of trouble to book a table for three because Janet had asked her to. It was her condition for coming, so they didn't get lumbered with unwelcome guests, and here was Janet overriding her.

Zelda didn't give up. 'Do join us for tonight, Primrose, but,' she turned to Janet, 'when we've eaten I shall go and see the purser and ask what went wrong with my booking of a table for three.'

Janet shook her head. 'It's serendipity, Viv.'

It's a cock-up, Janet. Viv couldn't speak her thoughts.

But Zelda could speak hers. 'I haven't explained well, Primrose, but we three are widows...'

'But so am I, as I said.' Primrose gave a pained little smile. 'So I know exactly how you all feel.'

No, you don't. No one knows exactly how someone else is feeling.

It was a thing of Viv's. We never know *exactly* what someone else is feeling and it's presumptuous to say you do. We don't know what's going on in someone else's head or heart. We get close sometimes and those moments are wonderful and bonding, but most of the time we're miles apart. We all grieve differently. They'd discovered that when they met fleeing from a ghastly bereavement group, united in their determination not to get stuck in their grief, like the dreary women there. And now Janet was grieving for Alan, her second husband, differently to the way she'd grieved for Malcolm, her first.

'Viv, choose.' Janet broke into her thoughts, nodding at the menu and they all perused as the waiter hovered. Crikey! How did you choose from this lot? It all sounded delicious: crab and shrimp Skagen, risotto of wild mushroom, terrine of pork knuckle, cobb salad with avocado, green salad, beef consommé, roasted cauliflower soup, and that was just for starters.

Janet was the first to make up her mind. 'I'll have the roasted cauliflower soup.'

'So will I,' said Primrose.

'And the penne pasta for main,' said Janet.

'So will I,' said Primrose, looking more relaxed by the minute.

'I should have made introductions.' Janet sat up straight when the waiter had taken their orders. 'I'm Janet Loveday, and these are my very good friends, Viv Halliday and Zelda Fielding.'

'I'm very pleased to meet you. Thank you so much for making me welcome.' Primrose smiled and Viv smiled back because she didn't want to be downright rude, but she didn't want to be too welcoming either. Zelda seemed to be thinking along the same lines. Her usually ready smile looked forced and she wasn't her chatty self. Janet though was chattier than she'd been for a long time, aided no doubt by the fizz she'd already downed. And when the wine waiter arrived she ordered a bottle of Chablis to go with the starter and a bottle of red for the main course, after verifying that what they didn't drink would be kept for the next day.

'In the unlikely event that we don't drink it all.'

'Not for me, thank you.' Primrose covered her glass with her hand when the waiter brought the white and started to fill their glasses. 'I am, I'm afraid, an impecunious widow, travelling steerage, so I won't be partaking of alcohol.'

'Oh, please,' said Janet. 'Have one on me. Or two. I am not an impecunious widow. I'm very pleased to say my first husband left me comfortably off. Cheers, Malcolm!' She raised her glass.

Janet was tipsy! She didn't usually go around revealing to strangers how well-off she was.

Zelda, clearly anxious, intervened. 'The mushroom risotto is delicious.'

Fortunately, Primrose and Janet went back to reminiscing about the delights of Edinburgh, discovering that they grew up there at about the same time. They were both baby boomers, born soon after the Second World War had ended, and were teenagers there in the early sixties.

'My friends and I used to meet in the Kardomah café.' Janet looked happy remembering.

'So did I!' said Primrose.

'We shopped for clothes at Top Shop in Princes Street.'

'So did I!'

'My husband went to the RHS.'

'So did mine!'

The RHS, Viv gathered, wasn't the Royal Horticultural Society she was familiar with, but the prestigious Royal High School for Boys in Edinburgh. Janet and Primrose's boyfriends, subsequently their husbands, both went there. Their lives did diverge a bit after that and they concluded that they hadn't met each other while young, well, not knowingly. Primrose said she'd been to a private girls' school called St Margaret's. She'd met her husband, Mal, at dance lessons which the school put on for sixth formers, inviting boys from the RHS to take part. Janet said she'd been to Firrhill, a girls-only state secondary school, where they didn't do risky things like mix with boys. She'd met her first husband Malcolm in London when she was training to be a nurse.

'He was at the London School of Economics.'

'But so was Mal!'

They were off again, so-did-he-ing about the sixties student scene in London.

It was like a weird game of Snap.

7

VIV

Janet ticked them off when they returned to her suite for coffee.

They had been unfriendly, she said. She'd seen their eye-rolling and feared Primrose had too. She'd expected better from them. Primrose was a widow like themselves, a single woman travelling alone, and she'd deserved a warmer reception.

'She declined my invitation to join us for coffee, saying she didn't want to outstay her welcome.'

Slumped on a sofa next to Zelda, enjoying petits fours and coffee served by Janet's lugubrious butler, before Janet dismissed him, Viv kept quiet.

Zelda, she was pleased to see, wasn't accepting Janet's criticism.

'I was carrying out orders,' she said. 'You said you wouldn't come if you had to eat dinner with other people, and I went to quite a lot of trouble to make sure you didn't have to. You explained that it was customary to eat with the same passengers each night, and I got the company to say we could have a table for three. I must have spent at least an hour being passed from one person to another to get them to agree and put it in writing. And I think they should keep their promise.'

Janet conceded the point and said she was grateful for all the trouble

Zelda had gone to. 'But I was wrong and I've changed my mind. We should be welcoming to new people.'

Maybe, but not her. There was something that didn't ring true about the woman, though hard to say what. Zelda obviously felt the same way, but Janet was saying she didn't want her to lodge a complaint with the purser.

Viv felt for Zelda, who must be torn. If she agreed with Janet there would be one less thing for her to do – that must be tempting, no one likes complaining – but they would be stuck with Primrose for the next six nights. If she insisted on their table for three she would upset Janet.

'The company should do what they'd agreed to do.' Zelda stuck to her guns. 'It's as simple as that.'

'But it isn't.' Janet stuck to hers. 'The situation has changed. We've met an interesting new person, and we've done a good deed by offering her the hand of friendship.' She picked up the Daily Programme from the coffee table. 'Now, what are we going to do for the rest of the evening?' Clearly the subject was closed as far as she was concerned. 'How about going to listen to the Animus String Quartet? They are playing Schubert in that magnificent lobby area on Deck 2 at 8.30.' She was proffering an olive branch, knowing Zelda loved classical music, and Zelda accepted, though still not happy from the look on her face.

They finished their coffees and went down to the lobby using the lift again. They were all tired – it had been a long day – and there were a lot of steps between Deck 11 and Deck 2. Viv really wanted to go and collapse with a book somewhere, but thought hostilities might break out if she left Janet and Zelda on their own. Janet was chatty but Zelda was monosyllabic. Seating for the recital was informal, she was pleased to see, not upright chairs in rows, but leather armchairs casually grouped round coffee tables. There weren't many listeners and they easily found three chairs together beside a white grand piano not being used, and quite close to the quartet, who had already started playing. Viv put herself between Janet and Zelda and relaxed a bit when they seemed to be enjoying the music. Her position gave her a good view of the lobby and her attention drifted to passengers wandering in and out. There was a constant flow of people, many of whom lingered a while to listen or gaze up at the huge Christmas tree, which extended beyond the balcony up to the next deck, before climbing up the grand staircase to view it from the top.

Janet and Zelda seemed absorbed by the music. Viv had no idea what it was as her knowledge of classical music was minimal, and mostly gleaned from Classic FM. She could recognise and name only a few famous pieces. This wasn't one of them but it was a bit of a tear-jerker, she realised when she tuned in, not what you wanted, well, not what she wanted right now. Oh no. A tear was trickling down Zelda's cheek.

The cellist was a good-looking bloke, she found herself thinking, like that black actor – what's his name? – in *The Wire*. He was quite a bit older than the other players, three youngish women. He was in fact more their own age, and she noticed a dog at his feet, a black Labrador she thought, wearing a harness, so he must be blind. As the violinists took up the theme, Zelda's fingers disappeared into the pocket of the caftan she was wearing, as if feeling for a dog-treat, which she always kept about her when she was at home. Viv couldn't help feeling apprehensive. This could be lovely for Zelda, a dog to talk to or even pat, or it could make her yearn for Mack and Morag, her own spoilt Westies, and wish she hadn't come.

The piece came to an end, to at first a thoughtful silence then a smattering of heartfelt applause. She turned to Zelda, now dabbing her eyes, to say she hoped the next piece would be more cheerful, but got shushed. Zelda nodded at the group who were beginning again.

Fortunately the next piece was livelier and so was the next. Viv enjoyed the music but, checking the time on her mobile, she wondered if Janet and Zelda would be up for some jazz next, as that was more her sort of thing. According to the Daily Programme – she'd downloaded a digital version onto her phone – the Animus Quartet finished at 9.15 and Jazz Club with the Steve Goffe Trio began in the Chart Room on Deck 3 at 9.30.

'What about...' She turned to Zelda when the concert came to an end, but Zelda was already on her feet, heading for the cellist's dog.

'What about what?' Janet was getting to her feet.

Viv explained her idea and Janet agreed it sounded lovely but wasn't sure about Zelda, who was now talking to the cellist. 'Do we wait for her? She seems otherwise occupied and hasn't patted the dog yet.'

'Perhaps you're not allowed to pat guide dogs,' said Viv. 'She seems to be getting on with its owner though, discussing the finer points of Schubert and Haydn maybe?'

'Or Labradors and West Highland terriers.' Janet picked up her bag. 'Let's leave them to it. I'll text her with our whereabouts.'

They made their way up the magnificent curved staircase, feet sinking into the sumptuous red carpet, pausing at the top to look down at the scene below. 'I feel as if I'm standing on the balcony at Buckingham Palace,' said Janet. 'Should I give a regal wave to the crowds below?'

'They'll think you're Her Maj,' said Viv and Janet laughed.

'Pity I forgot my tiara.'

Some people glanced up from time to time but to look at the star on top of the Christmas tree. At the bottom a tableau of characters from *The Wind in the Willows* was getting a lot of attention and so was an old-fashioned barrel organ belting out 'Silent Night'.

'What's Zelda doing now?' Viv spotted her still in the performance area.

'Picking up a chair?'

'But why?'

'So she can sit down next to the cellist?' Janet raised an eyebrow. Viv too. Zelda didn't do up close and personal with chaps these days. She'd given them up.

The three women in the quartet had gone, so it was just the cellist and Zelda and the dog, of course. And Janet was right, Zelda was putting the chair she'd been carrying close to the cellist's and they were soon in deep conversation. Well, that's what it looked like.

'Presumably he invited her to do that.' Janet was thoughtful. 'Bringing a chair to sit close by him, I mean. I can't imagine Zelda being that pushy.'

Unlike your new friend, Viv thought but didn't say.

8
ZELDA

Zelda was enjoying herself now, though she hadn't at first.

When she'd asked if she could pat the cellist's dog he'd said no, abruptly, and she'd been about to leave when he'd called her back saying sorry to sound rude but if she could hang on a bit he'd explain. He'd been putting his cello in its case, and she'd hung on though her eyes were filling up; a combination of the Schubert and missing Mack and Morag more than hurt feelings, she hoped. Up to then she hadn't realised how much she'd been missing her dogs, probably because she hadn't allowed herself to think about them, but seeing the man's beautiful black Labrador made her yearn for a bit of dog-contact. So, when the piece had ended, she'd hurried over to ask – she knew better than to pat without asking – and got a rebuff. There was no other word for it. He'd quickly relented. 'Thanks for asking. Most folks don't,' and stuck out his hand. 'Richard, pleased to meet you. Typical male, I'm afraid, not good at multi-tasking.' He nodded at the cello, now in its case. 'Sorry if I was crass.'

'Zelda.' She'd taken his hand and shaken it. 'Female, not into stereotypes and prone to barging in where I'm not wanted.'

'Not at all, well, not in this instance. Really. Draw up a chair and meet Billie, also female, who may be more into stereotypes than you are.'

That's when she'd got herself a chair.

Zelda had quickly learned that the dog was named after the jazz singer, Billie Holiday, and that she was excellent at her job, which was getting him from A to B without tripping up or crashing into anything. Job was the key word. Being a guide was Billie's job. She was a worker, but not a slave, so she had on-duty and off-duty time. She was entitled to time off, Richard said, and he gave her as much as he could, using her services only when he needed them. Right now though she was in work-mode, and when she was in work-mode she was totally focused on his needs and didn't need distractions.

'Like me wanting to pat her?'

He nodded.

'Sorry.'

'Don't be. When she's off duty she'll let you pat and fondle her as much as you like, but possibly not as much as she'd like. She loves fuss and attention and she'll probably roll over onto her back so you can rub her belly. I'm afraid she's a bit of a tart.'

'She doesn't look like a tart.'

She lay at his feet, eyes open, listening to his every word, ready to do his bidding.

'Not in a white harness with its Day-Glo yellow sleeve, she doesn't. But take that off and she's her own woman. That's a good thing to look out for, by the way. As a rule, if a dog's wearing a working harness and handle, and especially if the owner is holding the handle, the dog's on duty. If he or she isn't wearing a harness, or when the owner is holding an ordinary dog lead, then the dog's off duty.'

'I wondered why she had an ordinary lead as well.' It was attached to her collar.

Richard reached for Billie's handle as a couple of stewards came in and started to rearrange the performers' chairs and music stands. Richard had obviously heard them as he got to his feet and so did Billie. Then he called one of the men over and asked him to take his cello to his room.

'We're in the way now, Zelda. They're getting ready for the next show, and I'm dying for a pint. Fancy a drink in the Golden Lion?'

She said she'd love one, though she'd had more than enough at dinner, and followed, fascinated, as the dog led the way to the pub. Richard, she noted, gave the orders – 'Forward, Billie. Left, Billie. Stop' – which surprised her, though she wasn't sure why.

'One of the first routes I learned,' he said as they stood in the entrance to the pub, 'so one of the first Billie learned too.'

'You learned it first?'

'Yes, of course.' He seemed surprised that she'd asked. 'I had to learn to be able to show her. That's how it works. Guide dogs are wonderful, Zelda, and sometimes show amazing initiative, but they don't have GPS. Billie will know the way to the Golden Lion by the end of the week, because she'll have done it several times by then, and learned the way – from me. I had a few days aboard to learn the layout before you passengers embarked, by the way. I was assigned a steward to show me around and familiarise myself with the ship, so I could decide which areas I needed to know well. Definitely not all thirteen decks.'

It seemed obvious once he'd explained. The blind person needed to know where he or she was going to be able to instruct the guide dog. Of course! Dogs didn't have super-human powers, and nor did blind people, but together these two made a super-impressive team.

'Where would you like to sit?' He had an American accent, she'd noticed earlier.

There was a wide choice – booths by the window overlooking the sea when the blinds weren't down, tables with bucket-style armchairs around them in the centre, and high stools at the bar to their right. The Golden Lion was described in the Daily Programme as a 'typically British pub', and looked like an upmarket Wetherspoons. Brass rails gleamed at the bar, and the leather seating was polished to such a high sheen that she'd have to be careful not to slide off and land on the floor.

'There?' She pointed to an empty booth, forgetting he couldn't see.

'Er...'

'That booth, by the window, on the left.'

'Fine. Is it okay if I take your arm and give Billie a rest now?'

'Of course.' She felt privileged to already have his trust, as he let Billie's handle fall, picked up the lead with his left hand and tucked his right arm into her left. Aware of the closeness of him, the warmth and strength of his body, she led the way to the booth, where they separated, manoeuvring themselves in, he on one side, she on the other, and Billie lay down between them. Almost immediately a waiter came over from the bar and took their orders, Richard's a pint, Zelda's a mineral water.

Richard took Billie's harness off. 'I think she'd like a stroke now.'

'Me too. I mean...'

'I know what you mean.' He laughed. 'And she particularly likes her ears fondled.'

As she stroked Billie's glossy ears, feeling her blood pressure falling as she did, Richard told her that he'd joined the Animus Quartet at the last minute when they'd put out an SOS because their regular cellist had dropped out for family reasons. He'd applied for the post on impulse. The move had taken a bit of organising – he'd had to fly out to Southampton and start rehearsing at short notice – but the Cunard staff had been brilliant, so good to Billie. They'd taken care of all the travel arrangements, which were complicated when you had a guide dog.

'How could they not be, good to Billie, I mean?' Zelda loved dogs even more than she loved the cello, which she'd adored since the first moment she'd heard it. She was about to say so, when Billie licked her hand, and looking down she recognised a pair of black patent leather sandals walking past their booth.

Primrose the Invader.

'You were saying...' Richard prompted, '...when you first heard the cello?'

'Sorry. Got distracted. It was when I was still at school, on the way to school in fact, walking past a house. The sound stopped me in my tracks.'

He nodded. 'The cello reaches parts that other instruments don't, for me anyway, and says things there aren't words for. But is something the matter?'

She'd just glanced over her shoulder to check if it really was Primrose she could hear getting into the booth behind her.

'We can move if you like.' It was as if he could see.

'No, honestly, sorry. I'll explain later. Maybe.' She focused on him again. 'I think I recognise your accent. Where are you from?'

'Raleigh, North Carolina.'

'*Really*?' She couldn't believe it.

'No, Raleigh.' He laughed.
'But that's where my family live.'
'No! You sound so English.'
'I can explain that.' She started to, but got distracted again when Primrose was joined by someone else, another woman from the sound of her voice. Zelda carried on telling Richard about discovering that her dad was American, while reaching for her phone to switch her hi-tech hearing aids from Restaurant mode, which cut out background sounds, to Automatic to give wider coverage. She also glanced over her shoulder and recognised the woman Primrose was talking to. It was the same one she'd met by the lift, tall with a lot of strawberry-blonde hair piled on top of her head. Interesting. But when she turned back, Richard was getting to his feet, saying he had to be off.

'Oh. Please stay and have another drink.' She saw his glass was empty. 'My turn. And I haven't had my dog-fix yet.'

But he carried on easing his long lean body out of the booth. 'Thanks, but I've really got to go, so Billie and I will leave you to your sleuthing, Miss Lansbury.' And with that he put Billie's harness back on and took hold of her handle. Then with a 'Forward, Billie,' they set off for the exit.

I've blown it.

Miss Lansbury? She got it. He meant Angela Lansbury, the actress who played the sleuth in *Murder, She Wrote*. Well, he was no mean sleuth himself, picking up that she'd been listening to the people sitting behind her, more interested in them than him. That's what it must have felt like. But she wasn't, not at all. She liked him and his dog. She was fascinated by their relationship and wanted to know more. Mortified that she'd hurt his feelings, she considered rushing after them to explain, but she also wanted to know what was going on behind her.

Primrose and Strawberry Blonde had lowered their voices to an incomprehensible murmur. She needed to get her phone and turn up the volume on her hearing aids to hear what they were saying. Delving into her handbag, she saw her make-up mirror and got another idea. Looking into her mirror, as if checking her make-up, she got a good view of the other woman talking to Primrose. It was the same woman who had tapped her on the shoulder by the lift. She had a long narrow face heavily made up with a lot of eyeshadow, and pink-blonde hair piled high on top of her head which made her face look even longer and narrower. Mirror back in her bag, Zelda turned up the volume on her hearing aid to its highest setting, and tuned in.

The first word she heard was 'Janet' and then 'Daddy' as Primrose was giving a near verbatim account of her recent conversation with Janet. She was up to the point where Janet said she'd met Malcolm in London when he was at university when she yawned and said she'd tell her more later as she needed an early night. Strawberry Blonde said she needed another drink and there was some shuffling as if one of them was getting out of her seat. Zelda couldn't see who, but after a bit more shuffling behind her, she saw Strawberry Blonde heading for the bar, where she perched herself on one of the tall stools and started chatting to the bar steward. A man older than her came in soon afterwards and sat on a stool beside her. He got drinks in for both of them.

Interesting.

Zelda observed closely, discreetly she hoped, mulling over what she had heard. Daddy had been mentioned several times. She wondered for a moment if the man at the bar could be Daddy. He was quite a lot older than Strawberry Blonde but she was flirting with him, so no, unless this was very weird. Zelda examined the woman's features. She was taller than Primrose, with long legs now elegantly crossed, her silvery cocktail dress drawn up above her knees, beguiling the man who had joined her at the bar. Could Primrose and Strawberry Blonde be mother and daughter? Both women were blondes, one strawberry, one ash, but hair colour wasn't significant as both could have come out of a bottle. The more revealing thing was that they both had high cheekbones, enhanced in Strawberry Blonde's case by the liberal use of blusher. Zelda estimated that Strawberry Blonde was in her early fifties, maybe late forties. Primrose was in her late sixties, like Janet, so they could be mother and daughter if Primrose had had her in her teens. Whatever, Primrose was looking less and less like the lonely passenger she'd claimed to be when she'd gate-crashed their table.

9
JANET

Janet was back in her luxurious suite after enjoying listening to the Steve Goffe Trio with Viv. It was the light traditional jazz she liked, but the comfortable seats and the low lighting in the sophisticated Chart Room cocktail bar, 'like the night sky which had guided navigators of yore' – to quote the programme – had made them both feel sleepy. It had been a long day, and she didn't need to see the waves hitting the bows, which she could do through the bay windows at the far end of the room. She didn't want to be reminded that they were on the high seas, heading for the Atlantic Ocean, if they weren't there already. She was happy to pretend she was in a luxury hotel on dry land. After half an hour of the group's playing and a delicious 'celestial cocktail' recommended by the barman, they'd decided they needed their beds more than they needed music. They'd messaged Zelda to tell her what they were doing, and headed for their rooms.

First, after closing the curtains to hide the waves, she'd enjoyed a warm bubble bath, to soothe away the cares of the day, not that there had been too many of those, thanks to Zelda's organising skills. The mix-up over the table was a blip and Zelda had over-reacted, but it would all turn out for the best, she was sure. She had done the right thing insisting that Primrose join them. She had been wrong to make that silly proviso in the first place, limiting not only who she met but also Viv and Zelda's choice, expecting them to put up with her low-key company every night. They had been stalwart since Alan died, so supportive, but now she must start branching out and take the pressure off them. It was good to widen their circle and she was already feeling the benefits. She'd enjoyed reminiscing about old Edinburgh with Primrose.

She was in bed in her pyjamas when a phone rang, flummoxing her for a few moments. At first she thought it was her mobile which was plugged into a socket by the wall charging, but it wasn't. Then she realised it was the landline on the other side of her bed, if landline was the right word. Sealine? She picked up the phone just as it stopped ringing. But it rang again.

'Is that Mrs Janet Loveday?' It was Reception.

'Yes, it is.'

'Will you accept a call from passenger Mrs Carmichael?'

'Mrs who?' She regretted taking her hearing aids out.

'Mrs Carmichael.'

'But I am Mrs Carmichael, sorry, was. Mrs who did you say?'

'Mrs Carmichael. Mrs Primrose Carmichael.'

She must have misheard. The man on the other end of the phone had a foreign accent.

'Could you spell that please?'

'P for Papa...'

'Sorry, I mean Carmichael. Please spell Carmichael.'

'C for Charlie. A for Alpha...' He spelled out Carmichael, exactly as she had spelt her name when married to Malcolm. This was bizarre. 'Do you want to accept the call, madam?'

'Y-yes.'

'Janet.' It was of course Primrose. 'I'm sorry to call you at such a late hour, but I just wanted to say how sorry I am for intruding at dinner tonight.'

'You didn't, Primrose. You really didn't.'

'I did, Janet, I was tactless and your friends resented it. I understand and won't intrude further.'

'But you must. I mean you didn't intrude. I'm sorry about my friends.

They're not usually like that and they'll understand when I explain. Please join us for dinner tomorrow evening.'

'If you're sure?' Primrose sounded uncertain.

'I am sure, Primrose. Thank you for phoning, though it wasn't necessary to apologise. Good night.'

Primrose *Carmichael*. How did she get to be Primrose *Carmichael*? By marrying a Carmichael obviously, like she'd married a Carmichael. But as soon as she put the phone down she regretted not mentioning it. Why hadn't she? It was an amazing coincidence, that was all, and perhaps not so very amazing. Carmichael was a common name, in Scotland anyway, not so common in England when she'd married Malcolm, but not unusual. Something else niggled though. Mal and Malcolm. Primrose had called her late husband Mal, which was surely short for Malcolm. *We were both married to Malcolm Carmichael*. That *was* an amazing coincidence. Now memories of Malcolm's philandering past came back and a silly thought, a ridiculous thought came into her head. *Malcolm wasn't that bad*. Janet reached for one of the books she'd brought with her, a thriller with an intricate plot which needed her full attention.

10

VIV

'That woman is *not* a solo passenger!'

Viv was sitting up in bed, relaxing against the pillows, reading the next day's Daily Programme when Zelda nearly fell into their cabin in her eagerness to share.

'She's a liar.' Zelda, shoes off, was looking around the room, for her suitcase at a guess.

'Over there.' Viv pointed to the case-stand near the door. 'The steward took it off your bed before he turned it down, and put a heart-shaped chocolate on your pillow. He's in love with you obviously. I've unpacked my case but left you most of the wardrobe.' She had travelled light, much lighter than Zelda, even with the clothes Libby had insisted she borrow.

'I didn't like her from the start.'

There was no need to ask who Zelda was talking about. Getting ready for bed, she proceeded to give a blow-by-blow account of her evening's sleuthing in the Golden Lion, including its run-for-the-exit effect on the dishy cellist and his dog. Viv hoped Zelda was as resolutely single as she'd been saying she was for some time because if she had romantic ambitions in that direction she had definitely blown them sky high.

'That woman is not what she says she is. For one thing, she's here with her daughter. For another, this meeting with Janet is not a chance encounter. I'd put money on it.'

'So what are they up to?' Viv decided not to ask for evidence, well, not tonight. She was worried about Janet though. 'What are we going to tell her?'

'Nothing tonight.' Zelda got into bed and put out the light. 'And "what are they up to?"' she said from the darkness. 'I'm not sure but I'm going to find out.'

* * *

Thursday, 17 December

'Nothing,' she said again in the morning, when Viv asked what they should tell Janet. 'She wouldn't believe me. She thinks I've got a down on the woman.' Zelda still couldn't say Primrose.

'We,' said Viv. 'Janet thinks *we've* got a down on Primrose, that we're being unfair.' They were sitting in bed drinking tea, analysing what Zelda had seen and heard the night before. 'Nice pyjamas, by the way.'

They were apricot satin, very Zelda. Hers were red with pandas on them, a present from the grandchildren. Viv had woken up first and put the kettle on. It was now 7 a.m. according to the mobile in Viv's other hand and the clock on the table between the two beds. But *really*, Viv couldn't help thinking, it was 8 a.m. because the clocks went back an hour each day, automatically it seemed. So she'd had eight hours' sleep. They had, she thought, slept well considering what was on both of their minds.

Viv agreed with Zelda that things looked iffy. How else could that odd encounter be interpreted? The talk of 'Daddy' was revealing. It did sound as if Primrose and Strawberry Blonde were mother and daughter.

'So, what do we do?' Zelda wanted action.

'Do a bit more investigating? Get more evidence that they're up to no good? I agree we shouldn't tell Janet yet.' Viv didn't like to think of Janet doubting Zelda's word. 'You're as honest as she is, and that's very honest.'

'Yes, but...' Zelda put down her cup. 'Janet knows I'm honest, she won't think I'm lying, but she will say my perception is coloured by my dislike of the woman. And by my failing hearing. She thinks I guess when I don't hear every word and fill in the gaps. Just like she does, I should say.'

'Like we all do,' Viv agreed. 'But how do we find out more, Miss Marple?'

'Miss Lansbury, that's what my one-time drinking companion called me.' She looked a bit rueful, Viv thought, as if she might be regretting something, but if she was she dismissed it with a shrug. 'Observe? Keep a look-out? Take a photo if we see the two of them together?'

'Easier said than done, I fear. Do you know how many passengers there are aboard this boat?' Viv didn't wait for an answer but picked up the Daily Programme. 'There are, it says here, 2,691 passengers on this voyage and 1,253 crew. Those are our Nautical Facts of the Day, by the way. The population of this ship is bigger than the village of Elmsley, but spread vertically over twelve decks. We're living in a floating high-rise, Zelda, with the inhabitants engaging in a hundred or more activities night and day. Our chances of finding those two in the same place at the same time, when one of them is pretending to be a lonely widow, are... well, needles in haystacks come to mind.' Viv perused the programme. 'Listen, events start at six in the morning and go on till 12.30 at night. So Primrose and Strawberry Blonde – relationship yet to be confirmed – could be anywhere, together or separately at any time of day. Right now, for instance, they could be in their cabin or cabins – sorry, staterooms – listening to "Wake up with Paul!" or they could be on their way to Power Deck Walk on Deck 7, which, by the way, I was thinking of doing myself.' Viv got out of bed and found her tracksuit. 'Or they could be heading to Catholic Mass in Illuminations on Deck 3, or,' she handed the programme to Zelda, 'they could already be eating breakfast in a variety of eating places – five at least – on one of several different decks.'

Zelda reached for her mobile. 'How about we message Janet and say we'll meet her for breakfast at nine in the Kings Court Buffet on Deck 7?'

'And play it by ear?' Viv pulled on her tracksuit top.

'Agreed.' Zelda started typing. 'I won't say anything, well, anything of consequence, about last night till you join us.'

'Agreed.' Viv pulled on her trainers and headed for Deck 7. By nine o'clock and after power-walking ten blowy laps of the promenade deck, about three miles, her mobile calculated, she was ready for the full English breakfast. The other walkers, about twenty of them, had set a brisk pace, pushing against the wind for half the distance, carried along by it for the other half. There hadn't been much time to think as they'd walked, but as she headed for the Kings Court Buffet she decided they should be open with Janet. She'd encourage Zelda to tell her exactly what she'd seen and heard and leave Janet to form her own conclusions.

Would her sweaty tracksuit be acceptable, she wondered, hesitating as she reached the door to the restaurant. Yes, others similarly garbed were already eating or getting food at the buffet. It was self-service and informal. A group of men with wet hair looked as if they'd come straight from the pool next door. Ah, there were Janet and Zelda already at a table near the plate-glass window, staring out to sea, watching the waves. They hadn't got food yet. They weren't talking and looked tense. Zelda had told her what she'd heard last night. She looked guilty. Viv could tell.

11

ZELDA

But Viv was wrong.

Zelda hadn't told Janet anything. She was silent because Janet had just told her something which made her mouth fall open. She'd then clamped it shut to stop herself blurting out, 'That clinches it! They're frauds!' And she'd only kept quiet because she'd agreed with Viv that she wouldn't tell Janet what she'd heard last night till Viv was there.

'It gives you a perspective, doesn't it?' Janet, sitting opposite Zelda, chin on her hands, was gazing out of the window at the grey waves.

'What does?' Zelda asked, though she guessed the answer, because she couldn't think of anything else to say.

'The ocean,' said Janet, 'the vastness, the immensity, the never-endingness of it. Don't you think it makes all our troubles seem trivial?'

'No, I don't actually.' Zelda knew the theory but didn't go along with it. And she was surprised that Janet who claimed to abhor cliché went along with it. Gazing out at the grey waves, miles and miles of them, making their relentless way to America and beyond, didn't make the slightest bit of difference to how she felt about anything, least of all the ticking timebomb that was Primrose Carmichael.

Primrose *Carmichael*.

Zelda couldn't get the name out of her head. She'd been filled with foreboding ever since Janet had told her about Primrose's late-night phone call. Primrose Carmichael, married to Mal Carmichael, who went to the same school as Malcolm Carmichael, who went to the same university as Malcolm Carmichael, who did the same job as Malcolm Carmichael, Janet's stingy, two-timing late, *philandering*, lying bastard of a husband.

There were too many coincidences.

Where is Viv? Ah! At last! Here she was heading for their table, looking as if she'd been blown round the deck by a hurricane. Her faded auburn hair, white-streaked at the front – she wouldn't let Zelda's girls give her a rinse – was almost horizontal. Her face was red and raw, showing every broken capillary. *Moisturiser, Viv, moisturiser.*

'Ten laps, just over three miles,' she gasped, bent double, still puffing.

'Sit down.' Zelda patted the seat beside her. 'Janet's got something to tell you.'

'And you've – got – something – to tell – her, haven't you Zelda?' Viv straightened up with difficulty.

'Not yet. Later.' Janet insisted they get food and drink from the buffet first. 'And don't think you're going to hear anything life-changing from me, Viv. I've thought it through and this isn't as big a deal as Zelda seems to think.'

'You don't know what I think,' Zelda fought back.

'I do, Zelda – I'm not completely without imagination – and I'm sure you're wrong.'

When Janet at last told Viv what Primrose had said, that she had been married to Mal Carmichael, Viv's eyebrows shot to her hairline, but Janet still didn't seem that concerned. If she'd had fears of a more alarming explanation, she'd done a very good job of dismissing them. Now she seemed to think that the similarity, the *sameness* of their names was just another thing she and Primrose had in common.

'I think it's possible that Mal and Malcolm are related. Not closely, not brothers, because you wouldn't give brothers names so alike and anyway, Malcolm didn't have a brother. He was an only child. But they could have been cousins, something like that, which might account for their going to the same school and university.'

Primrose still seemed to be flavour of the month.

'Your turn, Zelda.' Viv gave her a hopeful look.

Zelda knew that Viv was keen to *scotch* – her word – Janet's *love-in* – her word again – with Primrose. But she proceeded cautiously, simply reporting what she had seen and heard in the Golden Lion, without expressing an opinion, so Janet could make up her own mind. She kept her feelings under tight control and spoke in what she thought was a neutral tone but she might as well have accused Primrose of murder.

'I think you're making a lot of very little, Zelda.' Janet sipped coffee.

'Zelda's not making anything of anything, Janet.' Viv took a pause from her full English. 'She's just telling you what she saw and heard.'

Thank you, Viv.

But Janet saw no significance in the many mentions of *daddy*, the seeming closeness of the relationship between Primrose and Strawberry Blonde or the similarity of their cheekbones. When Viv pointed out that Primrose had said she was a lonely solo passenger, who had envied them their camaraderie when she saw them at the Sail Away party, she said, 'And nothing Zelda has said suggests Primrose wasn't telling the truth.'

Janet was in see no evil, say no evil, hear no evil mode and nothing was going to budge her.

Zelda didn't push the point and instead she dug into her delicious eggs Benedict. Janet, eating the same, paused to say it would make her very happy – and she knew they wanted to make her happy – if they would look kindly on Primrose as a fellow widow. 'I liked her. We have so much in common.'

Too much, perhaps.

But Zelda didn't voice her worst fear, not even to Viv, because it was too awful to think about. Janet's first marriage to Malcolm Carmichael hadn't been happy. He'd kept a lot from her, which she'd only discovered after his death and it had taken her a long time to come to terms with it all. Could she come to terms with further revelations? This was Operation Cheer Up Janet, Zelda reminded herself, not Drag Janet Down to the Depths. If Janet wanted them to welcome Primrose they should give it a go. Janet was eating more enthusiastically than she had for months, Zelda was pleased to see. Viv, now wiping her plate with a piece of bread, seemed to have come to the same conclusion.

'What are we going to do for the rest of the day?' Viv had put the digital version of the Daily Programme on her phone, and now produced it from her tracksuit pocket. She read out the options and, after a bit of discussion, they decided to stick together for their first full day aboard. Janet said she thought the Tanzanite Seminar in the Chart Room at eleven sounded interesting. Viv wrinkled and quickly unwrinkled her nose. Zelda knew she wasn't into jewellery and a tanzanite was a very rare precious stone, but pleasing Janet was the order of the day. Zelda was in fact quite keen, so they all agreed on that and on a talk about the night sky in the ship's planetarium at two, after lunch in the Britannia restaurant. And, said Viv, if they survived another meal without a heart attack, she'd quite like to hear the lecture on Vivien Leigh, as she'd been named after the film star. She thought it might be time to find out exactly why she was such a disappointment to her mother.

'Just joshing!'

She was. Zelda checked her face, and so, she saw, did Janet. The days were long past when Viv let her demanding mother get her down.

* * *

For the rest of the day, Zelda kept a look-out for Primrose and Strawberry Blonde, feeling only slightly guilty. Yes, she had agreed to 'look kindly' on Primrose, but that didn't stop her keeping an eye out for anything suspicious. She didn't see the two together at any point, but Strawberry Blonde was on the front row for the talk on the tanzanite in the Chart Room, and she led the way when after the talk ended the audience were invited to the jewellery boutique, 'to see the beautiful blue stone in gold, silver and platinum settings with no obligation'. Zelda said, 'See you later,' to Viv and Janet who were chatting to someone and followed her prey at a discreet distance. She found her peering into a glass cabinet full of jewellery, now with an elderly man in a flowery short-sleeved shirt at her side. Tanzanites, Zelda had learned from the talk, were a thousand times rarer than diamonds and were reputed to have a good effect on the heart, but the astronomical prices nearly brought hers to a standstill. Strawberry Blonde was very interested though. As Zelda took a step backwards, she saw her take hold of the elderly gentleman's skinny arm with one hand and point with the other to the centrepiece, a very flashy brooch.

Gold digger then – or should that be tanzanite digger?

Before she left, Zelda took a surreptitious photo on her mobile, to share with Viv.

12

VIV

Viv took a sneaky look at the photo as she sat down at the table that night. Yes, there was a resemblance. It was the cheekbones, like little shelves underneath the over-made-up protruding eyes. Strawberry Blonde went in for blue eyeshadow, Primrose a light grey tone. The younger woman's hair was piled on top, Primrose's cut in a chin-level bob, but they could well be mother and daughter. Viv, not into fashion, wasn't one to notice what people were wearing, but she thought Primrose looked much the same as she had the previous night. Garbed in black, except for a white bow at her throat, she made Viv think of a black widow spider. Had she eaten her husband?

Try harder. Be fair.

Viv, like Zelda, had resolved to look for Primrose's good points, to *look on her kindly* as Janet had requested. Janet had ticked them off again over lunch. They shouldn't have taken against Primrose, because she'd asked to join them. Primrose had been assertive and proactive, qualities The Muscateers usually admired.

So when Primrose greeted her warmly with 'Good evening, Viv!' Viv replied in a friendly manner. When Primrose said, 'Have you had a good day? What have you been up to?' Viv awarded her a merit mark for being interested in other people. And another for being a good listener when

Janet took it upon herself to tell her what the three of them had been doing. And yet another for her enthusiasm when Janet said they'd been to the planetarium. 'But I was there too!' she gushed. 'Wasn't it wonderful?'

She is not gushing. Viv ticked herself off.

'Wasn't the *Stars Over the Atlantic* film fascinating?' Primrose continued with enthusiasm. 'But why didn't we see each other?'

Zelda replied, without a hint of sarcasm, that it might have been because it was dark inside the cinema, or because they'd been to different performances. There had been several showings of the film throughout the day. As Primrose digested this, Janet struck a slightly negative note, saying that actually she didn't think the ship's planetarium had been quite as wonderful as the planetarium in the Science Centre in Edinburgh. That brought forth a 'Nor did I' from Primrose and another round of teenage reminiscences on the joys of Edinburgh.

Viv looked at Zelda. Zelda looked at Viv.

When is Janet going to mention the Carmichael coincidence? She had said she would.

Now they were onto the coffee bars they used to frequent. This was old ground – they'd done coffee bars before. Janet said the Kardomah was her favourite, and that she'd had her first ever spaghetti Bolognese there. Primrose started to say all too predictably that the Kardomah was her favourite too when Janet suddenly took a deep breath.

'Primrose, I have to say I was rather taken aback last night when Reception asked if I would take a call from Primrose Carmichael.'

Primrose blinked several times before saying, 'Oh, er... why?'

Blinking, did that indicate deceit? Viv, observing closely, tried to remember which signs showed that someone was lying. Primrose's 'Why?' didn't feel genuine. Did she really not know that Janet once had the same surname?

'Because,' said Janet, 'that was my married name too, when I was married to my first husband.'

'Really?' Primrose's eyes opened wide. 'You were Mrs Carmichael too? That's *amazing*. Are you sure? Sorry, silly question, of course you're sure who you got married to. Oh. Well, I never.' She lifted her glass to take a sip of water, then put it down again. 'And,' she said casually – too casually perhaps? – 'didn't you say his name was Mal?'

'Malcolm,' said Janet. 'I always called him Malcolm. He didn't like abbreviations.'

Janet and Primrose went quiet then, Viv too thinking what to say next. Zelda was quicker. 'What's Mal short for in your case, Primrose?'

'Malcolm, er... I assume.' She gave a little shrug.

'Don't tell me you don't know!' Zelda didn't disguise her incredulity.

'I-I-I always called him Mal.' She looked uncomfortable. 'He liked Mal.'

'Yes, but what did he put on official documents? What did he say on his wedding day?' Zelda put a little laugh into her voice. 'You know how it goes. *I something-or-other take you something-or-other to be my awfully wedded wife.* Was it a surprise when he said his full name? It sometimes is, isn't it? Right in the middle of the service. You think you're marrying good old George, and discover you've got an Ebenezer.'

Viv watched.

Primrose looked like a contestant on *Who Wants to Be a Millionaire* faced with a difficult question. Her hand moved towards her mobile, which was on the table. She looked as if she wanted to phone a friend, or more likely a daughter, but then, thinking better of it, she put the phone in her bag.

'I, er, must confess, I do sometimes have memory problems.'

The waiter arrived to take their orders and they all studied their menus and when he had gone Primrose was the first to become chatty again, talking mostly about the food, how difficult it was to choose, etcetera. Then suddenly, out of the blue, when their meals had been served and they were all eating, she asked Janet how her first husband had passed away. 'If you don't mind me asking.'

I mind you asking. Viv deducted a mark for poking her nose into things that had nothing to do with her.

'Cancer,' said Janet.

'And when was the sad event?'

Event! What an odd choice of words!

'It was 2008.' Janet answered minimally, making it clear she didn't like the subject.

'Prostate, was it?'

Viv wanted to prostrate Primrose, but once again Zelda was quicker.

'When did your husband die, Primrose? And what of?'

Spot on, Zelda!

But Primrose said her duck á l'orange was perfect. Did she really not hear Zelda's questions? Janet got the Daily Programme from out of her bag. 'Let's move on, shall we? What is everyone doing tonight?'

Viv said she might go to Jazz Club at nine, and Zelda said she'd go with her. Janet said she fancied an early night with a book, but they were all welcome to join her for coffee in her room after dinner, before they went out. Primrose, looking keen to get away, said thank you but no thank you. She was going to the Early Evening Trivia Quiz in the Golden Lion. 'I took the bold step of going to a meeting for solo travellers this morning, and six of us have formed a team.'

'Well done,' said Janet, not too upset, Viv thought, that her new buddy wasn't coming for coffee. Maybe Primrose realised she'd struck a wrong note or several, because when dinner finished she was the first to her feet, saying she didn't want to outstay her welcome.

You already have, Viv managed not to say, before she scurried away. Zelda too got to her feet. 'See you later. Won't be long.' She'd gone before she or Janet could ask why, in the same direction as Primrose.

Janet said, 'Did Primrose leave something behind? Is Zelda trying to catch her up?'

'Maybe,' said Viv, but thought Zelda was on a mission.

13

ZELDA

Viv was right.

Zelda had been observing Primrose throughout the meal too and had come to the same conclusion that Primrose was up to no good. Zelda had seen her eyeing her phone, her fingers moving towards it, as if she was itching to make a call when she was questioned. Questions made her uncomfortable. She was happier asking the questions, fishing for information, even happier when she caught a fish or two, like the cause of Malcolm's death and the date. Happy might not be the right word. Primrose had been anxious. She had a script, Zelda thought, and she was okay when she could follow it, not so okay when other people's enquiries knocked her off-piste – to mix metaphors.

Now Zelda was following Primrose, unobserved, she hoped.

At first it looked as if she was going to the Golden Lion, as she'd said, but she hurried past it to the lifts. What now? Where was Primrose going? Zelda waited till she got in, then hotfooted it up the stairs to Deck 3, arriving at the same time as the lift. Hanging back, she saw other people and then Primrose getting out. They all seemed to be heading for Illuminations, the venue the three of them had been to earlier that day. It housed the planetarium but it was also a cinema where, billboards showed, a film called *Paranoia* was about to begin. *Paranoia*! How appropriate! Zelda was feeling paranoid on Janet's behalf.

Primrose, she was sure, was out to get her.

But what should she do now? Primrose was hovering, looking around, looking at her watch, looking at her phone. She seemed to be waiting for someone, but suddenly changed her mind – because she'd had a message on her phone? – and went into the cinema.

Zelda considered her options. She could follow Primrose into the cinema and see who she sat with. If she was going to do that, she'd better be quick, as it would be dark in there, and once she'd sat down it would be hard to find her. She could go and see the film herself and see who she left with at the end, if she stayed till the end. Her hunch was that Primrose was meeting Strawberry Blonde to pass on the info she'd extracted from Janet over dinner. She did some calculations. It was nearly eight o'clock. The film, starring Harrison Ford, lasted 106 minutes, and would therefore finish at 9.46. It might be better to come back then and see who came out. Meanwhile she could go to the Golden Lion and wait for a bit to see if Primrose really did join her new friends for the Early Evening Trivia Quiz, which began at 8.15. She did fancy another drink. A couple of glasses at dinner hadn't quite hit the spot, and another glass of red would be welcome.

She headed downstairs, and to her surprise, there was Primrose in the pub already.

Her new quiz mates were greeting her, making room for her in one of the side booths. Mr Flowery Shirt, seen earlier in the jewellery boutique, was among them, the sole male. Another link with Strawberry Blonde! Primrose had moved fast, very fast. She must have made a quick visit to the cinema and then come down again in the lift. So what had she gone into the cinema for? Now Zelda wished she had gone in and tried to see who she'd met there. The quiz was about to begin. The compere was calling the teams to order and quiz sheets were being distributed. Zelda went to the bar, bought a bottle of Malbec, and took the lift up to Janet's suite on Deck 11.

* * *

Viv opened the door when she knocked.

'Is that all you went for?' Viv eyed the bottle.

'Tell you later,' Zelda murmured as she saw Janet approaching.

'You'll tell us now.' Janet led the way to her kitchen for glasses. 'All for one and one for all, may I remind you? We do not have secrets from one another.'

There was no escape so, once seated on comfortable sofas, Zelda told them both exactly what she'd seen, trying to give them facts only, voicing no opinion, showing no emotion, despite the tongue-loosening effect of the delicious red. But once again Janet wasn't impressed.

'How suspicious!' She was sarky when Zelda came to a close. 'Primrose did exactly what she said she'd do. She met her new friends and participated in a quiz.'

'And the quick in and out at the cinema? And the fact that she knows Mr Flowery Shirt too? What do you make of that?' Viv, pouring herself a refill, pushed for a different interpretation.

'To remind another member that the quiz was about to begin? Mr Flowery Shirt perhaps?' Janet held out her glass. 'Or simply pass on a message?'

'About what, for instance?' Viv was trying very hard to make Janet think.

But Janet had moved on to the delights of the wine. It was better, more full-bodied than the plonk they usually drank. Well worth the money. Viv, Zelda was relieved to see, mouthed, 'Talk later.'

14

VIV

'Right, spill,' said Viv as soon as they were in the corridor outside Janet's suite, after receiving assurances that Janet really did want a quiet night in with a book instead of coming with them to hear the Steve Goffe Trio. 'I know what you saw. I want to know what you think.'

Zelda began with her observations of Primrose at dinner. 'She was itching to tell someone what she'd learnt.'

'That's what I thought!'

'So I wondered, "Who does she want to tell?"'

'So did I!'

'So I followed her.'

'Good for you! And?'

They'd reached the lifts and Zelda hadn't yet said anything Viv hadn't guessed.

'Lift or stairs?' Zelda asked.

'Lift if we don't want to be late. We'll do stairs tomorrow. It's getting on.' Viv pressed the down button.

But it was the wrong call. The lift was crowded, making further talk impossible. It was nearly nine o'clock, and clearly a lot of people were heading for the same gig. When they got out of the lift at Deck 3, they only had to follow the crowd to reach the Chart Room where the group were playing. Chart Room sounded dull like a classroom, Viv thought, as they shuffled past walls covered with maps and diagrams, most of them comparing *QM2*'s dimensions with other famous monuments including the Giza Pyramids and Tower Bridge and, well, almost anything. The liner was three times as long as St Paul's Cathedral is tall and four times as long as something else was wide. Entrancing it was not but Zelda actually seemed interested. Or she didn't want to divulge her thoughts while others could hear.

Viv, keen to discuss, hoped there would be time before the gig began.

The Chart Room was, she was pleased to see, a very welcoming bar and a sophisticated nightclub. Low lighting cast a golden glow over comfortable-looking leather seats, clustered informally round the room. They found two together close to the stage where the trio were already tuning their instruments.

'Quick.' Viv turned to Zelda. 'Tell me in thirty seconds flat what conclusions you came to, after your sleuthing, Miss Marple.'

But Zelda's attention was elsewhere. It took a repeat of the question to extract from her that she thought Primrose had gone into the cinema to consult with Strawberry Blonde, and probably did, though only briefly, and that she planned to go back to Illuminations when the film ended to see if Strawberry Blonde came out.

'What time does the film end?'

Zelda didn't answer.

Viv glanced sideways to check she'd got her hearing aids in, which she had. 'I said what time does the film end?' She tapped Zelda's hand because she obviously wasn't listening.

Zelda was transfixed by a dog, or maybe its owner.

The group, comprising a pianist, a percussionist and a cellist, had started to play a Dave Brubeck number, 'Take Five', probably their most famous piece, and they were playing it well in Viv's uninformed opinion. The only one snag was the hypnotic quality of the repetitive rhythm, which would send her to sleep if she didn't pay attention, and she needed to stay awake, because if anyone was going to see who came out of the cinema it would have to be her. Viv reached for her phone to take a surreptitious look at the Daily Programme and see what time the film ended:

9.46. She would have to keep an eye on the time, because Zelda was otherwise engaged.

Then it clicked. This was the cellist who'd played in the Animus Quartet last night, the one who'd invited Zelda for a drink, and been ignored while she listened in on Primrose and Strawberry Blonde. But he had her full attention now and Viv could see why. He had a dog, always a plus with Zelda, but he was easy on the eye too, as well as talented. He was one of those men who become more attractive as their hair recedes a little, exposing a brainy forehead, glowing now with his exertions, veins prominent. When the piece ended and the applause had died down, the young fair-haired pianist stood up and thanked the audience and then said that he wanted to thank all his fellow players, but in particular the versatile cellist, Richard Williams, who had stepped in at the last minute because their regular bass player had suddenly been indisposed. There was another round of applause, and Zelda clapped enthusiastically.

'Is that him?' Viv asked a stupid question.

'Yup.' Zelda clapped on.

'A man of many talents?'

'Yup.' She kept on clapping.

Zelda looked smitten. Who was she smitten by, was the question, the man or his dog?

Viv glanced at her phone – half past nine. 'You stay here,' she said when she managed to get Zelda's full attention. 'I mean when the gig's over. Don't worry about checking on you-know-who. Go and do some bridge-building. Ask the man if you can stroke his dog for an opener. I'll do the sleuthing tonight.'

15

ZELDA

Zelda appreciated Viv's offer as she was in a bit of a tizz.

It wasn't just that she was longing to pat Billie and didn't know if Richard would let her, it was also some other unfamiliar feelings. Billie was in work-mode anyway, wearing her harness as she lay at Richard's feet, so there was no point in asking. And even if Billie was off duty, he'd probably refuse her, after the way she'd behaved in the Golden Lion, giving the impression she was more interested in the people behind her than she was in him.

Not true!

The music hadn't helped. 'Take Five' had got to her, stirring up feelings she didn't want or need, and the hypnotic rhythm was still in her head, insisting that something exciting was about to happen; making her want it to happen. She was in a state of suspended animation. Her pulse was racing, for heaven's sake, and not for Billie. She'd had these feelings before, of course, which is why she didn't trust them. They had led her astray too many times. If she fancied the man – she did, there was no point denying it – so what? She'd fancied men before, though not for a long time, and what had that led to? Heartbreak. Again and again. Music reached parts that even wine didn't reach, that was the trouble, and music and wine together

– she'd had both tonight – could be disastrous. What did that character in *Private Lives* say about music taking you to places you didn't want to go?

I'm not going there!

The group were starting to play again, fortunately a jauntier piece. Good. With luck she'd start to feel jaunty too. The pianist was playing the opening chords, Richard and the percussionist, listening attentively, were waiting their turn to come in. Billie looked as if she was listening too.

All I want is my dog-fix, a bit of time with Billie. Yes, when the gig ended she would take her courage in both hands ask Richard if she could pat Billie either now or later, and apologise for being rude when they'd last met. And if that went well she'd ask him to join her for a drink to make amends. She owed him one, after all.

'I'm off.' Viv was sliding out of her seat. 'Good luck.'

'You are coming back?'

'Of course.'

And she did about twenty minutes later as the group's final piece came to a close. Clearly pleased with what she'd found out, she sat down again. 'She *was* in the cinema. She came out on the arm of a man, another older chap, not Mr Flowery Shirt, and I think she was almost certainly in there when Primrose popped in and out.'

No need to ask who she was talking about.

'Now I'm going to see if she meets up with Primrose.' Viv got up again. 'Don't think she'll have gone far if she's still with the old chap. He doesn't move fast. You stay here and get your dog-fix. I'll carry on sleuthing.'

Watching her go, Zelda, still clapping the group, was torn. She wanted to stay and see Richard and put things right with him if she could, but she also wanted to help keep track of Primrose and her maybe-daughter.

Viv was clearly enjoying herself.

* * *

Here goes. It's now or never.

As she approached the cellist, now surrounded by a group of admirers, Zelda told herself that the worst that could happen was that he'd say no. So what? She'd survive. She waited on the edge of the group as first one person, then another, told him how much they'd enjoyed his playing, and questioned him about his dog. She heard him acknowledge their praise with thanks, and politely explain to the ones that asked that no, they couldn't pat Billie or give her dog treats as she was working. Then he interrupted one of the chattier ones to say that he was sorry but he'd have to stop her there as another performer was due to arrive, and he had to get out of the way. With that, he turned away to put his cello into its case.

Zelda was about to take a step forward when he said, 'It's not convenient right now,' nodding in the direction of a steward standing at the side, ready, she assumed, to take the instrument to wherever he wanted it taken.

Push off, that's what he means. But rashly she said, 'It's me, Zelda.'

He said, 'I know it's you, Zelda,' without stopping what he was doing.

Reckless now, she ploughed on. 'I'm sorry if now's not a good time, but I need to say that I'm sorry about how our last meeting ended. I feel bad about it and I'd like to buy you a drink and try to explain. If not now, well, er... later...' She tailed off, disheartened by his lack of interest. He was intent on doing up the catches of the cello case, feeling for them with his long fingers, snapping them shut one by one, snapping *her* shut.

I should go.

But then he looked up and said, 'I guess you'd like to pat Billie?'

She nodded then remembered he couldn't see and said, 'Yes, please.'

'Later then.'

What did that mean? Tonight? Tomorrow? Never? Was he accepting or declining her invitation? As she hovered, the steward approached and Richard asked him to take his cello to his room. Then Billie stood up and Richard reached for her handle. 'Where were you thinking of drinking?'

16

ZELDA

Of course she said she'd go anywhere he wanted and Richard said that here in the Chart Room was fine, quieter than the pub, so better if they wanted to talk. He then said something to Billie that she didn't catch and they – man and dog – led the way to a couple of chairs, more comfortable than they looked, by the curved window at the far end of the ship – the bows? Upholstered in blue velvet, the chairs were either side of a low table and a lamp in the middle cast a golden glow. She caught sight of their reflections in the window, leaning towards each other, looking romantic which it wasn't. The blue and gold décor was elegant, sophisticated even but the atmosphere in the rest of the bar was just as convivial as in the Golden Lion. Not so much here though. Quite full, it was obviously a popular place for late-night drinking, but most people were in the middle of the room, or at the bar, so they had the area near the window to themselves. It was a good choice for privacy. She could say what she'd come to say, without being overheard. He could say what he wanted to say, if anything, but first she must get her dog-fix. Richard loosened Billie's harness and she settled herself between them, her head near Zelda. 'She likes you,' he said, and feeling honoured she reached for Billie's ears. Bliss. She could feel her blood pressure falling, till turning her head she caught a glimpse of a wave, crested with silver by the ship's headlights, crashing against the bows.

Suddenly she was Kate Winslet aboard the *Titanic*.

'No worries. No iceberg.' His voice broke into her thoughts as the bar steward arrived at their table. Could he read her mind?

'You started. Better have a drink to steady your nerves.'

'Yes, but my turn, okay?'

Richard ordered beer. She went for one of the bar's famous Zodiac Cocktails, and they came quickly. Her cocktail, called Free as a Bird, was described in the menu as 'a free-spirited concoction reflecting Sagittarians' optimistic spirit'. Delicious, it was a mix of brandy, peach liqueur, lime juice and vanilla syrup. She told him she wasn't a Sagittarian but it gave her four of her five fruit and veg a day. He laughed, though not completely getting it, she thought, and when she started to explain her rudeness last time, he waved away her worries.

'No, hear me out, please,' she insisted. 'I don't usually listen in on other people's conversations, not when I'm with someone, though sometimes, because I'm nosy, I do when I'm on my own. But, to get to the point,' she lowered her voice because another couple had moved onto the next table, 'the woman in the booth behind me that night, well, she had gate-crashed our table at dinner saying she was a poor widow travelling alone who didn't know anyone. And yet there she was talking to someone she obviously knew very well, so clearly she'd been lying. I was cross, that's all – and interested. Why would she lie? Sorry. Again. But finished. Now I'm all yours.'

He raised an eyebrow.

'Oh no! I didn't mean…'

He shook his head. 'I think that before you got distracted you said that when we got to New York you were heading for North Carolina?'

She couldn't fault his memory.

'So why North Carolina?' He took a mouthful of beer.

'My dad lives there.'

She gave him a bit of her family history, including the bit about her father being a GI based in the UK during the Second World War. Then he gave her some of his.

'I think my dad was also a GI based in the UK in World War II.'

'You've never found out?' She was incredulous.

He shook his head.

'But your dad and my dad could have been in the same squadron. They might have known each other. You can find out, you know. What's your dad's name?'

'Richard Williams, same as mine. What's your full name, by the way?'

'Zelda Fielding, but that's...' She didn't really want to say that was her name by her third marriage, so changed course. 'I was born Griselda Mayhew, but quickly became Zelda. My mum, unmarried at the time, didn't take my father's name because he'd gone back to America before I was born. My dad is Samuel Eliot Richardsen.'

He said, 'I know some Richardsens.'

'Where do they live?'

A second Free as a Bird helped their conversation along. Richard ordered the next round along with a bowl of water for Billie, and he switched from beer to a cocktail called Stout Independence. Was he making a point, she wondered? They ascertained that although he lived in the same town as her family, he didn't know her dad or Cynthia, her half-sister, but he did know some of the places she'd been to with them. When they'd finished their second drink, he said that if she didn't mind he'd call it a day as he had rehearsals early next morning, and she felt dismissed, though he did say, 'Let's do this again sometime,' as he got to his feet.

Was he just being polite? Probably. She waited a moment, wondering if he would ask her to take his arm to give Billie a rest. When he didn't, she thought of offering but then thought that might offend his spirit of stout independence. She'd picked up that if Richard Williams wanted help he'd ask for it. If she offered, he might think that she thought he was incapable of finding his own way back, like a drunk or, heaven forbid, that she was importuning him. *I'm all yours.* How stupid was that! She heard her own words in her ears and felt herself blushing all over again as she watched him putting on Billie's harness and taking hold of her handle.

'Good night. Forward, Billie.' He was off before she'd said good night back, without as much as a touch of his hand or a peck on the cheek.

As she made her way back from Deck 3 to their cabin on Deck 11, she hoped Viv would still be awake. There was so much to talk about! She was all at sea, ha ha! Her admiration for Richard grew as she navigated flights of stairs and narrow corridors.

Unfortunately Viv was fast asleep but she'd left a message, hand written, on Zelda's pillow beside the heart-shaped chocolate.

Hope you had a lovely evening. Stayed awake as long as I could cos bursting with news. They're sharing! They're in a cabin together on Deck 6. I saw them both go in!!! More in morning.

Who? What? It took Zelda a moment or two to work out what she meant.

17

VIV

Friday, 18 December

Viv was bursting to tell Zelda what she'd found out. How long was she going to sleep? As she made tea next morning, none too quietly, she recalled her evening's exploits.

After leaving Zelda to sort things out with the dishy cellist, Viv had looked into the Golden Lion where she'd seen Primrose taking part in another Trivia Quiz, just as she'd said. Janet would be pleased. Deciding to stay till the quiz ended, she'd got herself a drink and tucked herself into a booth some way away, but where she could keep an eye. At the end of the quiz, when Primrose had said goodbye to her fellow quizzers, she'd followed her, at a distance of course, to see where she went next – the lift. Reluctant to get in with her, she had hotfooted it up the stairs as fast as she could, and three flights later, now out of breath, she had seen Primrose emerge from the lift on Deck 6. The next bit had been trickier, following her along a narrow corridor with cabin doors on either side till she'd opened one of them and disappeared inside. Would anyone join her, that was the question, or was there another person already inside? She'd had a hunch all evening that Primrose and Strawberry Blonde were sharing and guessed that the younger woman would be later to bed. So she'd waited, near the lift, and her hunch had proved right!

'Are you brewing that tea or stewing it?' Zelda was wide awake. 'I'm all ears.'

A rapid update followed as they sat side by side in their beds, with Zelda avid for detail. 'What time was this?'

'It was 11 p.m. precisely when Strawberry Blonde got out of the lift.'

'*And*?' Zelda prompted. 'What did you do next?'

'I watched her as she made her way down the corridor, stopping once to take off her stilettos – her feet were clearly killing her – and then I followed as discreetly as I could, and I'm almost certain she went into the same room that Primrose did.'

'*Almost certain*?' Zelda pulled a face.

'I'm as sure as dammit, Zelda. I followed her as far as I dared, nearly to her door.'

'But you're not 100 per cent sure it was the same door?'

'N-no.' That she had to admit. All the cabin doors looked the same and she hadn't got close enough to see the numbers.

'I buy it, Viv. I bet you're right but it's going to take more than that to convince Janet that the two are sharing. She will say they could have gone into neighbouring cabins, that you were mistaken, and that...'

'...I'd got a down on poor Primrose colouring my perceptions?'

'Exactly.'

'So?' Viv got out of bed with her empty cup.

'We keep schtum till we've got more evidence.' Zelda got out of bed too, to get herself another cuppa, while Viv had first dibs at the shower.

They were all meeting for breakfast at nine. Viv didn't like not being open with Janet and nor did Zelda, but they agreed it would be counter-productive to share with her at the moment.

Breakfast might be difficult.

* * *

Janet was cheery, too cheery for nine o'clock in the morning.

Viv hoped the effort wasn't killing her as they embarked on another five-course marathon breakfast. It was Day 3 already, Janet reminded them, wielding the Daily Programme, and they mustn't waste a moment. She'd started planning her day. What did they fancy? There was so much going on. She'd ruled out the talk on Nutrition and Ageing – 'Not what I need at the moment!' – but was definitely going to the talk by Dr Jeffrey Hoffman, the famous astronaut who had mended the Hubble Space Telescope. Janet was into space exploration, Viv remembered with renewed surprise. She'd been on lots of courses about it. Firmly of the opinion that the money could be better spent here on Planet Earth – notwithstanding the huge advances in non-stick saucepan technology that it had brought about – Viv usually glazed over when Janet regaled them with not-so-interesting facts. Viv didn't need to know that every major galaxy was anchored by a black hole, and wasn't sure what a black hole was if it hadn't been dug with a spade.

But now she listened happily as Janet enthused about the famous scientist Viv had never heard of. How lucky they were to be able to see and listen to him in person, and see footage of the three space walks he'd made, and learn all about Hubble's greatest discoveries, which included helping to pin down the age of the universe to 13.8 billion years, which was roughly three times the age of Earth!

'It's all right, Viv, you don't have to come,' Janet said when she'd finished. 'I know you're not interested.'

'I'll come.' Zelda sounded almost as keen as Janet.

'And so will I. All for one.' If it was totally boring she'd switch off and think about something else, like asking Primrose how her husband had died. Again. When she'd first asked Primrose didn't seem to know, which was more than a bit odd.

18

VIV

The talk was surprisingly fascinating.

Viv found it hard to concentrate on what she really wanted to do – keep a look-out for Primrose and Strawberry Blonde. It didn't help that it was dark most of the time. The presentation was in Illuminations, the cinema where the two of them had had their last secret rendezvous. Would they turn up for the famous scientist? Probably not, Viv thought, but she kept a look-out, easy when the lights were up, impossible when they were down for the film footage, which was even more fascinating than the talk. Dr Hoffman, now an attractive silver-haired septuagenarian, was an articulate speaker. How proud he must feel watching his younger self floating around in space carrying out amazing engineering feats. At the end, along with Janet and Zelda, she joined the long queue to buy the man's book – Patrick would like it – and then another to get it signed. Dr Hoffman was flanked by his wife or partner, who looked ready to ward off any over-enthusiastic space-groupies. Wise woman.

There was no sign of Primrose.

* * *

The three of them went their separate ways after a coffee, agreeing to reconvene in the Kings Court Buffet for lunch at one. Janet said she was going back to her room to start reading Dr Hoffman's book. Zelda headed for a talk on Secrets of Great Hair in the Winter Garden – hoping for tips to pass on to the girls in the salon – and Viv took herself to a class called Yoga – Basic Moves in Canyon Ranch Fitness Centre. She was missing the exercise she got from gardening, and thought yoga might be what she needed. She didn't see Primrose or Strawberry Blonde in yoga and Zelda texted that she hadn't seen either of them in Secrets of Great Hair. They weren't at lunch either.

Mid-afternoon though, when Janet was in a Watercolour Art Class and Zelda was chilling out back in the cabin, Viv saw Primrose coming out of the Chart Room with another woman. Stepping to one side, because she'd been on her way in for a cup of tea, Viv saw Primrose say goodbye to the woman, and then walk toward the staircase linking Decks 3 and 4 where Strawberry Blonde was clearly waiting. They had a few words before going their separate ways, Primrose up to Deck 4, Strawberry Blonde towards the Veuve Clicquot Champagne Bar on Deck 3. Their exchange had lasted seconds – the word *furtive* came to mind. The two of them were definitely in cahoots. For the first time ever, Viv found herself wanting Primrose to join them for dinner – so she could put her on the spot.

* * *

Primrose was already at their table in the Britannia restaurant, presiding it looked like. What a bloody cheek! 'Do sit down.' She had her back to the gigantic tapestry of the *QM2*, and had clearly been looking out for them. Like a spider looking for flies, Viv couldn't help thinking. She was in black as usual.

'How are you, Primrose?' Janet greeted her warmly. 'What sort of day did you have?'

'I had a *lovely* day, thank you,' the spider replied, 'and I hope you did too.'

Janet and Zelda both said they had, and Janet gave her a rundown of hers. Primrose said she was sorry she'd missed the Dr Hoffman talk but she'd been in the library swotting for the next quiz from the latest Guinness Book of Records.

Viv saw an opening. 'Did you win, Primrose? I think I saw you coming out of the quiz this afternoon. Was it in the Chart Room?'

'Yes, it was,' she looked thoughtful, 'but sadly our team was wiped out. Never mind, the game's the thing, isn't it? Taking part and all that.'

They all agreed that it was but Viv decided to push it.

'Then I saw you chatting with someone who looked so like you, she could have been your daughter.'

Primrose fidgeted in her seat.

'You both had the same wonderful bone structure.'

Primrose picked up her menu.

Janet glared at Viv. 'Let's make our choices, shall we?'

The next few minutes were spent perusing menus and discussing dishes, with Primrose obviously relieved by the change of subject.

But Viv could tell she was worried. A nerve under the distinctive cheekbones jumped up and down as she said it was so hard to choose and what was Janet having? Janet said she might just have a starter, as she really couldn't eat another full meal, and Primrose said she would too. Of course, they were playing Snap again. It was chicken and leek terrine with beetroot salad and mustard mayonnaise for both of them, with maybe a dessert to follow. Primrose put her hand over her glass, when the wine steward brought the Pinot Grigio Janet had ordered earlier.

Janet said, 'Please, Primrose, we're friends.'

Primrose uncovered her glass and the steward filled it, and then just as the glass reached her lips, Zelda said, 'Have you got children, Primrose?'

Primrose spluttered, spraying wine, fortunately white, over the tablecloth.

Perfect timing! Thank you, Zelda.

Janet offered her napkin. Primrose accepted, and while they were dabbing, Viv signalled her thanks to Zelda, who gave her a smiley I-don't-know-what-you-mean look back. Janet then beckoned the waiter who topped up Primrose's glass and they began to eat. Janet said the terrine was delicious. Primrose picked at hers silently and emptied her refilled glass quite quickly. They were halfway through their starters when Primrose paused, a piece of beetroot on the end of her fork, and said, 'I'm afraid I must confess to a wee white lie.'

They all stopped eating. Was this going to be in vino veritas, Viv wondered as Primrose took a deep breath. 'I am not, I need to tell you, travelling alone, and yes, Zelda, I do have children, a child, a daughter.'

Janet said she was sure Primrose had her reasons for not telling them before.

Primrose said that indeed she had and she hoped they would understand. There was no way she could have afforded to come on this trip by herself so she was in fact travelling with her daughter, Isabella, who had spotted the bargain and booked the trip, and urged her to come with her.

'But,' she paused while the waiter refilled her glass, 'Isabella did not want it to be known that she was travelling with her mother. She thought it would cramp her style, so I agreed to pretend that I wasn't. Sadly,' she took a sip of her wine, 'Isabella has never found true love in her life and hopes to meet a special someone on this trip, so I didn't want to argue with her.'

She said Isabella could be difficult. Janet said her son could too. Primrose said she thought Isabella's problems were the result of childhood trauma. She hadn't been the same since her daddy died. Janet said Grant hadn't got that excuse.

How? How did her daddy die? Viv hoped she'd come to that.

They got more of her story as the meal progressed. Mal, Primrose's husband and, of course, Isabella's daddy had died when they had been living with her parents in Edinburgh and Mal was working in London. The plan had been that he would come back to Edinburgh when he had his degree, get a good job and buy them their own little house. 'But that never happened.' She found a tissue and dabbed her eyes.

Viv felt a pang of sympathy. Poor Primrose must have been in her twenties when she was left alone with a child.

'My parents stepped into the breach fortunately, because I went completely to pieces and may have neglected Isabella for a while. The three of them became very close. They adored their wee granddaughter and maybe even spoiled her to make up for her loss. And she of course adored her nanna and pops, who gave her everything she asked for and paid for her education. We carried on living with my mother and father and I'm afraid I let my father, who was an accountant, look after my financial affairs till he died six years ago, so I'm not very good with money...'

She paused for a moment while the steward cleared her plate, beginning again as soon as he'd gone, though Janet assured her that they all understood now, and she really didn't have to. But she was like a burst dam and the words came rushing out. She now relied on Isabella to help her with matters financial, though she wasn't sure that was wise, because Isabella wasn't very good with money either. Sadly she wasn't a liberated woman like the three of them which is why she admired them so much, and she really didn't think she could do her own banking now because they were closing all the branches and as for internet banking she hadn't a clue.

Pause, at last, for main courses to be delivered, well, for those who were having them. Then, when she and Primrose weren't eating, Janet told her that her career, well, her second career had been in banking, when she gave up nursing to be PA to Malcolm, her first husband, who was a bank manager. She could therefore recommend one or two internet-only accounts that were easy to handle if Primrose was interested. 'And I'm sure you are capable of managing your own account if you'd like to learn. I could help.'

Primrose said she was sure she couldn't.

Did she do anything for herself? Viv wondered. Surely she had her own bank account, for her pension to be paid into, and as a single parent she must have worked for a living. She would have needed a bank account for her wages to be paid into. She'd never mentioned a job though. It was one of quite a lot of things they didn't know about Primrose. Was Zelda having similar thoughts? She looked thoughtful, as she tucked into her sole meunière, so it wasn't a surprise when she asked one of her astute questions.

'Did you say it was your daughter's idea to come on this trip?'

'Yes,' said Primrose.

'Why?' Zelda smiled her sweet smile. 'Why did she invite you when she knew you would cramp her style?'

Primrose looked like a rabbit facing a weasel.

'What an odd question.' Janet glared at Zelda. 'Not to say rude. Primrose has already said they needed to share costs, just like you and Viv.' She picked up her menu, then put it down again, saying she didn't want a dessert, 'But you're all welcome to join me in my room after dinner for coffee and petits fours.'

Viv held her breath, not sure if she wanted Primrose to decline so they could analyse the evening's revelations in her absence, or accept so they could question her further.

'Thank you, Janet,' Primrose accepted. 'On this occasion I would love to. There is something else I'd like to share with you.'

What was she going to say now?

19

JANET

Janet felt sorry for Primrose and shocked by Viv and Zelda's rudeness.

It was unfortunate that Primrose had lied, but understandable in the circumstances. Poor lady to lose her husband when they were both so young, leaving her with a child to bring up alone. Primrose had had a difficult life. But what was she going to say now? Fearing further harrowing disclosures, Janet opened the door to her suite with trepidation.

Primrose followed her to the kitchen but Viv and Zelda went straight into the sitting room area and collapsed onto a sofa. What on earth had got into them? She almost wished they'd declined her invitation and couldn't believe she was thinking this about her closest friends. But they were acting out of character. What was Zelda *doing* asking that odd question? Putting Primrose on the spot.

James the butler had already made the coffee but then left as she had requested when she'd texted him earlier. She really didn't want him standing around, like a latter-day Jeeves, while she entertained her friends. Having a butler wasn't her style, whatever the others said about her lady-of-the-manor tendencies. You couldn't talk freely with a butler at your elbow, and she'd much rather pour the coffee herself, which she was doing when Primrose suddenly thrust her phone in front of her face, making her overfill the cup and pour coffee onto the worktop.

'Mal and me on the happiest day of my life.' Primrose sighed.

It took a few moments to look again at the photo Primrose was holding in front of her and recover, because for several seconds she had thought she was looking at a photograph of her own wedding to Malcolm. How had Primrose got hold of that, she'd wondered.

Now she could see why. The groom did look remarkably like Malcolm and the bride looked a lot like she had done on her wedding day. A very young Primrose wore a traditional white gown, fifties-style, high-necked, small-waisted with a sticky-out skirt, just like the one she had worn. The groom wore a kilt like Malcolm had. The photo was black and white so she couldn't be sure, but it looked as if it might be the Carmichael plaid, blue and green with a red and yellow stripe. But it was the face that still disturbed her a bit. Primrose's Mal looked so like Malcolm on his wedding day, though younger. Malcolm had been in his mid-twenties when he married her. She recalled Primrose saying that her Mal had been a student when they got married.

Primrose was putting her phone in her bag. 'Have you got any photos of your wedding, Janet?'

'No.' Janet's answer was automatic as she cleaned up the spilt coffee with kitchen paper. For the last seven years she had been trying to forget her first husband. She'd binned all the photos of him that she hadn't sent to Grant when he'd asked for some to show the grandchildren. But, she had a thought as she carried the tray of coffees into the sitting area, there might be one on her phone. And she suddenly felt she *did* want to compare hers with Primrose's and assure herself the two men were different. Aeons ago, when she thought she was happily married, she'd posted one on Facebook when someone on there started a wedding day feature.

Primrose followed her into the sitting room where Viv and Zelda were now sitting upright, looking very alert.

'Help yourself, everyone.' Janet put the tray on the coffee table and sat down opposite them. 'There are petits fours as well.'

'Do sit down, Primrose.'

She was hovering, which was irritating.

'Well,' Viv reached for a cup of coffee, 'can Zelda and I know what made you gasp back there?'

'Gasp? I didn't.'

'Yes, you did. We thought you'd dropped the pot.'

'It was this.' Primrose, now sitting beside her, reached across the table, holding out her phone. 'My wedding photograph, which astonished Janet for some reason.'

As Zelda took Primrose's phone from her hand, looked and then handed it to Viv, Janet found the photo she was looking for on her phone, posted on Facebook at some point. She was relieved to see that though Malcolm looked a lot like Mal, the resemblance wasn't as marked as she'd first thought. Malcolm had a lot less hair for a start. It was receding by then and he'd been bald by the time he was thirty.

Now she admitted she might have gasped. 'I was taken aback because Primrose's Mal looked so much like Malcolm, and I still think they could be related. If I didn't know that Malcolm was an only child, I would say they were brothers. What do you two think?' She held out her phone so Viv and Zelda could see – and Primrose snatched it from her hand. There was no other word for it.

Viv swore.

'S-sorry.' Primrose seemed surprised at herself, but held onto the phone.

Janet had thought of Primrose as a passive person, like she had been when she'd been married to Malcolm. Anything for a quiet life, had been her motto. That's why she had empathised with Primrose. She used to let other people make decisions for her and she'd thought Primrose was the same. But now she was seeing a different side, one she hadn't seen before. Or maybe she had? She remembered that 'May I join you?' on their first night. She'd admired her assertiveness.

Pushy, Viv had called her, and pushy she was now. And grabby, though now sounding more polite. 'May I?' Primrose reached out for her own phone, now in Zelda's hand, and studied both photos intently, looking from one to the other. 'Yes,' she said as if thinking aloud. 'Yes. Y-yes. Like this, I think.' She pressed her finger on Janet's wedding photograph.

'What the hell are you doing?' Viv swore again.

Janet couldn't believe what she'd just seen, Primrose forwarding the photo to herself – or someone else?

'I thought I'd like a copy, that's all. Hope I did it right. I'm such a silly.' Primrose handed the phone back to Janet with an expression on her face that Janet had never seen before.

It was a turning down of the bottom lip that said *I don't like you*. It didn't last long but the message was clear. Then she stood up, smiling. 'I really must be going.'

'I think you should.' Viv stood up too.

'So nice of you to invite me, Janet. Good night, everyone.' Primrose picked up her handbag, headed for the door and left.

What was all that about?

Janet was glad to see her go but she wanted her friends to stay. Shaken, she needed them by her but Viv was heading for the door too.

'Where's Viv going?'

'Where do you think?' Zelda got to her feet.

'Not you too?'

'No, I'm just closing the door!' Viv had left it open. 'Have you got any brandy?'

'Not sure. Why?' Janet went to look in the minibar.

'Because you look as if you need it. What's the matter?' Zelda followed her into the kitchen.

'I can't say.' Janet found three small bottles of cognac in the minibar, and carried them back to the sitting room with shaking hands, and then went back for glasses.

'I th-think Primrose thinks something *preposterous* about Malcolm,' she said after a gulp.

'A brother he never told you about?' Zelda was well versed in family secrets. She'd discovered several of her own. 'I wouldn't worry about that too much. Malcolm might not even have known he had a brother. Babies were hushed up for all sorts of reasons in those days. Perhaps...' She was about to come up with another theory when Viv came back, nearly falling into the room.

'Just as I thought.' She collapsed onto a sofa. 'Straight to Isabella as we now know her to be called, as fast as she could scurry on those strappy little black sandals. The woman was waiting in a booth in the far corner of the Golden Lion, trying to look invisible. They'd obviously planned to meet as soon as Primrose had the info she'd come for.'

'And?' Janet braced herself to hear what she'd been dreading.

'What are the two of them up to, Viv?' Zelda handed her a drink.

Janet took a deep breath. 'Tell me, Viv. What did you find out about Malcolm?'

20

JANET

'Those two are definitely in cahoots.' Viv looked triumphant.

'Is that all?' Janet felt like a flabby balloon.

She'd been pumped up in a state of suspended animation, waiting to hear her worst fear being realised and it hadn't happened. Viv hadn't discovered anything, only confirmed what she and Zelda already suspected, and what she, Janet, now believed was true. Primrose and her daughter had an agenda. What was on it? That's what they needed to know.

'Are they still in the Golden Lion, do you think?' Janet had to know exactly why Primrose had been so disturbed by her wedding photograph, and why it had turned her against her.

'They were when I left.' Viv, cognac in hand, looked relaxed. 'We know now that there's a pattern, brief meetings to pass on info, then they go their separate ways.' She made them sound like a couple of spies. 'I couldn't get close enough to hear what they were saying because the booths both sides of theirs were occupied. That's why I came back.'

Not good enough, Viv. I've got to know what they're up to. Resolved, Janet put her undrunk cognac down and got to her feet. 'I'm going to see if they're still there, on my own if you're not up for it. I need to talk to Primrose.'

Viv looked at Zelda. Zelda looked at Viv, and Viv put down her glass. 'All for one!' she declared, leading the way. But when they got to the Golden Lion, only minutes later because they took the lift down, there was no sign of Primrose or Isabella. The corner booth was empty.

Primrose could be anywhere on the ship, on any one of the thirteen decks, at any one of the myriad of activities taking place night and day.

'Coming in, ladies?' The bartender spotted them standing in the entrance.

'Primrose might come back later.' Viv voiced Janet's hope.

And some soft drinks were free, Zelda reminded them, and were probably a good idea.

'They were here.' Viv led them to the corner booth where the two women had conspired – her word – and the bartender came over for their orders.

Janet sat down facing the main entrance, feeling grateful for her friends' support, but in a state of limbo. On the other side of the table, Zelda was perusing the Daily Programme.

'What's on? We mustn't waste the evening.' Janet spoke to convince herself as much as the others. 'I need something to take my mind off my worries.'

If anything can.

'How about *World War Z*, a film in 3D?' Viv read from Zelda's programme. 'The world is plagued by a mysterious infection turning the whole human population into rampaging mindless zombies. Investigator Gerry Lane treks across the world braving horrific dangers to... Okay,' she laughed as Zelda sighed, 'not that. Just joshing, but it does give perspective?'

But it didn't. Janet felt her world was about to crash.

The barman brought their drinks and they sipped fizzy water, feeling virtuous, but their mood stayed flat. Viv and Zelda wouldn't discuss her fears. There was no point in surmising, they said which was unlike them. They were both usually 'better out than in'.

Zelda said, 'We're going to find out sooner or later, and when we do, we'll deal with it, whatever it is. There's nothing we can't handle. Meanwhile let's find something to do to give ourselves a lift.' Zelda picked up the programme again. At nine o'clock there was live music right here in the bar – a pianist called Patrick Patton was playing light classics – and there was pre-recorded Strict Tempo Music in the Commodore Club on Deck 9. 'Or,' she read aloud, 'acclaimed dance couple, Nadia and Volodymyr from *Strictly Come Dancing*, are giving a special floor show in the Queen's Room at 8.30. How about that, Viv?'

Strange but true, Viv was a big fan of *Strictly*, though she never danced, not even at parties. Viv said she'd give it a go and Janet said she would too, to show willing and because she'd just seen Richard the cellist and his dog standing in the doorway. Zelda hadn't see them and nor had Viv because they both had their backs to the entrance where he was standing but Janet saw him clearly and thought his arrival was an interesting development. Also a diversion. Was he looking for Zelda, she wondered? Was Zelda hoping he'd arrive to hear the classical pianist? Perhaps the evening could be salvaged from disaster after all, for Zelda if not herself.

'The cellist and his dog are here,' she murmured, giving a nod to where they were standing.

Zelda glanced over her shoulder and quickly turned back.

'I'll invite him over, shall I?' Janet went to get up.

'No!' Zelda shook her head. 'I've seen him two nights running now. He'll think I'm chasing him.'

Viv rolled her eyes, then looked over her shoulder. 'Do you think he needs a helping hand?'

'No,' Zelda sounded nervy. 'He knows the layout, so he'll be thinking about where he wants to sit, that's all, and when he's decided he'll tell Billie, that's his dog, where to take him. He'll give her instructions. He doesn't need help.'

Zelda seemed to know a lot about guide dog protocol.

'And if he wanted to see me again he'd have got in touch,' she added, picking up her water.

'How would he do that exactly?' Viv asked.

'By phone like anyone else,' Zelda near-snapped, 'though his is specially adapted for Braille.'

Janet got to her feet, aware she was trying to take her mind off her own fears as much as anything. All this waiting for things to happen was doing her head in – to use a Viv expression.

'Where are you going?' Zelda looked alarmed.

'To invite him to join us, of course. No harm in that, is there? He can say yes or no. I'd like to know the man better even if you don't.'

* * *

Richard Williams was charming in a non-smarmy way and Janet liked him at once. When she introduced herself and explained she was a friend of Zelda's he immediately said that any friend of Zelda's was a friend of his and probably Billie's too. He accepted her invitation with pleasure, saying he'd been hoping to find Zelda in the bar. She told him where the three of them were sitting, and he gave the dog instructions, just as Zelda had said he would, talking to her in a friendly encouraging voice, urging her on. It had reminded her of the way Alan talked to Kenny Dog Leash, no bad thing. He was a kind man.

The bar steward came to their table immediately and greeted Richard by name. He ordered a beer, and Janet told him there was a place beside her opposite Zelda, or would be when she sat down. She introduced him to Viv, then tucked herself into the corner of the booth opposite her, and waited.

Zelda looked icy.

Fascinating. Richard greeted her with a 'Hoped I'd find you here,' then he took off the dog's harness and placed it on the seat beside him. 'You're off duty now, Billie. You can relax.' Janet liked the way he spoke to his dog and to Zelda. 'She's all yours now, honey, if you'd like to fuss her.'

'I don't think so. All mine, I mean, she's very much yours, Richard, but oh!' Zelda seemed to thaw as the dog went and laid her head on her lap.

The dog's personality changed too, it seemed to Janet, as soon as her harness was off. In working mode she'd been attentive and alert to Richard's every need, loyal and dutiful, quiet and calm, totally committed to her role as helper and guide. Out of harness she was puppy-like, waggy-tailed and playful. Clearly enjoying being the centre of attention, she was delighting in Zelda's touch as she fondled her ears. Who was enjoying this most, Janet wondered, Zelda or the dog?

Richard sat down as the barman brought his beer. He'd come to hear Patrick Patton, he said, an excellent pianist who he'd got to know on this trip. Were they interested too? He looked round the table as he spoke, but it seemed to Janet that Zelda was the one he wanted to say yes.

Promising.

She caught Viv's eye, which wasn't difficult because they were sitting opposite each other and Viv was clearly trying to catch hers.

'Zelda's the classics fan, Richard,' Viv stood up, 'though she might need to be reminded that a recital is about to begin, if she's still drooling over Billie. Janet and I are off to see that pair from *Strictly* in the Queen's Room. Might even go to the dancing class afterwards.' Viv finished her drink. Then the two of them gathered their bags and departed, leaving the trio together.

21

ZELDA

Zelda was cross with Viv and Janet, especially Janet.

Though delighted to have Billie's heavy head on her lap, she felt she'd been manoeuvred into this closeness with Richard, who'd probably come in for a quiet drink on his own. It was embarrassing. Janet had been too pushy, like her new pushy friend, or perhaps her former new pushy friend. One possibly good thing about the evening was that Janet seemed less enamoured by Primrose now the odd business with the photographs had opened her eyes a bit. In fact she seemed more worried than ever about what she was up to.

Billie moved her head and looked up at Richard, who was looking at her intently, at *her*, not Billie. Had he just said something she'd missed? Now she feared a repeat of their first meeting. In a minute he'd get up and walk away, *leaving her to her sleuthing*. But she wasn't sleuthing and – oh dear, this was complicated – she wanted him and Billie to stay but Billie was on her way back to his side.

He fondled the dog's ears. 'It's okay, Billie, you're off duty. I was talking to Zelda. I said, "Are you all right?" You can go back.'

Billie came back.

'Sorry, I...' She hadn't heard 'Are you all right?'

Richard covered her hand with his. 'Zelda, what's on your mind? Tell me if you can.'

You, she nearly said but didn't. Did he look at everyone like this? she wondered. She felt his close attention.

'Sorry again,' she was aware of his hand covering hers, 'I just don't know where to start.' Dog talk seemed safest. Billie's head was back on her lap. 'She's beautiful.'

'Can't disagree.' He took his hand off hers and picked up his beer.

'A Labrador, isn't she?' She stroked her ears.

'Yeah, she's a Labrador, the breed best suited to me, I think. I've had sheep dogs and retrievers, three of each, all good dogs, but yeah, I think Billie's special. What kind are yours?'

'Westies, West Highland terriers. They're small dogs but highly intelligent and fiercely loyal.' She was impressed that he remembered she had more than one dog. What would Mack and Morag make of Richard, she wondered, remembering how they'd seen off her last two suitors, if that was the right word. 'I'm missing them as I've already said, and can't help worrying about them.'

'Are they in kennels?'

'No, they're with my stepdaughter and my grandson.'

'I hope they're getting on.'

'So do I. Albert's a toddler and tends to think they're cuddly toys.'

'They don't like cuddles?'

'Not when they're having their dinner.'

He said that Billie, trained to put up with almost anything, liked to enjoy her meals in peace, which of course, being a Labrador, she wolfed down. 'Then she asks for more! Like me.' He held out his empty glass as the barman appeared.

* * *

A fresh beer in his hand, Richard changed the subject, but back to one they'd touched on before. 'How's the detective work going?'

'Do you really want to know?' She had a delicious glass of Pinot Grigio in hers.

'I'm intrigued and not above a bit of gossip, I can assure you. Update me, please. Is the gate-crasher in league with the gold digger?'

Gold digger – had she called Primrose's daughter a gold digger in his hearing?

'Do you mean who I mean?' she had to ask.

'I think I do,' he said. 'The one behind you on Thursday night with the rasping voice?'

'I'd call it a hiss. But how...'

'...do I know? Well, I listen, I'm good at that, and staff, the stewards, they see everything, and *they* gossip, and I listen to them. Nothing much goes on that they don't know about. And Carlos in the jewellery boutique knows more passengers' finances than most. Is that useful?'

'Sure is!'

He tilted his head slightly to one side.

'What's up?' It was her turn to ask.

'Nothing,' he smiled, 'just the way you said *sure is*, like an American.'

'Oh.' She did that sometimes when she liked someone. It was a bit of a giveaway. She picked up on their accent or their intonation or even the words they used. It helped when she was learning foreign languages, but only if she liked the teacher. 'Has Carlos come across her of the rasping voice?'

'He has.' He took a sup of beer. 'She's in and out of the jewellery boutique all the time, desperate for cash, he thinks. She tried to sell him a not very good ring on day one and he had to explain they don't buy, only sell. Since then she's lured a couple of old guys into the boutique to woo them into buying her expensive items of jewellery.'

'Were they wooed?'

He laughed. 'Not sure. I'll ask for an update.'

'She's gate-crasher's daughter and they're sharing a cabin. Viv tracked them down.' Zelda described Viv's exploits, and he laughed again.

'Sounds as if they're up to no good.'

'That's what we think, even Janet now, because...' She hesitated, wondering how much to tell him. 'We think, well, I think, that they know more about Janet than they've picked up on this trip. I think they're here because they knew Janet would be here too and they've got something on her late husband, her first, that is, which, if it's true, could devastate her.' She didn't say precisely what. 'Janet's late husband and Primrose's have similar names, possibly the same, which is weird.'

Richard nodded and put down his glass, feeling for the edge of the table as he did, reminding her briefly that he couldn't see, then spoke thoughtfully. 'I may be able to find out more, but we need to be 100 per cent certain that we are talking about the same people. Can you tell me their names? As I said, staff see everything, in and out of rooms all day cleaning and tidying.'

'Oh no!'

'What?'

'Nothing.' She'd left her knickers on the floor.

He laughed. 'And the suspects' names?'

'Primrose and Isabella Carmichael.'

He took a mouthful of beer. 'I miss a lot visually, Zelda, but sometimes pick up on things that others don't. Think of me as a bat, using echo-location to get my bearings. I can tell when there's someone in a room, and if they speak, which direction they're looking in.'

That explained a lot.

'And people often don't see me, or if they do they think I don't know that they're there. They forget I can hear.'

'Then they're stupid...'

'Patrick's tuning up. Let's enjoy the music, shall we? And if you're worried look at my ears. I'm a long-eared bat, not a vampire.'

22

JANET

It was eleven o'clock when Janet returned to her suite, tired and she hoped squiffy enough to fall asleep, but not so squiffy she'd wake up two hours later. She'd had a convivial time with Viv, watching the *Strictly* floor show in the stylish Queen's Room and too many cocktails had helped her worries subside. A bit. At a tenner a time, the White Peach Bellinis, the cheapest item on the menu, had been an expensive amnesiac but as Viv had said frequently, 'What the hell, you only live once!' Nadia and Volodymyr had been very entertaining, giving it their all, and had even got them onto their feet at the end of the show, for a lesson on the Argentinian Tango. You cannot worry while attempting to do the Argentinian tango. They'd left when Nadia invited them to stay on for the Black and White Ball which was about to begin.

Earlier on Viv had dismissed her worries about Primrose not liking her. She thought the expression on her face wasn't necessarily dislike, but so what if it were? That would be a plus. They would be back to their original table for three. Viv had advised taking the – 'mad cow?' – by the horns and asking Primrose straight out what had upset her about the wedding photograph. 'What can she tell you that's worse than you know already?'

God knows, Janet thought, as she pulled on her pyjamas. You would have to have been married to Macolm to understand the enormity of that question. She had learned a lot about Malcolm since he'd died. Going through his clothes had been revealing. Slowly she'd realised he'd been a serial philanderer and stasher-away of money. It had made grieving for him complicated and difficult. But she'd been pretty sure she knew all about his family whom she'd visited a couple of times. They had come south for the wedding. Well, his mother and father had but no other family members. No aunts or uncles or sisters or brothers or grandparents. Malcolm didn't want a big wedding. Nor did she. That's why they'd married down south in the town where they both worked, and went to church. She'd assumed he was an only child because he had never mentioned a brother or sister, and his best man had been someone he'd worked with in London.

But he might have had a brother, even a twin, whom he hadn't told her about, who he didn't even know about. That seemed to be the most likely theory considering how alike Mal and Malcolm were. Viv had so-what-ed? again. She'd shrugged her shoulders. Perhaps the brother had been given away before Malcolm was born, because he'd been born out of wedlock. Or the family didn't talk about him because he'd done something they were ashamed of. Stranger things had happened. Viv was a big fan of *Long Lost Family* and *Who Do You Think You Are?* She'd shrugged again. 'So what if Primrose was married to Malcolm's brother, Janet? That makes you sisters-in-law. That's not the end of the world, is it? You like her, don't you?'

'I thought I did.'

She'd also shared with Viv her recurring worry since discovering Malcolm's philandering past, that he might have fathered more children and one or more of them would turn up and demand compensation. Viv had sympathised with that – this was close to home – but said this couldn't be the case here as Mal and Malcolm were obviously the same generation. She had reiterated that it would be best to ask Primrose straight out what her problem was. 'Do it tomorrow night at dinner while Zelda and I are there to lend support.'

Plan in place, Janet had a drink of water and got into bed feeling slightly better than she had earlier in the evening, though she hadn't shared her biggest fear. Too tired to read, she was reaching to put out the light, when there was a disconcerting knock at the door.

She lay quietly for a bit hoping it was a mistake, that someone even more squiffy than she was had knocked on the wrong door as they meandered down the corridor. With a bit of luck they would realise their mistake or get fed up and move on. But they didn't. Whoever it was knocked again. Insistently. They called her name.

It must be Viv or Zelda, she thought at first, though it didn't sound like either of them.

'Janet! Are you awake?'

A shiver ran through her as she thought she detected an Edinburgh accent. But the door muffled the sound, so hoping she was mistaken she got out of bed. It was most likely Viv or Zelda she still thought. One of them must have locked herself out of their room and couldn't make the other one hear. Her assistance was needed, a bed for the night maybe, and there was a spare in her suite. Tentatively, she went to the door, aware she was in her pyjamas.

'Who is it?'

'Primrose.'

She took a step back.

'It's very late, Primrose. I've gone to bed. Let's talk in the morning.'

'But I need to talk to you now, Janet.' She sounded upset.

'Need.' The word tugged at something deep inside her. It always did. She opened the door a crack, and that she realised, but only later, was silly. There was Primrose, her face creased with anxiety, and standing behind her, towering over her, was Isabella, a feathery black fascinator topping her monumental hairdo. Mother and daughter both wore long, glittery evening dresses, as if they were on their way to a glamorous event. They were of course, the Black and White Ball. She remembered Nadia's announcement. Primrose was in her signature black, Isabella in white except for her feathery head gear which made her look like a crow.

'W-what do you want, Primrose?'

'We'll come in first, shall we?' Isabella opened the door so Janet had to step aside, and Primrose scurried in after her. Surely they wouldn't stay long. Janet felt at a disadvantage in her cotton pyjamas. But Isabella flung herself onto a sofa.

'Over to you, Mummy,' she patted the seat beside her, 'but shall we have a nightcap first, Janet? I've heard the minibars in these suites are well-stocked.'

Janet wondered where she'd put her mobile before getting into bed. She needed Viv or Zelda here or both.

Her phone wasn't in the kitchen where she hoped she'd left it charging. As she got glasses, and then a bottle of Pinot Grigio from the fridge, and water for herself she remembered she'd plugged it in by the side of her bed.

'Here, help yourselves.' The glasses tinkled alarmingly as, with shaking hands, she put the tray on the coffee table in front of her uninvited guests. 'I, er... need the loo.'

But when she got to her bedroom, she found her phone with the battery still flat and not charging. And neither Viv nor Zelda answered when she rang them on the fixed phone by the bed. Returning to the sitting room, she found Primrose perched on the edge of the sofa next to Isabella, who looked as if she'd settled in for the night. Laid back, literally, her arms were stretched along the back of the blue sofa, red nails hooked like bloody claws.

'Tell her, Mummy.'

Primrose twirled the wedding ring on her finger. 'Let Janet sit down first, dear.'

Janet sat down opposite them.

'I don't know how to say this.' Primrose fidgeted.

'Just tell her.' Isabella leaned forward to refill her glass from the bottle on the table.

'Yes, tell me, Primrose.' Janet braced herself.

'Well.' Primrose shuffled in her seat. 'First of all I must confess to another wee fib. When I said I was a widow like you, it was because I *felt* like a widow like you and I very much wanted to join your merry throng, and part of me thought I was one—'

'Get on with it, Primrose.' Janet couldn't take much more.

'Sorry,' said Primrose, 'this isn't easy...'

'For me neither, Primrose, and there was no need for you to lie. I always think honesty is the best policy. If you'd simply said you were a woman on your own...'

'Mummy, just tell her.' Isabella looked at her watch.

Janet finished her sentence, '...I would still have made you welcome.'

'You're very kind, and I wish I had.' Primrose picked up her glass and took a sip. 'I wish I'd said right from the start what is the honest truth, that I didn't know if I was a widow or not. I felt like a widow because I'd been told I was a widow, but I've always clung to the hope that Mal was alive and well. Somewhere. And that he'd come back and find me. Us. Find us.' She looked over her shoulder at Isabella.

'But you said Mal died young?' Janet waited for another 'wee fib'.

'B-because that's what I thought, that's what I'd been told,' Primrose nodded, 'when he disappeared.'

'Disappeared?'

'Give her the facts, Mummy.'

Primrose took a deep breath. 'Mal married me, in 1965, rather hurriedly I'm afraid, because I must admit I was a few weeks pregnant with Isabella, and my parents urged us on. As I've said, we were childhood sweethearts and I was still at school when... but that doesn't matter. Mal was a student in London but keen to do the right thing. His parents weren't so keen, but we had a proper church wedding with bridesmaids and everything. Then, after a short honeymoon on the Isle of Skye, Mal went back to university to complete his degree, but he kept in close touch and came to see us frequently. He visited every few weeks – my parents who we were living with paid for his train fares – till, suddenly, he didn't. He'd got a job, a very good job he said, too good to turn down, in a bank in London, so Isabella and I would have to move south to be with him. But before we could he vanished.'

'Vanished?' Janet was trying hard to follow.

Primrose nodded. 'I last heard from him in 1971, in a letter. We wrote letters then, didn't we?' she said wistfully. 'But nothing at all since then.'

I married Malcolm in 1971.

'Get to the point, Mummy.' Isabella looked at her watch again.

'So, what we would like to know is, when and where you were "married" to Malcolm' – she did inverted commas in the air – 'if you were married to him, I mean.' Primrose looked apologetic.

'*If* I were married to Malcolm?'

'Yes. We'd like to see your marriage certificate, if you have one.' That was Isabella.

'Of course I have one. It's at home.'

'Mummy is saying,' Isabella emptied her glass, 'that when Daddy "married" you,' she did the inverted commas in the air thing too, 'he was already married to her. So, in fact he wasn't married to you, even if you do have a marriage certificate.'

Janet went cold and shivery.

'You're saying that M-Mal and M-Malcolm are the same person?' It was her greatest fear.

'Got it in one!' Isabella clapped mockingly.

'But...' Something rational roused in Janet. She needed evidence. 'I'd like to know how you reached that conclusion.'

'Isn't it obvious?' Isabella refilled her glass.

'Sadly, dear Janet,' Primrose now had a tissue in her hand, 'I fear we have both been deceived.'

Isabella spelt it out. 'My father was a bigamist. He was married twice, at least.'

'But he married me first, darling.' Primrose patted her daughter's knee. 'You're not er... one of *those*.'

'Yes, Mummy, Daddy was married to you, in a legal marriage, for which we have proof. That's why we need to sort a few things out with Janet, but it can wait till morning. Come on.'

'Why not now?' Janet had questions needing answers. 'What do you want from me?'

'I'm sure you can work that out.'

The pair were halfway to the door, swooping out as they'd swooped in, like ugly sisters off to the ball.

23

ZELDA

Saturday, 19 December

'The bullies.' Zelda was mortified that Janet had had to face the obnoxious pair alone. Now she was in the Britannia restaurant with Viv, waiting for Janet to join them for breakfast, and the SOS Janet had written last night had only just pinged in.

'Come on.' Zelda got to her feet, unable to wait any longer. They hadn't ordered yet. 'We've got to go and find her.'

Viv, even quicker, reached the lift first and they shot up to Deck 11. Fortunately Janet had given them a key because when they knocked and rang, she didn't open the door. They shouted for a bit, but when there was no response Viv opened it and burst in. They found Janet in a near-catatonic state, an empty brandy bottle by her bed.

'I had to do something to get some sleep,' she said, struggling to sit up when they'd roused her. 'That's all. I wasn't trying to do myself in.'

'Why didn't you ring us?' Zelda held a glass of water to her lips and Janet gulped. 'I tried, both phones, but nothing doing.'

Viv found Janet's mobile by the bed charged now, and between them both they extracted the story of the ghastly night visitors. 'Bullies,' Zelda said again. She wanted to throw them overboard.

'They're after your money, Janet. That's what this is about.' Viv was certain.

'Yes.' Janet was tearful. 'And if they're right about Malcolm, if Primrose was married to him and I wasn't, then she's *entitled to* his money.'

Janet had inherited quite a lot.

'Hang *on*!' Viv was stern. '*If* is a big word. You sound as if you're swallowing their story lock, stock and barrel. But we're not believing what those two charlatans say without examining every shred of their so-called evidence. There are gaps, gaping holes here, no evidence at all in fact. Get up. Get dressed. Eat.'

Janet got out of bed.

Zelda wished she felt as confident as Viv, but did promise to probe further using the internet to find out as much as she could.

A five-course breakfast, including eggs Florentine, helped to perk Janet up a little, though she only picked at it. So, maybe, did Viv's probing questions.

'Tell us about your wedding day,' she said as she bit into a blueberry muffin. 'With as much detail as you can remember.'

'It was on 17 July 1971 – in the Presbyterian church in Bedford. We'd already bought a little house in the town, though we weren't living in it of course. It wasn't like it is now. It was all "wait till you're married" and we were both in lodgings living unsullied lives. Malcolm, like me, was a regular at the church. He had become deputy manager of the local branch of Barclays and I was working as a nurse at Bedford Hospital. Ours was a traditional wedding service, all love, honour and obey in a white dress, well I was.'

'And?' Viv prompted.

'It went okay, including the moment when the minister said, "If any person present knows of any lawful impediment to this marriage you should declare it now."'

'And?' Viv prompted again.

'Well, there was that moment, slightly tense, when people hold their breath, waiting to see if anyone is going to say something, then that gasp of amused relief when no one does.'

'No one did?'

'No one. Definitely.' Janet shook her head. '*And* we'd had banns read before announcing our marriage. There was plenty of time for people to object if they wanted to.'

'Banns?' Viv obviously wasn't conversant with the rites of the church.

'You have to have your banns, your intention to marry, read out in church for three consecutive Sundays before the wedding so people can object if they want to.'

'And no one did?'

Janet shook her head emphatically.

Viv asked Janet why she didn't get married in Edinburgh, her hometown, as most people did back then.

'Malcolm didn't want to. Oh.' Janet looked stricken again. 'That doesn't look good, does it?'

'Why not? Sorry.' Viv was apologetic. 'I mean why didn't Malcolm want you to get married from home? What reason did he give?'

'He said he didn't want a big wedding with lots of relatives, and a lot of expense. We had decided to pay for our wedding ourselves, because my parents weren't well-off or in the best of health. They did come down for the wedding though, both our parents did. They all stayed in the Swan Hotel where we had the wedding breakfast after the service.'

'So, it wasn't a secret?'

'Not at all. There was a photo in the local paper and everyone read local papers then, and Malcolm was keen to establish himself as a pillar of the community.'

'Janet,' Viv was encouraging, 'this is looking all right and proper to me. I don't think it would have been possible for Malcolm to marry Primrose in Edinburgh in 1965 and then marry you six years later in Bedford without someone catching on. I'm no expert, but weren't records kept?' She looked at Zelda. 'You are the expert. Isn't there a national registration office, something like that, where all the certificates for births, marriages and deaths are stored?'

Zelda nodded. 'It's in Kew, and was then, but I think they would have been for England only, and maybe Wales. There was a separate office in Scotland.'

'But surely there would have been some cross-checking?'

Zelda wasn't sure. She wasn't an expert. The wedding was in the early 1970s before all the records were computerised and correlated. Her head was full of conflicting thoughts and mixed feelings. She *so* wanted to prove that what the ghastly pair claimed wasn't true, but proving anything would take a lot of poring over documents, if she could find them. She counted on her fingers. It was their fourth day aboard, Saturday, 19 December. They would arrive in New York on Wednesday, 23 December, in the early morning. They only had three and a bit days to prove Primrose and her daughter wrong. If they didn't, Janet's holiday and theirs would be ruined. For years now Zelda had been delving into her own family history, but it had been a long slow process, and she'd discovered some unwelcome facts. What if research revealed that Primrose was right? That Janet's Malcolm *was* a bigamist. Janet would be in bits.

'Zelda,' Viv broke into her thoughts, 'we need your skills. Urgently. Can you get Janet's marriage certificate off the internet while we're still on board?'

'If I can get onto the internet.' Internet connection was hit and miss, that was the trouble. So was Wi-Fi and she didn't know why. Were the two connected? The three of them had been keeping in touch on their mobiles using the ship's Wi-Fi package, and sometimes connection was instant, at others delayed, like last night when Janet's SOS didn't reach them till morning. They couldn't always get online in their rooms, and had to seek out public spaces where the signal was better. The weather and the ship's position probably played a part. She must be positive though. If she could get online she'd be able to get hold of birth certificates as well as marriage certificates and... she was having a new train of thought. If she could prove that Primrose's Mal and Janet's Malcolm were not the same person as the ghastly pair alleged, but two separate individuals, their plan would be scuppered. So, she needed to find birth *certificates*, plural, one for each of them.

Quickly.

Operation Cheer Up Janet wasn't working. Determined to dispel her worst fear if she could, Zelda drained her coffee cup. There was, she thought, a computer expert on the staff, and some sort of computer centre with equipment you could use. Reading documents on her mobile would be difficult. She needed a bigger screen to read the small print and decipher hard-to-read handwriting. Getting to her feet, she pushed back her chair. 'I'm off. See you both later for coffee, with useful info, I hope. Janet, don't despair. I'm on the case.'

With, she hoped, a bit of help from an impressive man and his dog.

24

ZELDA

Where was Richard?

You don't need Richard. Ask at Reception.

As she walked out of the restaurant, Zelda realised she couldn't message Richard, much as she wanted to, because she didn't have his phone number. Why hadn't he offered it to her, she pondered. *So I can't pester him?* Stop! Fed up with herself for worrying that she was about to give him too much attention, when only yesterday she'd been agonising about not giving him enough, she paused to think. What would he be doing soon after breakfast? Walking Billie, most likely. Yes! She remembered him saying that he walked her on a particular deck, where dogs were allowed. Which deck though? She got out her mobile and googled 'walking dogs on *QM2*'. Scrolling down, she quickly learned that the kennels were on Deck 12 and dogs could be visited and walked by their owners up there, but only at certain hours. That wasn't helpful though, as it didn't say exactly where they could be walked or what the certain hours were. Also, Billie slept in Richard's room, he'd said, but not where his room was.

He doesn't want me to know. She carried on googling.

There was a lot of information about where dogs were not allowed to go. Most decks were out of bounds, even for guide dogs. That didn't seem fair. Scrolling again, she was assured that dogs on *QM2* were very well looked after. The 'Pets on Deck' programme included:

> a range of pet-friendly services and amenities such as fresh-baked biscuits at turn-down, a choice of beds and blankets; a QM2-logoed coat and a complimentary gift pack featuring Frisbee, name tag, food dish and scoop and a complimentary portrait with their pet owners.

What would Mack and Morag have made of that, she wondered with a pang, if she had been able to afford the fortune it cost to bring them with her? Oh dear, they wouldn't have liked the next bit. Cats were allowed in the kennels too, at a price of course, and other small animals, *and* – this was astonishing – there were cats on the loose, three ship's cats, 'kept to keep down vermin'. Vermin? Rats and mice on the *Queen Mary*! That wasn't in the fancy brochures.

She scrolled down to 'Exercising your dog'. This looked as if it might be helpful.

> The shielded, open-deck area, fitted with a lamppost and fire hydrant is available to exercise pets on the Sun Deck on Deck 13.

At last! She hurried to the lift, once again breaking the rule The Muscateers had made at the start of the voyage, to keep fit by using the stairs. But needs must. There was no time to waste, and she was in luck. There they were, standing by the first door to the outside deck that she came to, Richard and Billie, and a few other people. But they weren't going anywhere. A steward in a red uniform was barring their exit. 'Sorry, everyone,' she heard him say as she approached. 'No one's allowed out today.'

Wet playtime, she half-expected him to say next.

'Why not, Joshua?' Richard asked for everyone.

'Storm blowing, Richard, Force 8 gale. Captain's orders. Don't want you and Billie blown overboard.'

The two of them obviously knew each other. Storm blowing? Really? The ship felt steady as the proverbial rock, or did till she looked through the small round window in the door the steward was locking and saw white-crested waves rolling towards her throwing up spume. Then suddenly she couldn't see anything through the window.

'Well?' Richard's hand touched hers. 'What do you think?' He said he'd just asked if she'd like a coffee.

She said she'd love one and wondered how he knew she was there.

He said he'd recognised her perfume as if she'd asked the question.

'B-but what about Billie's walk?' She still felt his fingers on her hand, though they were now holding Billie's handle.

'She'll get a walk as we walk. Let's go to Sir Samuel's Lounge down on Deck 3. If we take the stairs she'll get lots of exercise. And don't worry about her relieving herself' – she'd been about to ask – 'she did one before we set off. Guide dogs go when instructed, Zelda, and she has her own facilities. There's a box outside my room filled with mulch and she does it there when I say the word. I won't say what the word is or you might get an unwelcome surprise.'

'Wow! Can I teach mine that?' She was impressed, again.

'Doubt it. Billie learned as a pup, from her puppy trainers, not me. I take no credit. Forward, Billie. We're going to Sir Samuel's.'

It was one of the routes she knew, he said, as they made their way to the stairs, as it was one of his favourite places.

* * *

'So, what did you want to see me about so early in the morning, Zelda?'

They'd settled themselves in comfortable leather seats in the middle of the room well away from the windows at her request. She really didn't want to see those waves. The wood-panelled bar had a calm country club atmosphere, and there were only a few other passengers drinking coffee.

Nevertheless she lowered her voice as she asked him about the computer expert she thought he'd mentioned earlier, and told him why she needed the man's services, while trying not to disclose more of Janet's private life than she needed to.

Richard said he knew the man as he took Billie's harness off, but then Billie became her liberated doggy-self again, licking Zelda's hands and putting her head in her lap, so she spent the next few minutes getting her dog-fix. Richard ordered coffees from a motherly female steward who appeared as soon as he sat down. Great service was one of the perks of being blind, he said, when the lady had taken their orders. He never had to wait long, well not on *QM2*.

'Perks?' She had never, ever, met a man less sorry for himself, but before she could say so he said, 'So, how can I help? What do you want from me? No, don't apologise' – she'd been about to – 'you have to know what you want if you're gonna get it.'

'The name of the computer expert?'

'That's easy. Gary Mitchel.'

'And where do I find him?'

'Connexions, that's the name of the computer centre and it's down on Deck 2. Gary's the manager.' He sang Gary's praises, but also reminded her that other staff knew a lot about passengers that might be useful for her quest. He mentioned Carlos in the jewellery boutique again, then Joyce, the motherly steward, who brought their coffees.

When she'd gone, he said that Connexions was a fully equipped internet room with twenty workstations for the use of passengers, and it was in high demand. Twenty computers wasn't enough and they were in constant use. You had to book sessions and it cost a bit, but Gary was on hand to help with problems which he could usually solve. He also ran courses, including one on Ancestry, so he might be very useful.

Zelda was now keen to get going, for better or worse. Knowing what she did about Janet's first husband tempered any optimism about the outcome. Malcolm had been like an iceberg, she'd gathered from Janet, cold, well to her, and two-thirds hidden below the surface.

'It's open now.' Richard seemed to sense her eagerness to leave. 'And it would be good to get there as soon as you want.'

'Oh, sorry. I...'

'Stop apologising, Zelda. You're not hurting my feelings. Finish your coffee and go. I've got stuff to do too. I'd come and introduce you to Gary, but I have a rehearsal. Tell you what, I'll tell him you're on your way.' He picked up his iPhone to message, his fingers moving fast on the keyboard, specially adapted, he said, for him to write in Braille. She'd noted a gadget below the keyboard.

'Thank you.'

'Thanks premature, I'm afraid. It hasn't gone. I'm getting "try again later". The Wi-Fi must be down.'

He said he thought the bad weather was responsible, and sounding more computer savvy than she was, he went on a bit about satellite availability. Rain was bad too, he said, as it caused signal interference, and there was plenty of that. Even at this distance from the window she could see huge raindrops battering the glass.

She drained her cup.

'Before you go...' He picked up Billie's harness and the dog moved to his side.

'What?' She braced herself for the gentle brush-off, the *I'm sorry but I'm going to be very busy for the next few days*, and picked up her bag.

'I was hoping that you might be free for dinner one night before the end of the voyage?' He straightened up after putting on Billie's harness.

Tonight! she managed not to say. Just.

'Because if you could be free one night, I'll book a table. Sunday or Tuesday would suit me best as I'm not playing those nights, well, not till later in the evening, so we'd have longer to talk, but tonight or Monday if that's all you can do...'

'T-tomorrow then?'

'Great.' He lifted Billie's handle. 'Sunday then, for the avoidance of doubt, as the lawyers say. Let's get arrangements in place now in case the internet is still down. Oh, you'll need this when normal service is resumed.' He put his hand in his pocket and handed her a business card. 'Is seven o'clock in the Queen's Grill okay with you? It will be quieter there. I hope Connexions will be open, by the way. Gary tends to close the shop if systems are down.'

I've got a date! I've got a date!

Zelda floated down the stairs to Deck 2 and managed to find Connexions, but read the sign on the door before she reached it. 'Closed' in large letters, 'till further notice' in smaller letters underneath. What now? She reached for her phone to text Viv and Janet to ask them where they were, before remembering that she couldn't do that either. Then the ship's intercom crackled overhead and she heard the captain saying that weather conditions were worsening. Gale Force 8 had risen to Gale Force 9 on the Beaufort scale but they mustn't be alarmed. The *Queen Mary*, he assured them, was built for conditions exactly like these. Outdoor activities were cancelled but most indoor events were taking place as usual. He requested passengers with balconies to keep balcony doors closed, otherwise it was business as usual. 'Keep calm and carry on,' he urged them 'and have a nice day.'

Keep calm? How could she when her heart was beating like a demented food mixer? She had a date, a date, with an *amazing* man!

25

VIV

Viv and Janet were in the Golden Lion when the announcement came over the Tannoy. They were sitting in a booth by the window, watching the rain battering the glass, while waiting for a steward to bring drinks, coffee for Viv, tea for Janet, though Viv had been tempted to order something stronger to lift Janet's spirits and her own. Janet was hard work at the moment, not good company, she'd said so herself. After breakfast she'd wanted to head back to her luxurious quarters to be miserable alone, but Viv had persuaded her to come to the pub, thinking a chat in cheerful surroundings would take her mind off her troubles.

But it hadn't.

Janet might as well have been sitting in a prison cell. Deep in gloom, she seemed unaware of the gleaming brass fittings and warm wood panelling, or her comfortable, well-padded banquette. It was perhaps a mistake to be sitting so close to the window, where they could see the waves crashing against the side of the ship, but not hear them fortunately thanks to the triple glazing. It felt odd though, like watching a film with the sound turned down.

'Viv.' Janet was leaning towards her, across the table, her voice barely audible. 'What if I'm an unmarried mother?'

'I don't think it shows yet,' Viv whispered back, joking and getting it completely wrong.

Janet carried on in hushed tones. 'What if I have to tell Grant he's illegitimate?' The whispering wasn't necessary, there was hardly anyone else in the pub.

Viv was sympathetic, up to a point. She had, after all, encouraged Janet to voice her worries on the 'better out than in' principle but the more she said, the more her worries seemed to mount.

'Viv, what if Grant stops me seeing Rocky and Woody? What if I never see them again?'

Grant was Janet's son who lived in New Zealand. Rocky and Woody were her grandchildren, a boy and a girl – Viv could never remember which was which – whom she adored. The effect on Grant seemed to be Janet's main worry, because he could deny her access to her grandchildren. Her relationship with him had always been fraught.

'If I have to give Primrose all Malcolm's money, Grant will have no reason to keep in touch.'

'You won't, Janet. It's your money. You helped Malcolm earn it.' But Viv was wasting her breath, Janet wasn't listening.

Where were their drinks? Had the barman forgotten? And where was Zelda? They needed her here, preferably with news of a Primrose-clobbering discovery that she'd made with the help of the man she'd rushed off to see, Richard the cellist, at a guess.

'Janet, Zelda's on the case.' Viv tapped her hand to get her attention. 'You were married to Malcolm and have a marriage certificate to prove it. Zelda's probably found it by now. *And* he left everything to you in his perfectly legal will, didn't he? She's probably found that too.'

'But he left everything to his *wife* in his will. If I wasn't his wife...'

Fortunately Zelda arrived at that moment and sat down by Janet. Unfortunately she hadn't got the Primrose-clobbering news that Viv hoped for, but she did say she was hopeful about getting some when the weather improved and the internet was back up. And she had a couple more ideas not dependent on the internet, for finding out if they were the same person, like finding Mal and Malcolm's childhood addresses. 'Because if we find they lived at different addresses, then we've proved they're two different people.'

'How though?' Viv wasn't sure she followed the logic. 'How do we find their addresses, I mean.'

'By asking, Janet, for a start, then tonight – if she turns up – we ask Primrose, in a casual sort of chatty way, where Mal lived. She should know as they were childhood sweethearts. So,' Zelda turned to Janet, 'where did Malcolm live as a boy? What was his address?'

Janet shook her head. She and Malcolm hadn't known each other when they lived in Edinburgh. They'd met in London.

'But what about his parents' address when you first got to know him? That might have been where he grew up.'

Janet said she'd probably got it in an old address book at home, but she couldn't remember it right now.

It didn't look promising, Viv thought. 'What's your other idea, Zelda?'

'Asking Primrose straight out, when she's off guard, maybe when she's had a glass or two, when her husband's birthday was? Then we compare it with Malcolm's.'

Janet was frowning.

'You do know Malcolm's birth date, Janet?'

'Yes, of course, Zelda. It was 19 October 1945.' It tripped off her tongue. 'But I'm not sure if Primrose would know Mal's.'

'Why ever not?'

'Because...' Janet frowned. 'She seems to have memory problems.'

Viv had doubts too. Janet had been married to Malcolm for nearly forty years. She'd have said or written down her husband's birth date umpteen times, so of course it tripped off her tongue. But Primrose had been married to Mal for seven years at most before he disappeared from her life.

'How was your cellist, Zelda?' Janet changed the subject.

'H-helpful,' said Zelda, sounding surprised.

'How helpful?' Janet was almost perky.

'Very,' said Zelda. 'That's why I'm optimistic...'

'Good.' Janet actually smiled. 'Now is someone going to ask the barman where our drinks are? And order one for Zelda?'

No one changed gear quite like Janet, Viv thought, literally or metaphorically. She remembered her driving before she got an automatic. Since breakfast she'd been in a very low gear crawling along, often reversing, now she was going forward at a pace, albeit jerkily.

'What's next for you and the cellist, Zelda?' Janet said when they all had drinks. 'And for the three of us. We've only got three more days aboard and mustn't waste a minute.'

'The cellist?' Zelda seemed amused, fortunately. 'His name's Richard, Janet, and he's asked me to have dinner with him tomorrow night.'

'Excellent!' Janet beamed. 'Therefore, we must interrogate my so-called friend from Edinburgh tonight if we are to have your assistance, Zelda. Now, I was thinking of going to this at 11 a.m.' The Daily Programme was in her hand and *this* was a talk called 'A brief history of the diamond and how it became known as a girl's best friend'.

Another change of gear!

Janet was making a huge effort, perhaps inspired by the beloved maiden aunt whose diamond ring she constantly wore. Aunt Em had been a VAD nurse in the First World War and Janet had often said she'd like to know more about the ring's provenance. She'd wondered if her aunt had once had a sweetheart, killed in the war perhaps, leaving her with a broken heart and an engagement ring. Janet was a romantic at heart, Viv thought. Beneath that brusque exterior she was as soft as a hush puppy.

'Diamonds are for me,' Zelda said as the barman brought their drinks. 'I'll go to the talk with you, Janet.'

'Me too,' said Viv.

It was a time for sticking together, and presenting a united front to Primrose and her daughter, whenever they turned up.

26

JANET

Janet wasn't thinking about diamonds as she sat in the stylish Chart Room trying to concentrate on the lecture. Determined not to drag her friends down to the slough of despond where she'd been rapidly heading, she'd brought them here as a distraction. She was tired. That was part of the problem and being awake half the night hadn't helped. In the early hours she'd become convinced that Primrose was right. It was hard not to believe her, knowing Malcolm as she did. What *didn't* she know, though? That was what was torturing her now. Had he had another wife, a *legal* wife and a little daughter when he married her? Remembering his fumbling efforts on their wedding night, she thought, with a small leap of hope, that it was unlikely. He had seemed as inexperienced as she had been. She'd assumed he was a virgin as their church said he should be, as she was. They had taken off their clothes and not looked at each other. Then put out the light and gone to sleep.

He never fancied me. I didn't fancy him. Why did we marry?

The lecture wasn't as fascinating as she'd hoped, or she was too tired to appreciate it. As the lecturer, a smart young woman with a sharp haircut and multiply pierced ears, enthused about diamond mining, which looked horrific, Janet tried to remember if Malcolm had ever talked about what he had been doing in the years before he met her. Had he been dashing back to Edinburgh while he was still at university to see Primrose and Isabella? He hadn't talked much about his early life, that was the trouble, or anything else, really, well, not to her.

Alan talked to me, too much sometimes. Alan fancied me. Alan loved me.

As a tear rolled down her cheek, a burst of clapping broke into her thoughts. The lecture had ended.

'What? Oh, yes.' Viv had nudged her and was now flicking her head towards the end of the row where Isabella sat wearing a snake-print jumpsuit. Not flattering, it made her look like a snake, accentuating her long, lean frame. Now, like a lot of others, she was getting up to leave.

'A moment, ladies and gentlemen...' The young man from the jewellery boutique came to the podium. Carlos, was that his name? 'Ladies and gentlemen, you've just heard a fascinating talk about the diamond. Now come and see some superb specimens in imaginative and luxurious settings. Downstairs in the boutique we have a fine selection for your delight, with of course no obligation to buy.'

Isabella had left.

'And,' the young man continued, 'do bring your pre-loved treasures to show us so we can tell you more about their provenance.'

Janet picked up her bag. That's what she'd come for. She really did want to know more about Auntie's ring, not what it was worth, though that would be interesting, but where it came from and how old it was. She would never sell it.

But I may have to.

As financial ruin reared its ugly head again, she got to her feet, told Viv and Zelda she'd see them later, and hurried off, ignoring Viv's 'Hang on, I need a pee first.' When she reached the boutique there was already a queue which of course went slowly past all the glass-fronted cabinets where the *fine selection of diamonds in a variety of luxurious settings* was on display, and there near the front was Isabella, surprisingly without a man in tow. She'd got to the counter and was talking to a member of staff, not Carlos, by the time Janet reached the cabinets herself, but suddenly it seemed she was by Janet's side, pointing at the centrepiece of the display, a large star-shaped brooch with a chunky solitaire diamond in a platinum setting in the middle. 'Buy me that and I think I could persuade Mummy to let the matter drop.'

'B-but why would I?' Janet was proud of her answer, which astonished Isabella. 'And why would you accept a rather flashy brooch from me, when you might have so much more to gain if you waited and consulted a solicitor?' Game and set, if not match, Janet thought, as Isabella slithered away in her snake suit. But in the doorway she turned and hissed, 'You won't be smiling, Smug-Face, when the writ's served in New York.'

27

VIV

'What was that about?' Viv saw Isabella leaving the jewellery boutique as she came in with Zelda. 'A writ's g-going to be served.' Janet was shaking. 'Fortification needed!' Viv took her arm and near frogmarched her to the Golden Lion, where she ordered a bottle of fizz. Janet was back to thinking Malcolm must have been a bigamist. Zelda didn't help, saying she hadn't come up with anything to refute the ghastly pair's allegations. The computer centre was closed owing to the bad weather conditions, all too evident when they looked out of the window.

'Shall we move?' Viv looked from one to another but got no reply, so she picked up a menu.

They were in their favourite corner booth but today it was far from ideal. Janet and Zelda both seemed mesmerised by the sight of the sea and when Viv saw the height of the waves crashing against the glass she got a shock.

'If I can have your attention for a minute.' Zelda called them to order. 'I know you're disappointed that I haven't found anything groundbreaking yet, but I'd like to share my thoughts. Firstly, I think that Isabella is bluffing about this writ. I mean, what would she accuse you of, Janet? You haven't committed a crime. Secondly, I think she's the one behind all this, not Primrose. She's the one demanding money with menaces.'

'Menaces?' Janet raised her head.

'She's trying to blackmail you, Janet. Pay up or else.' Viv topped up Janet's glass. 'I agree with Zelda. If she wants to get money from you on this trip, which I'm pretty sure she does, she's running out of time. Why would she be prepared to "let the matter drop" for a fancy brooch if she knew she had a case?'

'Because she knows that the wheels of the law turn slowly, so she wants to settle out of court?' Janet seemed determined to believe the worst.

Zelda shook her head. 'There's still no evidence that they have a case, not that we've seen. They need to prove that Mal and Malcolm are the same person, and I need to prove that they're not. If I can prove they are two different people, we demolish their case. That's why I need to get back to work.' She looked at her phone, tapped a few keys and said, 'Fat chance of that, still no internet.'

They rallied a little over lunch, sausage and mash all round, returning to Janet's earlier idea, that Malcolm had a brother or close relative he hadn't told her about and that Primrose had married him. Zelda thought this was worth investigating. 'He was perhaps the family's black sheep?' Viv raised an eyebrow.

'Sorry, an archaic phrase, Viv, not without irony, but what I'm saying is there might be a brother who the family is ashamed of for some reason, so they didn't talk about him. We're talking about completely different times, remember, when they threw men in jail because they were gay. My dad couldn't marry my mum because he was black and she was white. The fact that this Mal had fathered a child outside of marriage might have been enough for his family to disown him. But if there was a brother, I don't think he would have been called Malcolm, but he might have been called something else beginning with Mal. So, if we could come up with some other names it would be helpful when I start looking for birth certificates.' She got a notebook from her bag. 'Any ideas?'

'Malachy?' Janet perked up a bit. 'I think Malcolm's father might have been called that.'

'Malvin? Mallory? Malvolio?' said Zelda, laughing.

Unfortunately, that was all they came up with, then Janet, definitely perkier, suggested they find a book on the subject. 'In the absence of new technology, we need the old. A dictionary of names, something like that. And there's a library on board if I remember correctly.'

Viv consulted the plan of the ship she kept in her back pocket. 'It's up on Deck 8 at the far end the front, on the right-hand side.'

'In the bow, Viv,' Janet corrected her, 'starboard side.'

Yes, she was definitely perkier.

* * *

They went straight to the library after lunch, using the lift again, their spirits rising as they went up in the Perspex cube, festooned with fairy lights, looking at all the Christmassy scenes as they passed. Deck 8 was a contrast with busier decks. When they got out, they saw a long bare corridor lined with cabin doors.

'That way, I think,' said Zelda, pointing right, but they were only halfway down when she came to a halt, her hand clutching a cabin door handle. 'Sorry, I can't do this.' She looked ill.

Viv was also struggling, staggering from one side of the corridor to another, and when she stopped by Zelda she felt the ship's up and down movement making her stomach heave. Clearly, the ends of the ship, the *bows* she corrected herself, were less stable than the middle.

'Sorry. I've got to go back.' Zelda covered her mouth with her hand.

Viv soldiered – or sailored? – on, after Janet. Walking confidently ahead, she seemed to have found her sea legs. When they reached the library, they found the librarian, a young red-haired woman, head in hands, looking as if she was sleeping on her desk, her purple-rimmed glasses on the floor beside her. But she opened her eyes when Janet picked them up, and waved an arm in the direction of the glass-fronted bookcases, screwed to the walls, Viv noted. Of course. For turbulent times like these. The tables and leather armchairs were also fixed to the floor. Olwen, Viv read the lanyard round her neck, said she was new to the job. It was her first time aboard, and no one had told it would be like this. She asked Janet to put her glasses in the top drawer of her desk. Viv felt her own stomach heaving as she went in search of the reference section and managed to find a book about naming your baby. Janet, seemingly unaffected by the lurching vessel, was moving from shelf to shelf, piling books into a basket, but when they went to the desk to check the books out, Olwen waved them away. She didn't want to record any details, she just wanted to die, so they set off again on the perilous journey back to Janet's suite.

All was blissfully calm in Janet's sitting room. The difference was amazing. When Viv closed the floor-length curtains so they couldn't see the waves crashing towards them, they could pretend they were on dry land – till the captain's voice came over the Tannoy.

'We are experiencing turbulent weather conditions. A Force 10 gale fast rising to Force 11 is upon us but passengers are assured that the *Queen Mary* is built for these conditions and need not be concerned. Please, however, keep balcony doors closed and stay near the centre of the ship if you are experiencing nausea. The library, Canyon Ranch beauty and fitness centre and swimming pools are closed until further notice. Cookery demonstrations are cancelled but the Britannia restaurant and other eating places are operating as usual and so are the medical centres.'

Viv found Janet in the kitchen making tea, adding shortbread biscuits and slices of Dundee cake to the tray. Pleased with this development, Viv didn't comment as she followed her into the sitting room.

'Our task is to find alternatives to Malcolm beginning with Mal, yes?' Janet poured tea.

'Yes.'

That said, tea in hand, they settled down with their books, their feet up on the comfortable sofa.

'"The name Mal is primarily a gender-neutral name of English origin that means a follower of St Columba,"' Janet said after reading a few pages of a serious-looking tome. 'And it is also a suffix meaning ill-omened. Think mal-function, mal-practice and...'

'Mal-odorous,' said Viv, reaching for a shortbread. 'You should have known he was bad news.'

'If only I'd consulted a dictionary first.' Janet picked up her cup. 'What have you found in the *Name Your Baby* book?'

'Several different spellings of Malachy and Malcolm like Malachi with an "i" and Malcom without a second "l" and a lot of variations of both names, like Malik, Malek and Malo. As all of them can be abbreviated to

Mal, it's going to take Zelda ages to trawl through all the possible Mals who may or may not be alternative Malcolm Carmichael's.'

It was, she didn't say, starting to feel like a waste of time and possibly money, paying for all those certificates. Janet said she was keen for Zelda to start searching and wondered how she was feeling.

Viv got up, lifted the curtain and quickly let it drop again. Waves like mountains crashing against the glass did not bode well for internet research. Operation Cheer Up Janet this was not. Operation Cheer Up Viv this was not. That glimpse of the sea was stomach shrinking, body shrinking, boat shrinking. Suddenly she felt like a Lego person on a Lego boat bobbing about in the never-ending sea.

'Janet Loveday, we need a Wet Afternoon Plan!'

A WAP was something they sometimes did to cheer themselves up when they couldn't get outside on a dreary day. They did it together or separately, watching the same film at the same time, something escapist, not too heavy, glass in hand, exchanging comments by text or phone.

Janet looked up from her tome. 'You're right, Viv, but together as we have no internet.' She got up and headed for the minibar. 'You fetch Zelda. I'll fix drinks and see what's on.'

Viv found Zelda in bed reading, feeling okay now that she was in the middle of the ship with the curtains closed, but reluctant to leave her bed. Viv assured her that she'd felt no pitching or rolling as she'd made her way from Janet's rooms to theirs, so Zelda wouldn't feel any on the way back. She didn't mention the height of the waves.

'Come on, it's OCUJ,' said Viv. 'Operation Cheer Up Janet.'

Back in Janet's suite they found her in the middle of her huge bed, opposite a wall-screen, perusing the Daily Programme, pen in hand. There was she said, a choice of three films they could watch. '*Paranoia* where...'

'No!'

'*Phantom*, where a submarine is trapped below several fathoms...'

'No.'

'Or *Bridges of Madison County* where Meryl Streep has a four-day love affair with Clint Eastwood while her husband and children are away and...'

'Perfect!'

They watched it sitting on Janet's bed, knocking back prosecco. Could their granddaughters have had more fun on one of their girlie sleepovers? Viv asked Janet. She was sure they'd have had a lot less. There would have been at least one falling-out by now about something they couldn't remember next day. But there were no fallings-out between The Muscateers that afternoon. It was All For One big time. United in their determination to live for the moment, they lusted with Meryl and wished her well. Better to have loved and lost, they agreed, than never loved at all. And at six o'clock as they walked arm in arm down to the Britannia restaurant, Viv felt optimistic about life and love and everything.

Until she saw who was sitting at their table.

'Leave this to me,' said Zelda. 'Leave this to me, Viv.'

28

ZELDA

Zelda thought Viv might throttle Isabella, sitting by her mother, looking like a bird of prey, a bearded vulture she'd once seen in a zoo. It was the combination of pink-blonde hair, and the feathery orange cape hanging round her shoulders.

'I hope you don't mind,' Primrose, with her back to the *QM2* tapestry, blinked several times, as Janet sat down, 'but I've asked Isabella to join us.' She was playing hostess again.

I mind. I minded from the start. I should have stopped it.

Zelda noted that Primrose now wore black from head to toe. Even her pussycat bow was black.

'Do sit down, Viv and Zelda.' Janet tapped the chairs either side of her.

Viv looked as if she wanted to throw the invaders overboard, which was how Zelda felt. This was worse than the first night. The round table was now set for *five*... Where was the steward?

'Of course we don't mind.' Janet had reverted to her default polite mode, lying for them all, but also maybe reclaiming her role as host. 'You're welcome to our table, both of you. We have lots to discuss.'

Primrose touched her eyes with the lace-edged handkerchief she'd pulled from her evening bag. 'Thank you, Janet. I'm pleased to see you looking so well. Perhaps you too have seen the silver lining to the black cloud that has descended upon us?'

'Sorry?' said Janet.

'That I can now grieve and be a bona fide member of your group? That you no longer have to waive your rules, because I am Malcolm's widow.'

'Come again,' said Viv as Janet's mouth fell open.

Fortunately the steward arrived before Viv could leap out of her seat and throttle Primrose.

* * *

When the steward had taken their orders, a calmer Viv said, 'I think you're jumping the gun a bit, Primrose. There's absolutely no evidence for what you say.'

'As yet,' Isabella jumped in. 'But it's clear that my mother has been a victim of a cruel deception.'

'And so have I,' said Janet, recovering, Zelda was pleased to see. 'I have been a victim of deception if, I repeat *if* what you allege is proved to be true. And if, *if* it is true, you may take some comfort from the fact that my long marriage to Malcolm was not a happy one, Primrose. The Malcolm I married was nothing like the Mal you describe, which is why I find it hard to believe Mal and Malcolm are the same person. Malcolm was cold, controlling and mean.'

'Because you didn't bring out the best in him, obviously.' Isabella touched her mother's hand. 'Not like Mummy.'

Zelda saw Janet flinch as Isabella probed her sore spot. In her darkest moments, Janet blamed her own inadequacies for the failure of her first marriage.

'Malcolm was always kind to me.' As Primrose rubbed salt in the wound, Zelda wondered when she'd started calling her one-time husband Malcolm.

Primrose added more salt. '*Our* Malcolm, Isabella's daddy, was a warm, demonstrative, generous man, devoted to us till...' She reached for her handkerchief.

'Till?' prompted Viv. 'Till when exactly?' She was date-searching as planned.

'Till someone more attractive lured him away. I mean that as a compliment, by the way, Janet.' Her lack of self-awareness was breath-taking.

'Daddy was kind and patient,' Isabella chipped in. 'He always played ludo and snakes and ladders with me when he came to visit.'

'And chess?' Janet looked up. 'Did he play chess with you?'

Primrose laughed. 'Janet, Isabella was only six when her daddy left us.'

'But Malcolm taught Grant how to play chess when he was four.' Janet turned to Jacob, their favourite wine waiter, who was hovering. 'We'll have a bottle of Chenin Blanc to go with the starters and the Cabernet Sauvignon with our mains.'

It wasn't game, set and match, but Janet had scored a point, unrecognised by Primrose and Isabella. Janet was fighting back and Zelda wanted to hug her. Mal played snakes and ladders with his daughter. Malcolm played chess with his son. He had taught Grant when he was four, but he hadn't taught Isabella when she was six. It wasn't conclusive but did suggest Mal and Malcolm were two different people. Zelda saw Primrose studying her menu and touched her arm, hoping to catch her off guard. 'When was your husband's birthday?'

'The tw—'

But Isabella cut her mother off. 'Nineteenth of October 1945.'

That was Malcolm's birthday. Zelda knew that.

Janet's eyebrows shot up, but she didn't say anything. Had she noticed that Primrose had been about to give a different date? *The tw...* she'd said, before Isabella intervened. She must have been about to say twelfth or twenty-something.

'And when was your, er, "husband's" birthday?' Isabella made inverted commas in the air.

'The same.' Janet was curt.

There was no point in denying it, Zelda supposed, and it didn't prove anything. Isabella could easily have got that date from the internet if she'd been planning this deception, as Zelda felt increasingly sure she had. Ditto his full name, but she'd ask anyway.

'And what did you say Mal's full name was, Primrose?' Again Zelda asked the mother and again the daughter answered. 'Malcolm George Carmichael.' Primrose hadn't said what Mal's full name was when they'd last asked. 'Sorry, Primrose, I didn't catch that.'

'Malcolm George Carmichael.' She was reading from a script.

Isabella smirked, as their waiter Cesar brought their starters. 'The same as your, er... *husband's*, yes?' It was inverted commas in the air again. Then she licked her finger and held it in the air. 'Point made, I think.'

Primrose did have the grace to look embarrassed.

Talk turned to how delicious the food was. It was delicious, but Zelda, sure now that Isabella had come along to stop her mother speaking for herself, wondered what to ask Primrose next – and how to stop Isabella butting in. Now, perhaps, while a heaped forkful of shrimp Skagen was on its way to her mouth?

'What was Malcolm's address when he was a boy, Primrose, I mean when you were childhood sweethearts?'

Primrose looked to her daughter for guidance.

Isabella spluttered shrimps.

Zelda passed her a napkin.

Isabella wiped pink mayonnaise from her chin. 'Sh-she, Mummy, can't remember things like that.'

'Oh dear.' Viv, all concern, filled Isabella's water glass.

'Please.' Janet looked uncomfortable. 'Before we go any further, I'd like to make it clear, for the avoidance of doubt as lawyers say, that if it were proved that Malcolm was married to you, Primrose, before he was married to me, and that you were his first and only lawfully wedded wife, and therefore his lawfully wedded widow, I would do the right thing.'

'Too right you would.' Isabella gulped water. 'The court would see to that.'

She's behind this. Zelda was certain. Viv too. Zelda got a glimpse of a note she'd scribbled as she slid it across the table to Janet.

DON'T MAKE RASH PROMISES!

'Thank you, Janet.' Primrose did her eye-blink. 'I appreciate your kind offer, but it will be enough for me to know that I was Mal's first and only one true love. I have no interest in money.'

'Let's drop the subject now, shall we?' Janet leaned back so Cesar could take away her empty soup dish. 'Let's enjoy the rest of our meal. Here's Jacob with the wine.' When all their glasses were full, Janet raised hers. 'To a fair and happy outcome for all of us.'

But Zelda knew that wasn't possible. Somebody had to lose.

29

VIV

Viv wanted to go back and wring Isabella's leathery neck. She was the driving force behind this dubious claim. It was obvious now that Primrose was following instructions when she had the nous to follow them. As they made their way back to Janet's suite, Janet said she had thought so all along, but Viv wasn't pleased with Janet either. She had been far too conciliatory. Thank God the brazen pair hadn't accepted Janet's invitation for coffee, which she was making now in the fancy coffee machine that looked as if it might take off.

Viv looked for a tray. 'Janet, what exactly did you mean when you said you'd "do the right thing" if it was proved that Primrose was Malcolm's first wife?'

'That *if* – I'm glad you noticed my if, Viv – that *if* it is proved that Malcolm was a bigamist, I would share my inheritance with Primrose in whatever way the law deemed right.'

'We need lawyers.' Viv found a tray. 'Maggie and Nikos for starters.' Maggie was Janet's solicitor and next-door neighbour. Nikos was Libby's new partner, a retired legal something or other. Her hand reached automatically for her phone to message them, before she remembered she couldn't.

Janet put the coffees on the tray. 'Facts, we need facts, Viv, also sadly dependent on the internet access we haven't got. If Zelda finds the relevant facts, we may not need lawyers, though contacting Maggie and Nikos informally is a good idea. Where is Zelda by the way?'

'Here.' She came into the kitchen with her phone in her hand. 'Optimist that I am, I've been going round your suite, trying to get a signal. But no,' she shook her head before either of them could ask, 'I didn't find one, and I made the mistake of looking out of the window, though looking out isn't the right word. I couldn't see out there was so much foam covering the glass. Oh. Listen, another announcement, I think.'

They paused as the Tannoy crackled and the captain's voice came over the airwaves, as confident and reassuring as ever, but unable to deny that things were getting worse. They needn't worry, however, because *QM2* was built for all weathers, etc. She was the stablest vessel ever built, etc. The storm would pass as quickly as it had arrived, etc., but some activities like cookery demonstrations and theatrical performances had had to be cancelled because of instability, and the internet was still down. Gale Force 10 was rising to 11.

'Bloody hell! Isn't that a hurricane?'

Not far from it apparently, but amazingly Janet's suite seemed unaffected. When Janet carried the tray into her sitting room and put it on the table there wasn't as much as a ripple on the surface of the coffees, and the saucers were pristine. As she sank onto a sofa opposite Janet, Viv noticed her scribbled note on the tray, and Janet noticed her noticing.

'I wasn't making a rash promise, Viv. I was simply saying what I would do if I had to. Malcolm left everything to his wife in his will. If I wasn't his lawfully wedded wife, I'm not entitled to it.'

'Malcolm left everything to Janet Carmichael in his will, a named person, right?'

'We will have to wait and see.' Janet was infuriating.

Zelda tried a different and better approach. 'Do you want to disinherit your grandchildren, Janet?'

'Of course not!' Her face registered alarm.

'Well then,' said Zelda. 'Let's hold our collective nerve, and think about what else we can do. I still think Mal and Malcolm are two different people, from what you've said and what they've said. One man was generous, one was stingy. One was warm, the other cold. One played chess, the other snakes and ladders. Now all I've got to do is find documents to prove it.'

'Is that all?' Janet half-laughed, but Viv felt her doubts returning. The differences between the two men could easily be explained away. The evidence was thin. Janet and Primrose had different perceptions that was all. Also, one man could have treated the two women differently. He could have been warm to Primrose and cold to Janet, mean to Janet and generous to Primrose. And the fact, if fact it was, that Malcolm played chess with Grant and snakes and ladders with Isabella wasn't that significant. By all accounts Malcolm was a sexist sod who would have thought girls weren't clever enough to play chess.

The room had gone quiet except for the sound of cups being picked up and put down and the occasional tummy rumble, whose Viv couldn't say. They were all thinking but getting nowhere. Janet rolled her shoulder as if to relieve an aching neck, her tension all too clear, and then went into 'What will be will be' mode, a sure sign she was getting depressed. Zelda didn't look too cheerful either. Something had to be done.

Viv got up. Spirits must be lifted, and earlier on she'd noticed something at the back of Janet's minibar that might do the trick, a reminder of happier times.

'I'm going to raid your minibar, Janet, if that's okay?'

Minutes later, she was back with the bottle, three glasses and a dish of macaroons.

'Ta-da!' She put the tray on the table.

Zelda frowned. 'I think we've had enough.' But Janet was reading the label on the bottle and started to smile. 'Muscat! A stroke of genius, Viv!'

It was the sweet white wine that had given them their nickname seven years ago.

Zelda perked up too – the name had been her idea – as Viv gripped the bottle between her knees to get leverage and pulled out the cork with a satisfying plunk. Then Viv filled their glasses with the golden liquid.

'To The Muscateers!' They clinked. 'All for one and one for all!'

***

'Zelda, when do you think the ghastly pair got the idea of pursuing Janet?' Viv's mind was still active as she got ready for bed two hours later.

But Zelda, already in bed, was sleepy.

'I mean,' Viv looked around for her pyjamas, 'when exactly do you think they decided to come after her money?'

'Good question, Viv,' Zelda yawned, 'but can we talk about this in the morning? Your pyjamas are under your pillow, by the way.'

'I've looked and they're not.'

'Look again.'

'I don't think it was a spur-of-the-moment thing. It's too much of a coincidence that they turned up on *QM2* on the same day as Janet and happened to bump into her, and then discovered, in Primrose's case, that her husband had the same name, or nearly, as Janet's husband. Oh, here they are, you're right, but so neatly folded they're nearly invisible.' She pulled the bottoms on. 'And how many people say "let's see your wedding photographs" when they've only just met you? What I'm getting at is this, how did those two know Janet was coming on this trip?'

'Facebook most likely. Janet's on it now and then and probably posted that she was coming on this trip. That's the sort of thing people do. Sorry, Viv.' Zelda put out her bedside light. 'More in the morning, right?'

'Okay...' Viv pulled her pyjama top over her head and got into her own bed, hoping she would sleep. Facebook! How could people become so-called friends with people they didn't know and proceed to tell them when they were going on holiday, alerting them that their house was empty and ready to be burgled?

...Oh, was that a ping?

Zelda's light went on.

'What's the matter?'

Zelda was sitting up. 'My phone. I've got a text, from Richard. Luckily I heard it. Oh, no!' She started getting out of bed. 'Billie's not well. He needs me. I've got to go.'

'Shall I come too?' Viv started to get out too.

'No, I don't think so. He wants me.' She was pulling a sweater over her head. 'I'll text you if we need more help. Where are my trainers? Oh, I've found them.' She pulled them on and was out of the door before Viv could say, 'Text?'

* * *

The storm was over.

The captain came on the Tannoy to announce the good news. The wind had dropped as suddenly as it had blown up. They were now in calm waters. If they opened their curtains, they could see the moonlight on the water. He wished them all a peaceful night's sleep, unless of course they weren't sleepy. If they were night owls there was plenty for them to do, as events were now taking place as featured in the Daily Programme. Connexions would be open in the morning. The internet was already up and running, so they could send messages on their smartphones.

Viv dashed off a spate of texts and emails as quickly as she could. She didn't trust the Wi-Fi to stay connected. It came and went even when weather conditions were good. First she assured Patrick she was fine but worried about Janet and told him briefly why. Then she told Maggie and Nikos about Janet in more detail and asked for legal advice. Then she texted Janet, telling her about Zelda rushing off to Billie's aid, and lastly Zelda herself:

> Let me know if I can help with Billie? V x

As she waited hopefully for replies she drew back the curtain to look at the now amazingly calm sea, glimmering under a new moon, a sliver of silver in an inky, cloudless sky. Romantic, she couldn't help thinking, which turned her thoughts first to Patrick with a pang of wish-you-were-here-ness, and then to Zelda and Richard, with a small stab of suspicion. Why had Richard really called for Zelda so late at night? It then occurred to her that Zelda had rushed out to meet him without telling her where she was going, breaking The Muscateers' golden rule. They always told each other exactly where they were going if they were meeting a man, especially if it was one they hardly knew. She'd known Richard Williams for how long, three days? I'm going to see Richard, she'd said, but not where, but in the middle of the night, so probably his cabin. Where was his cabin? Viv didn't know, she realised with alarm, but Zelda presumably did and was heading there in her best apricot-coloured satin pyjamas. How ill was Billie? Viv began to have more doubts. Was Richard Williams using his worry about Billie being a bit off-colour to lure Zelda to his room? She thought back to the times she'd seen Zelda and Richard together. There was definitely chemistry between them.

She texted Janet again, hoping she was awake.

> Ring me as soon as you can. Wi-Fi's back on. Storm over. Zelda can get moving on the research IF she ever returns from Richard Williams's room! V x

Zelda hadn't returned by the time Viv put out the light an hour later and she hadn't texted. Viv did eventually get off to sleep but when she woke up, the first thing she noticed was Zelda's empty bed.

30

ZELDA

Zelda was in bed with Richard.

But it wasn't quite as Viv visualised. Zelda was one side of the bed, Richard the other. He was in the chinos and shirt he'd fallen asleep in; she was still wearing her satin pyjamas, though without the sweater. He was on his back, his mouth slightly open, she on her side, close to the edge of the bed, her hand hanging over the side, touching Billie.

It had been an eventful night.

First had come the text which galvanised her into action.

> Billie's not well. Please can you help? We're in 4016.

It had been like a starting gun. Independence was Richard's second name. He wouldn't have asked for help unless he really needed it. Zelda had shot down to Deck 4 and found his room easily because he'd been standing by the open door, no Billie by his side. Before she could ask, he'd turned and pointed to the dog's bed beside his own where she lay stretched out and listless, not like Billie at all.

Richard said, 'Zelda's here, Billie. She'll know what to do. You'll be all right now.'

Hoping his faith was justified, she'd gone into the room and knelt down beside the lovely dog, and stroked the top of her head, running her fingers through her silky fur. 'Hello, Billie, sweetheart, don't you worry, we'll have you up and running in no time. How long has she been like this?' she'd asked as Billie opened an eye but closed it again. Her nose felt hot and dry as if she had a fever.

'A couple of hours?' he'd said. She'd been tired before at this time of night, but never so tired that she hadn't come to his side if he asked her to, to take him to open the door for instance. Worse, she hadn't eaten her evening meal. There it was still in her bowl, untouched. He'd been so worried, he'd pulled the alarm cord and asked for the ship's pet master to come and help. The pet master, a qualified veterinary nurse, was in charge of the ship's kennels and other pet accommodation, but he couldn't be found, an apologetic steward said. He was off duty at eleven o'clock on a Saturday night and no one knew where he was.

'A vet?' she'd asked, hopefully. 'Isn't there a resident vet?' There were after all other pets aboard.

He'd shaken his head, and said he'd asked if there were any vets among the passengers and been told there weren't. Zelda had racked her brains. What, she'd asked herself, would she have done if it was Mack or Morag lying here, besides go out of her mind with worry? What *had* she done when either of them wasn't well?

She thought back to the last time Morag was ill – when she'd got a tick. The Westies were always getting ticks. They got them when they went for a run in the rougher areas of the park or open fields or the woods. They didn't bother Mack but Morag was allergic to them, and they made her quite poorly. Remembering when Morag had reacted badly, her hand reached instinctively for her handbag, where she usually kept a twister, a special pair of tweezers for removing ticks. Had she by some miracle left one there when she sorted her handbag pre-cruise, jettisoning everything she wouldn't need? It was a long shot that this was what was wrong with Billie, but the listlessness and high temperature and lack of appetite were familiar.

'Richard, when did Billie last go for a walk? I mean before you boarded *QM2*? When did you walk with her in long grass?' She explained about ticks and how the little beasts lurked in long grass. Parasites, they lay in wait till an animal passed by. Then they dropped from the blade of grass onto its fur or hair and burrowed down before sinking their claws into its skin to suck its blood – and in some cases pass on a lethal infection called Lyme disease. She hadn't mentioned that though. No need to panic him, he was worried enough. Instead she'd told him how Morag recovered really quickly once she'd found the tick and removed it. And oh – phew! – thank you God! – she'd found a twister at the bottom of her handbag, as Richard said he had taken Billie for a walk in a park before boarding the QM2 at Southampton. It had been her last chance to sniff around and feel the grass beneath her paws before they hit the sterile decks. 'But,' he looked stricken, 'I wish I hadn't.'

'No time for regrets, Richard. There's work to do. The sooner the better. Er... can you help?'

'Just tell me what to do.' He was already lowering himself to Billie's side and hers, using the bed to get his bearings.

She was kneeling by Billie's head, he tail-end. 'We need to part her fur with our fingers,' he'd be good at that she thought, 'feeling for the creatures. If you think you find one, tell me. Start at the back, and I'll start here. The most likely places to find them are on her face, or legs or chest for obvious reasons, so leave her tail for the moment. It will feel like a wart, though smooth, not wrinkly, more like a blister, but round, not flat.'

For the next ten minutes, all you could hear was their breathing, his, hers and Billie's and his calm, soothing voice from time to time. 'It's all right, darling. You're going to be fine, just fine. We'll have you up and running in no time at all. Don't you worry, my darling.'

Billie didn't respond in any way.

Then Richard's tone changed, lifted, really lifted. 'Found one, I think.' And leaning towards him she saw where his long fingers held the fur apart. And there it was, the little balloon of blood between the black hairs on Billie's white belly, one wriggling wire-like leg just visible.

'Well done. Hold it there.' She reached for the tick twister. 'And I'll try and I get this in place.'

The next moments were tricky. Thankful that she'd had lots of practice with Morag, she carefully slid the 'claw' of the tweezer under the tick's body and gently, ever so gently, started twisting. Slowly, slowly, catchee tickee, that was the way to do it. No rushing. It was vital to get all eight legs out. Leave one and all their good work would go to waste and Billie might not get better. She held her breath and Richard held his. If they'd been trying to defuse a bomb they couldn't have been any tenser. Then something changed. Hoping she wasn't imagining the slight slackening, she pulled, smoothly she hoped, and yes, there was the creature on the end of her tweezers, eight wiry little legs still wriggling. Phew! She held it aloft, forgetting Richard couldn't see, but he sensed her triumph.

'What do you do with it now?'

'Squish it.' She found a tissue in her bag and squished. 'Then we look for more.'

They began again and found two more quite soon, but it was gone midnight before they finally got to their feet, creaking a bit and laughing at themselves as they rubbed their backs and stretched their aching limbs. Then, when the tick bodies were safely squished and in the bin, Zelda asked Richard for crushed ice, which he got from the fridge, and she made little cold compresses by wrapping them in tissue. Kneeling again, she applied them to the swollen areas where the ticks had been. 'These should bring down the inflammation and make her feel better.'

'She's feeling better already, I think.' Richard was stroking Billie's ears.

'It usually takes longer than this. With Morag it's about four hours. With luck though her temperature will start to come down and she'll recover her joie de vivre.'

'Well, I think I just heard her tail wag.' Richard got to his feet. 'How long do those compresses need to stay on, by the way?'

'Till the ice melts, then I'll put some more on and leave you both to get some sleep.' She was ready to drop.

'Must you, go, I mean? Sorry, that's pathetic...' She knew it took a lot for him to ask, and she really wanted to stay, to be by Billie's side in case she needed to send again for the pet master and some antibiotics if she took a turn for the worse.

Richard glanced at the bed and so did she.

'Room for two, I think.' *She* said it. It was a big bed.

So that's what they did, he on one side, she on the other, each lying close to the edge, she, where he usually lay, she realised, with one hand hanging out so she could feel Billie on the floor beside her. Richard crashed out quickly on the other side. It took her longer to get off than him and she slept fitfully, waking often to check that Billie was still breathing and feel her nose, cooler each time she thought and maybe moister. Once in the early hours when she murmured 'good girl' to her she thought she heard her tail thumping the floor. Then she must have fallen into a deep sleep because it was light when she opened her eyes, wondering where she was. Seeing a cello by the wall filled her first with pleasure then alarm, till she remembered the events of the night before, and was alarmed again seeing the empty dog bed beside her bed. 'Billie, where are you?'

'It's all right, honey.' Richard's voice came from the kitchen area. 'Billie's with me eating her breakfast. Are you a tea in the morning person, or do you like coffee first thing?' Richard stood by the kettle, Billie by his side, her head in her bowl downing her breakfast with all the enthusiasm of a very hungry, healthy Labrador.

31

VIV

Sunday, 20 December

Viv was making tea when Zelda came in at half past eight, wearing the satin pyjamas she'd gone out in, with the sweater over the top. She looked much the same as she had last night in fact, except for the dreamy expression on her face.

'It's not what you're thinking.'

'I'm not thinking,' Viv lied. 'How's Billie?' That had to be the safest line of enquiry.

'Fine. Now.' Zelda smiled and shook her head, as if she could hardly believe what she was saying.

'Not very ill then?'

'Oh, she was, she was poorly, but I guessed what it was and had the remedy.'

'Richard was very grateful then?'

'Very.' Zelda beamed.

'Tea?'

'No, I've had a lovely cup of tea, thanks. I need a shower now.' She headed for the en suite.

'Breakfast? Have you had breakfast?'

'No.'

'The Britannia then, for the full five courses? None of us ate much dinner last night, if you remember?'

'Okay.' Zelda closed the shower room door and Viv reached for her phone to message Janet.

> Britannia at nine o'clock? Zelda currently on Planet Romance. Need to bring her back to earth to focus on your plight.

* * *

Zelda

Zelda returned to Planet Earth with a bump when they sat down for breakfast in the Britannia restaurant. She hadn't forgotten what she needed to do for Janet, and if she had then one look at her friend's face would have reminded her. Janet looked drained, as if she'd hardly slept at all, and she was still going on about recompensing Primrose if Mal and Malcolm were the same person and a bigamist.

'So, Zelda,' Viv was a tad teachery, 'you need to find birth certificates proving they're two different people, ASAP.'

'Yes, Viv, I know.' She hoped she didn't sound tetchy.

She opted for a Continental breakfast and was in Connexions by ten o'clock when it opened. It wasn't hard to find a free PC in the corner of a side room, affording her some privacy. Clearly, earlyish on a Sunday morning wasn't a popular time for getting in touch with friends and family back home or doing ancestral research. Nevertheless, it took her ages to find Janet's Malcolm's birth certificate despite knowing his date of birth, 19 October 1945, because there were lots of Malcolm Carmichaels, several born on the same day. She had to look closely to see where they were born and where they subsequently lived to track the right one down. She used a website called FreeBMD which Gary, the manager, very helpfully told her about. BMD stood for Births, Marriages and Deaths, he said, taking her for a beginner, and Free fortunately meant what it said. But she still had to upgrade her Wi-Fi package, that is pay more, to use the internet room more frequently. Gary was apologetic, but Zelda said that was okay, knowing Janet could afford it, and would reimburse her.

It was slow work, even though Janet had told her that her first husband's full name was Malcolm George Carmichael and that he'd been born at 14 Craddock Street, Edinburgh. But once she'd found his birth certificate, she had quickly learnt that his mother's maiden name was Eliza MacDonald, his father's Malachy George Carmichael, and that his father's occupation was railway engineer. But where did this get her? And what to look for next? Gary said that electoral rolls would show when and where Malcolm's parents were living for the following years, and therefore give young Malcolm's likely location, which might be useful, but they were on a different site. Censuses would have been even more useful, he said, but they weren't available for the 1940s yet. Zelda paused to think it out. Did she want to find out more about Janet's Malcolm, or try and find another Malcolm, father of Isabella? And wouldn't it be easier and possibly useful to find Malcolm and Janet's marriage certificate? She found that quite easily because she had both their names – Janet was Janet Elliot before she married – and it looked perfectly legal, she was pleased to see.

Deciding that her best bet was to find another Malcolm – or someone with a similar name – she went through the list of Malcolm Carmichaels again. The search page on FreeBMD had given several ways of doing this, but it was confusing. There was Exact Match on First Names, Phonetic Search Surnames, Match Only Recorded Ages and Identifiable Spouses Only. She'd used Exact Match to find Janet's Malcolm because she had his birth date, and his full name, but even that had come up with a batch of Malcolm Carmichaels, which she'd had to sift through to find the one she wanted, well, one of the ones she wanted. It took ages. The other one might be there, or it might not, and how would she know? She'd only got Isabella's word for it that Primrose's Mal's birth date was the same, anyway. Now she tried Exact Match again but spelling Malcom without the second 'l'. It was quite a common alternative spelling and her search came up with another batch of twenty Malcoms, born in Edinburgh on that day. This was doing her head in, even before she started looking for Malvins and Maleks and Malachys.

Getting up to stretch and roll her neck and give herself a break to clear her head, Zelda remembered gloomily that it had taken the best part of a year to track down her father. A *year*. Research was mostly slow, even without distractions like memories of last night. Sitting down again, she told herself she had two days, just two days, to find something that would stop Janet sinking into depression.

None of the Malcoms without a second 'l' seemed right, so she moved on to Malvin Carmichaels, then paused again. Would it be better to try Malachy, Malcolm's father's name, first? In those days, men liked to name their firstborn after themselves. Malcom might have had an older brother named Malachy called Mal for short. Could Primrose's husband have been Malachy, registered with the diminutive? It was common now but not then. Looking at the search options again, Zelda focused on Identifiable Spouses Only. She guessed that if she searched for Malcolm Carmichael married to Janet Elliott she'd get their marriage certificate, again. But what if she asked for Malcolm Carmichael married to Primrose? She didn't know Primrose's maiden name but as Primrose was an unusual name it might be enough. In fact, lightbulb moment, why not search for Primrose's marriage certificate? That would reveal her husband's name. Berating herself for not thinking of this earlier, she looked around to ask Gary for advice and saw him by the door talking to Richard.

'I thought we'd find you here,' Richard, with Billie by his side, called out. Thud. Thud. Thud. Was that Billie's tail she could hear or her own heart?

'How's Billie?' She hurried over.

'Pleased to see you. Look at her tail.'

It was still thudding against the floor.

'I'm pleased to see her too.' Her hand reached out, until she remembered the rule and withdrew.

'It's okay.' He took Billie's harness off. 'You can have your fix now, and she hers. We've come to remind you about dinner tonight, and maybe take you to lunch in the Golden Lion?'

Was it lunchtime already? She wasn't hungry but she'd like to see more of Billie who'd moved to her side and was licking her hand. Was that allowed, she asked.

'Sure, if it's all right with you.'

'Very all right.'

'Let's get going then. Can I take your arm and give Billie a rest?'

'Of course.'

'Great. You're off duty, Billie.' He linked his right arm with Zelda's left and she felt the warmth and strength of him through the fabric of his jacket. Thud. Thud. Thud. That *was* her heart, jumping around like a boisterous puppy, not Billie's tail.

'Okay?' He paused to check.

It was better than okay, but also disconcerting. She hadn't planned for these inconvenient feelings.

32

VIV

Viv and Janet were in the Commodore Club bar, sitting by the bay window watching the bow of the ship, throwing up a V of foam as it surged through the still astonishingly calm ocean.

'Was that yours or mine?' Viv heard a mobile ping.

'Yours, I think.'

It was Zelda, saying she was in the Golden Lion with Richard and Billie, who was once again a happy healthy dog, she was pleased to say. She and Richard were about to order lunch but would wait if Viv and Janet wanted to join them. They would be very welcome.

'Afterthought,' said Janet, sipping her cocktail, when Viv forwarded it. 'The "would be very welcome" bit. I detect insincerity. She's being polite.'

Viv, sipping too, agreed. She'd told Janet about Zelda's night-time adventure. Still stuffed after their five-course breakfast, they had decided to have a liquid lunch of one cocktail a piece, so were trying to make them last, which was difficult because they were delicious. Viv had gone for a rightly named Over the Top, a mix of gin, sloe gin, cherry brandy, fresh fruit and basil, Janet for a more restrained Yorkshire Pace Setter, a combination of cognac, ginger liqueur and black treacle with mixed spices.

'I'll reply for both of us, shall I?' Janet put her glass on the table in front of them. 'From what you said, they've got things to talk about, or not talk about.'

'Ask her if she found anything useful this morning.' Viv, a bit cross with Zelda, wondered if she'd actually been doing research.

'Wouldn't she have said if she had?'

'Maybe, but...'

'Viv, shush.' Janet touched her hand. 'Look who's just come in. Sorry, you can't. No, don't turn your head. It's Primrose, *by herself* and I've thought of something pertinent to ask her.'

Interesting, and good to see Janet showing signs of fighting back. She risked a glance over her shoulder and saw Primrose hitching her bottom onto one of the bar stools, then looking at her watch. Was she meeting someone here? Looked like it. Better get her over here before they arrived...

But Janet was onto it. 'Primrose! Come and join us! We're looking at the ocean, enjoying the calm!' Primrose looked at her watch again then got down from the stool and came over. Janet patted a chair beside her. 'Sit down, Primrose, and have a cocktail with us. Viv recommends the Over the Top, a veritable health food she says, with five of your five a day.'

Primrose sat down, but on the edge of the seat, looking uncomfortable. How long had they got before Isabella or anyone else appeared? And when would Janet ask her pertinent question? At the moment Janet was doing a sterling job of trying to put her at ease, preparing the ground Viv hoped, so Primrose would relax and be off guard. Janet sounded friendly and reassuring, chatting about the bad weather which Primrose agreed had been frightening.

Did Primrose and her daughter know Janet was coming on this trip, before they booked, and if so, how? That was what Viv wanted to ask. If they did, there was a good chance they had come with a purpose, because they had done some research beforehand, and discovered that Malcolm really was a bigamist perhaps. But why had they come on a cruise to tell Janet when they could have taken the legal route from the start?

The barman brought Primrose's drink and she took a gulp, still on the edge of her seat, looking nervous.

Pertinent question, Janet?

Janet was still going on about the weather, now wondering what it would be like in New York. She'd heard there might be snow and a bit of her hoped so. It would be so pretty. She was so looking forward to seeing the ice-skaters at the Rockefeller Centre and the famous Christmas tree and all the decorations, and to a walk, maybe a carriage ride in Central Park. Had Primrose ever been to New York? Primrose said she never had. No one mentioned Mal or Malcolm. It was as if last night's bombshell hadn't been dropped. Then suddenly Primrose put down her glass, empty now except for the debris at the bottom, and reached into a pocket for a handkerchief. 'I'm sorry, Janet, th-that this has happened, I mean. I *so* wanted to be your friend.' She dabbed her eyes.

Janet patted her hand. 'Que sera sera, Primrose.'

'Thank you, Janet.' Primrose tucked the handkerchief up her sleeve.

Viv couldn't wait any longer. *Whose idea was it to come on this trip?* was on her lips when Janet gave her a *leave this to me* look and called the barman over. 'Another OTT, please.'

As the clock behind the bar ticked loudly, Primrose started to look more relaxed, more so when her second OTT arrived. Janet's glass was still full, Viv noticed, when she said with a little shake of her head, 'Primrose, I still can't believe our paths didn't cross before, when we were girls, I mean. I've been wondering, did you know Helen Stathan?'

'Yes, we were friends at school.' Primrose nodded.

'I thought you might have,' Janet took a sip of her cocktail, 'because she went to St Margaret's too. She lived round the corner from me in Cobden Street and we were friends and went to primary school together. Then Helen passed the entrance exam to St Margaret's, and I didn't, so we went our separate ways to some extent.' She took another sip. 'Did Mal know Helen, Primrose?'

'Yes, she introduced us.'

'Oh, how?'

Viv held her breath.

They were chatting but this wasn't chat. Clever Janet.

'Helen asked me to form a double at table tennis at the youth club we went to. Mal was really nice looking and he had a brilliant backhand and, well, he was brilliant at everything really, and...' Primrose, her tongue loosened by drink, went on about the wonders of Mal, and Janet let her, only occasionally asking yet another question.

'And which youth club would that be, Primrose?'

'St Andrew's. It was attached to St Andrew's church.'

'Oh, I went there, to the church I mean, but also the youth club sometimes...' Janet stopped, startled by something, and glancing over her shoulder to where she was looking, Viv saw why.

It was Isabella, naked she thought for a horrified second, till she realised she'd shed the snake-patterned jumpsuit and replaced it with one in pale pink. She was at the bar, but looking in their direction and now coming over, clearly not pleased with what she'd seen. 'Mummy,' she reached Primrose and stood behind her chair, ignoring the others, 'I thought we were having a drink together before lunch.'

'Yesh, darling,' Primrose looked round at her, 'but I've just been having a little one with The Mush-cateers...'

Primrose was squiffy.

Isabella nearly tipped her out of her chair. 'Come on, Mummy. We need to find you a glass of water.'

* * *

'So,' said Viv later, 'what did you learn?'

They were back in Janet's suite, in the kitchen.

'Nothing definite, well, not *definitive*,' said Janet, ever precise as she made coffee, 'but I am increasingly of the belief that Mal and Malcolm are not the same person.'

'Evidence?' Viv hoped this was convincing.

'He never went to the St Andrew's youth club. Well, I never saw him there.'

'But you said you only went there sometimes.'

'That is true.'

'Anything else?' Viv wanted something *clinching*. Malcolm could easily have gone to the youth club when Janet didn't.

'Facebook. I know you don't approve, Viv, but I'm sure I was friends with Helen Stathan on Facebook for a while, and still may be.'

'So? Sorry, you've got to explain, not about so-called friends, I think I've got that, but how this Helen Stathan comes into things.'

'Well, I think Helen, who was a close friend of mine when we were very young, was the one who suggested we all post a photograph of our wedding day on Facebook. So that's where Primrose might have seen it. It's very probable that Helen and Primrose were Facebook friends because they knew each other at secondary school. Then when Primrose saw the photograph, she jumped to the mistaken conclusion that because her Mal and my Malcolm looked alike they were the same person.'

Viv didn't want to be discouraging as this train of thought seemed to be cheering Janet up, but what she'd found out wasn't game-changing. Were they inching forward? Possibly.

33

JANET

Janet wished Viv had been more enthusiastic about what she'd discovered. She was fighting hard not to let anxiety ruin the holiday, for Viv and Zelda as well as herself. When Viv went back to her room for a Sunday-afternoon zizz, Janet put her feet up and tried to relax on the sofa, but there were too many thoughts whirring in her head. Were Primrose and Isabella on Facebook? She reached for her phone to try and find out. Yes, they were and they 'followed' her. How long had they been following her? She couldn't find that out, but their bumping into her was looking even less like an accident. Suddenly being 'followed' seemed a bit sinister, as it would if she heard footsteps behind her when she was walking home on a dark night.

Janet wasn't like some people, posting every time they had a cup of tea. She didn't tell everyone her business and sometimes went months without posting anything. She waited till she had something interesting to say. *Like going on holiday.* Or till someone made a request for a special feature. *Like weddings.* She'd responded to one of those, and, she suddenly felt a bit sick remembering, she'd been invited to join a Facebook 'Cruise family' and joined because she'd thought she should. Now she wished she'd never heard of Facebook. Fortunately, a text pinging in broke into her negative thoughts. Even better it was from Maggie, her cheerful solicitor neighbour:

> Hi Janet, stop worrying! Zelda's told me about the ghastly pair and they sound like fraudsters. Enjoy the rest of your holiday and we'll sort it when you get back.

Feeling chirpier, Janet planned a pleasant afternoon for herself, and Viv and Zelda if they wanted to join her. A cream tea might be what they all needed. It was a long time since breakfast. She'd also like to go back to the jewellery boutique to try and find out more about Auntie Em's ring. Isabella had thwarted her last effort, with her nasty attempted bribe, but she probably wouldn't be there this afternoon. Janet consulted the Daily Programme. Cream teas were being served in the Queen's Room from 3.30 to 4.30 but it was only 2.30, so it made sense to go to the jewellery boutique first. She texted the others with her plans and set off, taking the stairs, anticipating the extra calories later.

It was quite a trek from Deck 12 down to Deck 3 and required switching from one carpeted stairway to another, so she had to keep her wits about her. There was absolutely no one else around to consult, and it felt odd being the only person using the stairs. On one of the landings, she thought she heard the cough of someone behind her but when she stopped to look there was no one there, and most of the time it was eerily quiet as the muzak coming through the Tannoy wasn't more than a hum and the thick carpet absorbed the sound of her own footsteps. And those of anyone who might be following her, she thought at one point, before telling herself to keep her imagination in check. It was quite a relief, nevertheless, to reach Deck 3 and the hustle and bustle of the Grand Lobby.

A brass band in front of the Christmas tree was playing 'O Come, All Ye Faithful' and there were lots of people milling around. In need of a bit of a breather – her knees ached – Janet looked for somewhere to sit, but all the seats were occupied, so she went straight to the jewellery boutique which she found busier than she'd hoped. And there didn't seem to be a free seat here either. The customer talking to Carlos at the counter was sitting on the only chair and there were others obviously waiting for his services. Deciding to leave and come back later, she turned to go when someone hissed in her ear.

'Second thoughts about what I said?' It was of course Isabella.

She followed me here.

'No.' Janet was abrupt.

'Okay-ay,' Isabella drawled, 'but I still like that brooch.' She jerked her head in the direction of the glass cabinet.

'As I said last night, Isabella, I will do the right thing if and when your case is proved. You must be patient. Now let me pass.'

'Okay-ay.' Isabella stepped aside. 'If you're happy with me sharing our fascinating story on Facebook that's absolutely fine by me.'

It took a moment for what she'd said to sink in.

'Just to be clear,' Isabella smirked, 'if you're okay with friends and family knowing about our, er... relationship, then I'll get someone else to buy me a present. Think about it.'

She slunk off.

* * *

Janet was shaking when she reached the Queen's Room and the elegant cream and gold décor did nothing to lift her spirits. Nor did the afternoon tea when it arrived, nor Viv and Zelda's well-meaning remarks.

'That was blackmail, Janet.' Viv topped up her gold-rimmed china teacup with Darjeeling, rather different to her usual sturdy mug of breakfast tea.

The dainty sandwiches and fancy cakes on the three-tiered stand sat untouched. on the table in front of them.

'I know, Viv, you've said.'

'You can't give in to her.'

'I know, Viv.' *But if I don't...* She didn't finish.

'You really can't, Janet.' Zelda joined in.

Janet nodded, though she was still shaking. Even her best friends didn't understand.

'Please,' said Viv, 'someone, eat something. We can't let this lot go to waste.' She waved her hand at the cakes and scones and neat little sandwiches. 'Janet's paying for them whether we eat them or not.'

'Sorry,' Zelda patted her only slightly rounded stomach, 'but I had lunch and I'm eating dinner with Richard in a couple of hours.'

'It's up to me then.' Viv helped herself to a scone and reached for the cream and strawberry jam. All around them people were munching away and murmuring, oohing and ahhhing with delight, looking as if they hadn't a care in the world.

Janet tried again. 'What if I...'

'No, Janet!' They spoke as one, Viv with a mouthful of scone.

'Hear me out, please.'

They did at least listen, their lips pursed, as she tentatively suggested that she buy Isabella something, not the super-expensive brooch she wanted, but a *little* something to give them time to find the information they needed to refute what she was claiming...

'No-o-o.' They shook their heads in unison.

Janet got it. You don't give in to blackmail. Of course you don't. They were absolutely right. If you gave into blackmailers they came back for more. They upped the stakes. She knew that and agreed, in principle. She was strong on principles, was usually the first to insist they abide by them. 'But,' she lowered her voice to a whisper to stop the people on the next table hearing her anguish, 'you don't know Grant like I do. You don't know how *vindictive* he can be. If he reads this on Facebook, or worse, if someone else reads it and tells him about it, he'll cut me out of his life.'

'Janet, you don't see the grandkids that often now, do you? Sorry, ignore that. That was insensitive.' Viv had the grace to look abashed.

'Thank you, Viv. I am well aware Rocky and Woody live in New Zealand, and therefore we don't see each other in person very often, but I do see and speak to them on Skype quite often and Grant is quite capable of preventing even that.'

'But why would he?' Zelda looked puzzled. 'I mean, even if the worst is proved to be true, why would Grant blame you for something his father did?'

'Because he's Grant' – she thought she'd told them this – 'he blames me for everything and thinks his father can, I mean could, do no wrong.'

A waiter arrived to ask if everything was all right and she almost cried out, no! When he'd gone, Viv changed tack. 'Let's be positive. Zelda, how's your research going?' She was willing Zelda to come up with something.

You could see from the meaningful look she gave her before reaching for another cake, but Zelda failed.

She said she'd spent the morning in Connexions and Gary, the manager, had been helpful pointing her towards different sites but she hadn't found an alternative Malcolm Carmichael whose location fitted, and didn't see how she could, well, not quickly, because it was a process of elimination. 'But,' she said, when Viv glared at her, and maybe even kicked her under the table, 'I have thought of another line of enquiry, marriage certificates. I've found yours, Janet, and it all looks legal and above board.'

'See,' said Viv. 'That's good.'

'But...' Janet stopped herself saying that the one she had at home, the original, also looked legal and above board, but that didn't prove it was.

'So,' said Viv, as if priming a pump for optimism, 'what's the next step, Zelda?'

'Finding Primrose's marriage certificate which will with luck show her married to her Mal, but not your Malcolm. A marriage certificate gives the groom's full name and his father's name and occupation, which should be enough to tell us whether he's Malcolm or not.'

'Clinching it!' said Viv, as if it were job done.

Zelda frowned. 'First, though, I need to know Primrose's maiden name. You don't happen to know it, do you, Janet?'

Janet shook her head. 'I didn't know her, remember.'

'But do you really need it?' said Viv. 'There can't be that many Primroses.'

'That's what I thought, but there are more than you'd think. It would take me quite a while to trawl through them all.'

'So we ask her, when she's not with her daughter, obviously.' Viv straightened up in her seat and scanned the room as if hoping to see Primrose having tea. If she had, Janet felt sure that she'd have got up and gone straight over and asked her there and then. But she didn't and next thing she was leaning forward, conspiratorially.

'We have a plan, right.' She reached for another scone and spread it with jam. 'As soon as we've finished tea we split up and go and look for her. Whoever finds her, asks her, casually, making up a reason for asking. For instance, I might say, *Hi, Primrose, just been talking to Janet who thinks she does remember you after all, and wonders what your maiden name was...* And if we don't find her, we try at dinner tonight. That will be just you and me, Janet, as Zelda will be otherwise engaged. If the daughter turns up too, one of us will distract her while the other questions Primrose. She can hardly pretend she can't remember her own maiden name, can she?' Viv was firing on all cylinders, fuelled by jam and cream.

Janet wanted to hug her.

'And,' said Viv, 'I've got another idea, more long term, but another clincher.'

'Out with it, Viv.' Zelda was smiling.

'Getting hold of Isabella's DNA so we can compare it to Grant's and see if they have the same father. I think our best bet is hair. It shouldn't be too hard to get one of Isabella's, she's got such a lot. I don't mind having a go at that. And if by any chance you've kept a lock of Grant's hair, in a locket or something...' She tailed off. 'What's the matter, Janet? Oh, no, don't cry. I've put my foot in it again, haven't I?'

'No, no you haven't, really. I'm a bit teary, that's all, but mostly because I was laughing, picturing you creeping up on Isabella to tweak a hair. And,' she wanted to hug her friends, 'there's nothing the matter, nothing important that is, because whatever happens now, however this turns out, if I lose my house, my money, everything, I've still got the best friends ever.'

34

VIV

Viv was fired up to fight Janet's corner, as she sat down in the Britannia restaurant for dinner that night, her back to the *QM2* tapestry, so she could see the others coming in. She had come early to prevent the pushy pair getting here first and taking control of the table as they had last night. Janet needed support. Her 'if I lose everything' outpouring was worrying. Now wasn't the time to consider defeat. They must fight the ghastly pair to the last ditch or document. Here was Janet now. They could finalise their strategy before the enemy arrived.

'Sorry I'm late.' Janet sat down.

'You're not. I'm early. You look great, by the way.' Janet wore a smart purple dress.

'So do you. That jacket's good on you.'

'It's Libby's, of course.' She'd just had time to pull on the brocade jacket before rushing down to dinner.

'Suits you. The red and gold picks up the red of your hair.'

'What's left of it. More pepper and salt these days, paprika pepper in a good light.'

'My frock's from Biba, a repro, not vintage, moiré velvet. Sorry, I know you don't care. I await instructions, revered M.'

Viv laughed, M she was not, but it was good to hear Janet making fun.

'I don't think we can be too specific about who does what. We'll have to play it by ear to some extent, but if we aim for me distracting Isabella while you chat to Primrose about old times and ask her the key question, I think that could work.'

'Agreed. Here's to us.' Janet went to raise her glass and saw it was empty. 'Oh no! I ordered a bottle of that delicious Chablis.'

The sommelier arrived as she spoke and poured a taster into Janet's glass. 'Are the other ladies joining you, madam?' Janet swirled and sniffed and tasted the wine, and nodded her approval. Then said she thought there would be four of them. 'Mrs Carmichael and her daughter will be here soon, I expect, but we'll have a glass while we're waiting.'

The waiter topped up Janet's glass and then filled Viv's, though filled wasn't the right word. She'd noticed that the posher the restaurant, the less the waiter poured into the glass, and the Britannia was posh so he poured a bare inch. Viv feared for Zelda in the even posher Queen's Grill...

'Viv.' Janet had a raised glass in her hand. 'Quickly, before they come. To success.'

They clinked, but as it turned out needn't have hurried. Ten minutes later, their adversaries hadn't arrived. They waited another ten minutes before they ordered food, by which time they were halfway down the bottle.

'Do you think they've got wind of our plan?' Janet, sotto voce, seemed to be the one playing M now.

'How could they?'

'Spies?' Janet checked her phone for messages. 'In the Queen's Room you mean, listening while we were having tea?'

'That's where we devised the plan.'

'Or is there a traitor in the camp?' Viv played along, keen to keep Janet's spirits up.

'Zelda, you mean? A double agent?'

Viv risked being serious. 'I have a Plan B.' She hoped she wouldn't have to use it.

Janet sighed but looked up from her phone.

'Call Isabella's bluff. Tell her to publish and be damned. Say, "Put it on Facebook. See if I care!"'

'But I do care, Viv. That's the trouble. I care very much. In my case it's not true what they say about not caring what people think when you get older. I don't want to be pitied or sniggered at behind my back.'

She went back to scrolling. 'It's my guess she's done it already and that's why they haven't come.'

'Have you found anything?' Viv guessed she was on Facebook.

'Not yet.'

'Well, stop looking. I think she will wait a bit before she resorts to that. She'd much rather have that brooch.'

'So...' Janet looked up quite sharply.

'No! That is not what I mean. You do not give her a thing. What we do is find her and tell her that if she posts false information about you, you will sue her and you already have lawyers onto it. You have heard from Maggie?'

Janet nodded as Cesar arrived with their starters. They'd both gone for the leek terrine with Melba toast.

'But what if...' Janet began again as Cesar departed.

'...it isn't false information?' Viv finished her sentence for her. 'What if Malcolm was even rottener than you thought he was? Then we'll deal with it. We've dealt with worse. Meanwhile we look at the positives, right? One, as we've said before, if those two had a case they'd take the legal route. Two, we're going to spike their guns with a few well-discovered facts, as soon as we've found out Primrose's maiden name, which we'll get back onto as soon as we've finished this meal. She's probably quizzing somewhere and we'll track her down. Three, sorry, can't think of one at the moment but give me time.' She reached for a piece of toast. 'This is delicious. Try it. The terrine is really good.'

But Janet pushed her plate aside. 'How much time have we got, Viv? Before the whole world knows that I wasn't married to Malcolm, and Grant is illegitimate, and I have to sell my house and I'm reduced to penury?'

'Janet, Zelda's on the case...'

But Janet wasn't listening – her fear had surfaced – and Zelda, as they both well knew, was currently otherwise engaged.

35

ZELDA

Zelda was in the Queen's Grill restaurant feeling torn. She was pleased to be here with Richard and Billie of course – she was under the table – but also guilty for leaving Viv and Janet to deal with Primrose and Isabella.

'Penny for them? Isn't that what you Brits say?' Richard's ability to tell when her attention wandered was disconcerting.

'Er... you look terrific.' He did, in white dress shirt and black dinner jacket, and she wasn't going to admit that her thoughts had been elsewhere. How easy it was for a man to look good, especially if he was good-looking to start with.

He laughed. 'So do you, I'm sure. Tell me.'

She was glad she'd dressed up. 'I'm wearing a grey silk dress, long and high-necked, which I'm pleased to say fits in rather well with the décor here. It's very theatrical, all red and cream and gold as I imagine it was in the 1930s on the first *Queen Mary*. These chairs are amazing. Their high T-shaped backs are upholstered in scarlet velvet and most of the clothes in my wardrobe would have clashed violently.'

'And does the grey of your dress pick up the grey in my hair?'

Now she laughed. 'Of course. They both have a silvery shimmer.'

He raised his glass. 'Don't forget your drink.'

'How could I? It's delicious.'

'What's the celebration?' she'd asked when he ordered champagne, Veuve Clicquot.

'Every day's a celebration.'

'You drink champagne every day?'

'No,' he'd shaken his head, 'but today's special. You turned up for a start.'

'You thought I wouldn't?'

He pointed to the paper menu in front of her. 'Let's choose then talk. Have anything you fancy, but I'd highly recommend...' he picked up his mobile and seemed to read from it, 'the "wild sturgeon caviar for starters with warm blinis and sour cream with accompaniments" unspecified but I expect they'll be okay.'

'How, how do you do that?' She knew the menus were online but...

'You'd like a demo?'

He got to his feet and came round to her side of the table, then standing by her, close but not touching, he showed her the screen of his mobile where the menus were displayed, and then pointed to a gadget underneath the keyboard which he touched with his long fingers, reading aloud as he did.

It was totally amazing.

She'd heard of Braille, of course, and thought she knew what it was, but it wasn't till she saw him running his fingers over the raised dots, translating them into words, that she realised how *wondrous* it was.

'Invented by a fifteen-year-old,' he said, 'Louis Braille. French, 1824.'

'Really?' She was in awe, and not just of the teenage inventor. 'I can't even touch type properly. I still look down at the keyboard.' She couldn't believe the speed at which his fingers moved.

'Needs must,' he said, 'but Braille isn't used quite so much these days. It's going out of fashion. The young prefer sound. They do this.' He pressed a key to demonstrate the audio version of the menu, switching it off when she'd heard a snippet. Then he went back to his seat, feeling his way by the table with his right hand.

Wow! she didn't say, sensing he didn't want applause, but *wow!*

Billie, thankfully, filled the slightly awkward silence that followed, by coming over to her side. The attractive spicy scent of Richard still lingered.

Off duty now, Billie's harness was beside Richard on a table thoughtfully provided by a watchful steward when they'd first come in. When their starters arrived Billie went and lay down beside the table, trained, he said, to ignore people eating.

You turned up for a start. His words came back to her as she tasted caviar for the first time in her life.

'What made you think I might not turn up tonight?'

'Because you didn't this afternoon.' He put sour cream on his blini.

'This afternoon?' Oh! She remembered the concert in the Royal Court. She'd said she'd go.

'I'm so sorry...'

He shrugged.

'But I completely forgot.'

'It really doesn't matter, Zelda. You're here now. How's the caviar?'

'Great, but it does matter, not doing what I said I'd do, I mean. I've got to explain. You remember the first time we had a drink together in the Golden Lion...' She stopped. Maybe this wasn't such a good idea.

'When you were listening to the couple behind you instead of being totally enthralled by me?'

'Yes.'

'And you thought they were up to no good?'

'Yes.'

'Go on then.'

'Really?' Most men would have been at least ruffled that she hadn't been totally enthralled by their company, but he seemed amused.

'I'm *asking* for an update, Zelda.'

They were onto their mains and a bottle of red by the time she'd finished and he seemed genuinely interested. He said he thought Gary, the Connexions manager, would be able to help even more if they did find Primrose's maiden name, and he wished he could help himself.

'I quite fancy being The Blind Detective. You know?' She didn't and he said there was a film of that name, which he hadn't seen of course, but he'd listened to the English version, dubbed from the original Cantonese. 'It was funny, and not entirely implausible. Like me, no more than me, the guy picked up on things sighted people didn't. Panned by the critics, by the way, but I enjoyed it.'

He went back to the prawns on his plate which needed a lot of sorting, and she went back to hers, following his lead as he seemed to know what he was doing.

It was a delicious but messy meal and at first sight, she hadn't been sure how to tackle it. But Richard had pulled apart a huge tiger prawn with his fingers, speared it with his fork, dipped it in the garlic and ginger soy sauce and expertly conveyed it to his mouth without dripping any of it down his dress-shirt front.

Competence is sexy.

'Another thing I can do is ask staff,' he said, when they were washing their fingers in the bowls provided. 'As I may have said before, they see *everything*, being in and out of people's rooms all day. And they talk among themselves about what they see.'

'Oh no, I'm very untidy.'

He laughed and said he couldn't be because he had to know where things were, then became serious, after wiping his hands on the linen napkin. 'May I have your hand for a moment?'

'Are you going to tell me my future?'

'No, but I can tell a lot about the present from a hand. You can say no if you like.' His hand was on the table, palm up.

She put hers on top of his, palm to palm. His was warm, dry and firm, his fingers strong, the tips slightly rough, hardened she thought by hours of contact with vibrating cello strings.

'And palm to palm is holy palmers' kiss.' The words came into her head.

'William Shakespeare?'

She nodded. 'Romeo and Juliet.'

'Good bloke.' He took his hand away, then thought better of it and reached for hers again, this time linking fingers, parting them slightly so she felt their strength. 'Can we with all our years of experience do better than that tragic young couple, do you think?'

36

VIV

Monday, 21 December

'So, how did it go? No, don't need to ask.' Viv was still in bed when Zelda floated in, wearing the long grey evening dress she'd gone out in.

'I need a shower first, Viv.'

'Bet you do.'

She dropped her bag on the floor and closed the en suite door.

Viv got up and put the kettle on. *Good for her. I hope it works out.* But how soon could she get the obviously loved-up Zelda back on the case? As she made tea for herself, and put a teabag in a cup ready for Zelda, she went over the night before, which hadn't gone so well for her and Janet. They hadn't found Primrose when they'd combed the ship after their meal and Janet's mood had gone rapidly downhill. At ten o'clock she had insisted on going back to her suite alone, convinced she was going to be publicly shamed and resigned to a life of penury.

Viv dashed off a text:

> Hi Janet. How are you this morning? Meet Kings Court Buffet Deck 7 for breakfast at 9? Unless you want to join me for a Power Deck Walk first? Ha ha!

Determined to do ten laps of the promenade deck before joining the others in her favourite breakfast place, she was in her jogging togs putting on her trainers when Zelda came out of the shower, cuddling herself in her fluffy white Cunard towelling robe. 'Might have to buy this,' she said dreamily.

No point asking her about Janet yet.

Viv told her about her plan for breakfast and Zelda said she'd join her. 'And Viv,' she said as she was going out of the door, 'contrary to what you're thinking, I was not completely off duty, last night, and I will be back on the case *momentarily*.' She said *momentarily* with an American accent.

Loved-up was the word.

On the way to Deck 7, Viv checked her phone to see if Janet had replied to her breakfast suggestion. She hadn't so Viv sent off another text, but when, panting and doubled over, she reached the Kings Court Buffet at nine o'clock Zelda was sitting alone, in a seat by the window, looking out at the choppy sea. Choppy, because there was a breeze, but still calm, Viv noted with relief, as Zelda turned round and saw her. Beckoning her over, she held up her mobile, which she passed to her as soon as she was sitting down. It was a text from Janet:

> Sorry but not fit company. Eating breakfast in room. J x

Viv checked her phone and found the same message.

'What do we do?' Zelda was fully engaged.

'Drag her out of her room and take her to something diverting. But breakfast first.'

Viv got up and headed for the breakfast bar, turning her back on the sea, which she was getting a bit fed up with if she was honest. There was too much of it, she decided, with a pang of yearning for her garden, colourful even at this time of year. The sea was too grey and relentless. She needed a touch of green or red, even brown would do. Shouldn't there be a sign they were getting closer to land by now, like a bird with a leafy twig in its beak? They were only two days from New York, after all. It was Monday morning and by this time on Wednesday they would be docking in the Brooklyn Terminal, or even making their way to the hotel.

Over breakfast, full English for her – she deserved it – healthy fruit and yogurt for Zelda – keeping fit in her own way – Viv reported on the failed fact-finding mission of the night before, including Primrose's no-show. Zelda was surprised. She said she'd been hopeful that things were going well in the Britannia because Isabella was in the Queen's Grill with one of her escorts. 'I assumed then,' Zelda lowered her voice because tables round them were filling up, 'that the unguarded mother was with you and Janet, spilling out what you needed to know.'

'Well, she wasn't, because, as I've said, she hadn't turned up. And we couldn't find her afterwards though we searched all the places she was likely to be, including the Golden Lion, where there was a quiz going on.'

'Isabella must have locked her in her room.'

'That doesn't seem...' *Totally far-fetched*, Viv was about to say, when Zelda returned to her current favourite subject.

'Richard was the one who realised she was there, actually.' She leaned across the table. 'He's got this amazing hearing. Honestly, Viv, if I turn my head away or look in my bag he *knows*... He says it's because the tone of my voice changes. He's very sensitive to tone, of course as a musician he has to be, and he's *very* funny, ha ha funny I mean, not odd funny. He's very *ordinary* in other ways, though *extraordinary* in others. He says I should think of him as a bat...'

Zelda, have you forgotten about Isabella?

'He's got this great sense of humour, Viv, and uses echo-location to know where someone is. So he knew I wasn't in his concert yesterday afternoon – I *forgot*, can you believe it? – but he also missed the smell of my perfume. It was when I didn't go to say hello to Billie afterwards, as I usually did, that he realised I hadn't turned up. Anyway, he recognised the gold digger by her voice, though he'd only heard it once, that time in the Golden Lion when he'd described it as rasping. We'd just had this rather intense exchange, about *Romeo and Juliet* actually, when he leaned forward and said quietly, "I think someone you're interested in is behind you, again." I risked a glance and saw her – that tower of hair does rather stand out – at a table with an old guy with a comb-over of about three strands... Well, I took a second glance to be absolutely sure Primrose wasn't there and I nearly texted you to say so. But then I stopped feeling guilty about leaving you to it because I thought you'd be fine interrogating Primrose by yourselves, and I started to relax with Richard...'

No need to say more.

'But by then Janet was going downhill.'

'So how do we get her up again? Honestly, Viv, I'm back on the case.' Zelda started to gather her things. 'Richard's busy this morning. He's rehearsing and he's preparing for a talk he's giving about guide dogs or seeing-eye dogs as they're called in America. It will be to raise funds for the American equivalent of the RNIB. So many people have stopped to ask him about Billie that...'

Viv stopped her. 'Sorry, Zelda, I love hearing about Richard and we'll all come to his talk obviously – great idea – but we need to get on. You with trying to find a Mal who isn't Malcolm – me stopping Janet throwing herself overboard. Sorry again,' she saw the look of alarm on Zelda's face, 'I don't mean that literally, but she's very unhappy so we've got to pull out all the stops.'

37

VIV

Viv was standing on one leg, Janet by her side.

Agreeing to come to a Tai Chi class was the only way she'd managed to persuade Janet to get out of bed. Janet had been trying to get her to come to Tai Chi for years, so she could hardly refuse when Viv said she was at last willing to give it a go. Inner calm was the aim, and it seemed to be working for Janet. She hadn't wobbled once.

Not so Viv.

'Now the other leg,' said Paulina, the young instructor whose long plait was even stiller than she was.

Viv changed to the other leg and wobbled even more.

They were in the Winter Garden, a glass building like a conservatory doubling as a café, where some tables and chairs had been pushed to one side to give the Tai Chi-ers space. Viv thought 'garden' was stretching the meaning of the word. How many gardens had wall-to-wall carpeting, for heaven's sake, albeit with orange lines in a pattern a bit like crazy-paving and a few pot plants? An olive tree and a couple of tree ferns did not a garden make.

Viv was bored.

Before standing on one leg she'd stood on two for what seemed an age, firstly with arms by her sides, then lifting them to ninety degrees and holding them there, then lowering them slowly to her sides again, not forgetting to breathe. You had to breathe in through the nose on the up, tensing the muscles and out through the mouth on the down, letting everything go. In was yin and out was yang or maybe the other way round. This was the first movement of The Form, according to Paulina, and it had to be done *slowly*. Tai Chi was all about slowing down and getting in touch with their inner qi or life force, which Paulina said was deep inside just below the navel.

Janet, eyes closed, by Viv's side, seemed to be well into it. Good. Viv just wished it was working as well for her, but her inner qi was telling her to bloody well go and do something useful, like finding Primrose and shaking her till she divulged her maiden name. How was Zelda getting on, she wondered, had she managed to find another Mal Carmichael?

Viv was also trying very hard not to fart and wondered if anyone else was. Did that account for the look of concentration on all their faces? It was easy enough when you were breathing in, 'tensing those muscles', not so easy when breathing out and 'letting everything go'.

'Let go of your negative thoughts,' said Paulina. 'Elongate your spine to the top of your head. Keep your chin level and in a line. Close your mouth, keeping teeth gently together. Let the tip of your tongue go up, lower your shoulders, down, down, down, loosen those elbows, and those wrists, let hands and fingers fall to your sides...'

Paulina had a monotonous or soothing voice depending on your point of view and trying to do all she said in the right order did indeed dispel negative thoughts, or any thoughts – but only when nothing interesting was happening. When a customer wandered into the café it was harder and here was one now, a woman Viv recognised purposefully steering her elderly escort towards a table on Viv's left-hand side.

Viv wobbled.

Yes, it *was* Isabella with three-strand comb-over man. Viv hadn't been sure at first because the hairstyle was different today, not piled on top but hanging down to her shoulders. Zelda would have been able to describe the style but Viv just saw DNA, long strands of easy-to-get-hold-of hair.

'Put your weight on your left foot,' said Paulina, 'lift your right and make a semi-circle...'

Sit down, Isabella. She was hovering near the table nearest Viv.

'Now raise your right foot.'

Isabella sat down and so did three-strand man.

'You are a crane,' said Paulina, 'a graceful bird. Now lift your wings...'

Viv lifted her wings and reached out but a bit too late. Isabella was getting up, changing her mind it seemed, wrinkling her nose and complaining of a funny *atmosphere* in the room.

Viv lurched, falling onto the table and sending a small pot plant flying into comb-over man's lap. But no harm done, he wasn't hurt or sprayed with soil as pot and plant were plastic.

* * *

'I didn't break anything.' Viv was relieved about that.

It had been embarrassing, that was all, well, that and a sore elbow and the shattered inner peace of anyone who'd managed to find it. Solicitous staff had quickly appeared to see if Viv was okay, then to straighten the furniture, and Paulina had called the Tai Chi class to a temporary halt. Viv had left at that point, after apologising profusely to the participants, and Janet had followed, worried about Viv at first but laughing when she saw the funny side.

They were in the pub now in their favourite corner booth and had just been joined by an apologetic Zelda, whose morning hadn't gone well.

'Nothing good to report, I'm afraid. All the computers in Connexions were occupied and Gary the manager was nowhere to be seen. I've started trawling through the marriage certificates of anyone called Primrose born in the 1940s on my phone, but it's slow work.'

'No worries, Zelda.' Janet was still feeling zen. 'Even those few minutes of Tai Chi have given me some inner calm. I'm starting to think Primrose and her daughter haven't got a case, because if they had, well, if Isabella had one – she's the one behind this, I'm sure – she would have done what she threatened to do by now.'

Wow! Operation Cheer Up Janet was working, if not quite as planned.

Viv was about to suggest Buck's Fizz all round to celebrate when Janet got a text and went very quiet and tense.

'What's the matter?' said Zelda, for clearly something was wrong.

'Grant,' said Janet, unzenned, holding up her phone to show them a text, saying:

> What the hell's going on, Mother?

38

JANET

Encouraged by Viv and Zelda, Janet messaged back:

> What do you mean, Grant?

This was after she'd checked Facebook for what she feared but didn't find. Phew! Isabella hadn't yet posted anything incriminating, well, not that she could see. Zelda checked too but couldn't find anything. Viv didn't because she didn't do Facebook, but she googled to work out what time it was in New Zealand, so Janet could ring Grant and speak to him. They were mid-Atlantic, maybe three-quarters of the way across, so there was a bit of guesswork involved. New Zealand was sixteen hours ahead of New York, she said, so if it was 11 a.m. in New York on a Monday morning it would be 3 a.m. on Tuesday in New Zealand. Aboard the *QM2* it was twelve noon by the ship's clock and the three of them were still in their booth in the Golden Lion about to order an early lunch before it got crowded.

Janet checked her watch, remembering that they had to turn their clocks back an hour each day of the voyage to align with New York time when they got there, in less than two days' time. She'd been doing it every morning as soon as she woke up but hadn't this morning. She did it now and calculated that they had forty-two more hours aboard before they docked in New York at 6.30 on Wednesday morning, a day and a half, that was all. She wanted to get on, to ring Grant and find out the worst, but he would be in bed. She asked the others what they thought.

'He's just texted you,' Viv looked up from the menu, 'which suggests he's awake.'

Zelda shook her head. 'Not necessarily. He might have written it last night, his time, and there's been a delay from the server. He hasn't replied to Janet's text, which he would have done if he'd been standing by his phone waiting for a call. She might wake him up in the middle of the night if she rings now, and he'll be grumpy.'

'A grumpy Grant I do not want, though that might be unavoidable.' It didn't take much to make Grant grumpy. Janet looked at the text again.

> What the hell's going on, Mother?

Something had upset him.

They discussed what it could be for a bit over light lunches, very light in her case as her appetite had gone. She picked at her leek and truffle terrine as Viv wondered if Grant's question might have nothing to do with what was worrying them. 'It might be a comment on the climate crisis, or war in the Middle East or even the cricket. I think New Zealand's suffering a bit at the hands of the Sri Lankans at the moment.'

Zelda said Grant might simply be cross because Janet was spending his inheritance on a luxury holiday.

Viv spluttered. 'If that's it...' and Janet held up her hand.

'Thank you, but this is pointless. Sorry if that sounds rude, but I just have to sit it out till I can talk to him. Grant's an early riser, so by my calculation if I ring about 4 p.m. our time I'll catch him. Sorry to sound weak and watery, but if one of you could be by my side when I do that, I'd be grateful for your support. Now, what are we going to do this afternoon?' Trying hard to summon some enthusiasm, she got the Daily Programme from her bag. 'Anyone fancy Singers in Concert? They're in the Royal Court Theatre, singing along with,' she quoted, '"the combined talents of QM2's musicians". Richard might be there, Zelda.'

But Zelda said she was going back to Connexions to have another go at finding Primrose's marriage certificate.

Thank you, Zelda.

Viv said she was going to go in search of Primrose herself. 'And I think we should join forces, Janet. Let's pop into the concert as Primrose might be there, but if she isn't we look in other places. If we find her alone, you get her talking and ask The Question. If Isabella's with her, we do distract and divide as we planned last night...'

Viv was trying to crank her up, like her old Range Rover on a cold winter's morning. 'Look,' Viv was on her feet now, reading the programme over her shoulder, 'there's a Trivia Quiz in here at three. We can come back and look in on that and see if Primrose is here. It's really odd how she's disappeared. Then at four o'clock we'll find a quiet spot and you ring Grant and I stand by ready to pick you up from the floor if he says, "Sorry, Mum, just joshing."'

'Ha ha, Viv.'

* * *

Grant sounded grumpy when he answered the phone, but grumpy, Janet told herself, was Grant's default mode when he was talking to her. He could be cheery with other people. She was sitting at a table in the café area outside Connexions with Viv by her side, her phone on loudspeaker so Viv could hear. Grant cut in, before she'd finished asking about Belynda and the grandchildren. 'Let's get to the point, Mother. This woman's got in touch with me, saying she has reason to believe she's related to me on Dad's side.'

As her heart stopped beating, Viv pushed a note in front of her.

Might not be HER. Ancestry? DNA?

Urged on by Zelda last Christmas, they'd both sent samples of their spit and £45 each to a company called Ancestry, to discover their genetic ancestry, and the results had been disappointing in her case, and Viv's. She'd been informed she was 87 per cent Celt with a bit of Viking thrown in, which she already knew. Viv was 91 per cent Viking and a tad Celt, and she also knew that. They'd both hoped for a more exotic mix, like Zelda, and now from time to time, quite often in fact, they got emails from far-flung relatives, usually second or third cousins twice removed, in America or Australia or Timbuctoo, asking if they could come and stay.

'Grant, have you ever sent any spit to a company called Ancestry?'

Grant said he wasn't in the habit of spitting.

'Oh.'

'Back to this woman, Mother. She says she's met you on that cruise you're on.'

Her heart stopped again.

'She says you can tell me more...'

Another note from Viv.

Tell him. Call her bluff.

But Janet couldn't. It would ruin everything and she might not need to. Instead she said, 'I think you're overreacting, Grant. I have met this woman but...'

He cut in again. 'She wants me to send her a photograph of myself so she can see if we look alike. She sent me one of herself. Looks nothing like me.'

Well, that was something.

'And she sent me one of you and Dad on your wedding day. Says she found it on Facebook...'

Viv took the phone from her hand, which was as well because her mouth had gone dry and she couldn't speak. It was all too clear what Isabella was up to. She was showing what she could do. She'd contacted Grant by some means or other knowing he'd get in touch with her, letting her know that she could tell Grant he was illegitimate if she didn't 'buy her a little something' to keep her quiet.

As if from a long way off, she heard Viv saying, 'Hello, Grant. This is Viv Halliday. I'm a friend of your mum who is indisposed at the moment. But please don't worry about her, or this, er... intervention from a third party. The woman you speak of, Isabella Carmichael, yes?... is to say the least dubious. This is most likely a scam. Your mum will, I'm sure, be in touch soon. Goodbye.'

Viv rang off and handed her back her phone.

'She knows.' Janet was convinced. 'She must have proof.'

'She's chancing her arm. This means she doesn't have proof.'

'You're just saying that to make me feel better. Sorry, Viv, but I'm going back to my room.'

39

ZELDA

'You heard *what*?' Zelda was open-mouthed.

What Richard had just said was gobsmacking.

Now he said it again. 'I heard her say "Daddy". She said, "See you soon, Daddy," when she rang off. She was on her phone.'

They were in the café outside Connexions, sitting at a table. Richard had texted her to meet him there, and she'd come straightaway. He was waiting and had already taken Billie's harness off and now her head was heavy on her knee. It was five o'clock, and at about half past four, he said, he'd just finished walking Billie round Deck 3 and he was sitting on a deck chair outside, about to phone home because reception was good there, when he'd heard someone approaching, a woman he thought, because she was wearing stilettos – the sound was very distinctive. He'd paused for a moment, waiting to see what she'd do – he liked quiet for his calls – and she'd stopped. He'd waited, thinking she might come and chat as people so often did, but she didn't. She sat down, further up on one of the deck chairs – close enough for him to hear it creak.

'How did you know it was her?'

He'd already said it was Isabella.

'When she started speaking, I recognised her voice.'

'And how did you know she was on the phone, I mean, that she wasn't speaking to someone sitting beside her?'

'There was only one voice, hers – and she said she was looking forward to meeting him in New York.'

'*What?*'

This changed everything – if it was true, if Richard had heard right. If.

'I could be mistaken,' he said, intuiting her thoughts as he had a disconcerting habit of doing, 'but I'm pretty sure I've got this one right.'

'Daddy?' she said. 'You're sure she said "Daddy"?'

He nodded, looking, she thought, rather pleased with himself. So he should be. The Blind Detective! She wanted to hug him but that had to wait, she must tell Janet and Viv about this straightaway. She got to her feet. 'Sorry, Richard, sorry, Billie, but I've got to go and tell my friends. This will help a lot.' She'd had a text from Viv earlier, saying Janet was feeling depressed after talking to Grant and had retreated to her room.

Richard reached for Billie's harness. 'Okay, but might it be better if I came too? So your friends can hear it from the horse's mouth, or even the dog's? Billie heard too.'

***

They went up to Janet's suite, after a bit of texting on Zelda's part, saying she had good news to impart. Richard said he'd never been up to Deck 12 before, so they linked arms for her to show him the way. Loving the closeness, she talked him through the route, as he'd asked her to do, so he could commit it to memory and teach Billie. They took the lift to be faster, and when they got there, Viv opened Janet's door and poked her head out.

'I'm letting you in only if you guarantee to cheer Janet up.'

'Here's my guarantee.' Zelda knew she was beaming as she pushed Richard forward.

They settled in Janet's sitting room, Richard and Zelda on one blue sofa, Billie's head on her lap, Viv and Janet on the other, opposite them, Janet looking more depressed than Zelda had ever seen her before.

'Wow!' said Viv when Richard had reported. 'This is the breakthrough we've been waiting for!'

Janet was still stone-faced.

'This is good news, Janet,' Viv stood up, 'a cause for celebration, and it's time for an aperitif if we're eating at six. Have you got fizz in the fridge?'

Janet said she had, a bottle of Cava, she thought.

Viv came back with four glasses and a bottle, which, after a moment's hesitation, she handed to Richard, who opened it with practised hands. Viv filled their glasses.

'To truth over lies!' She raised her glass. 'To fact over fucking fiction.'

Janet drew back in her seat.

Zelda and Richard raised their glasses, and so did Janet but only slightly. Zelda guessed what was going on in her head. She was having doubts but didn't want to say. 'Janet,' she said, 'go ahead. Ask Richard anything. He won't take offence. You won't hurt his feelings.'

Richard backed her up. 'My hide's as thick as a buffalo's, Janet. Ask away.'

'H-how can you be so certain?' Janet spoke hesitantly, voicing concerns that had occurred to Zelda too. Richard went through it all again, adding that his sense of hearing was enhanced because blind people's brains were wired a bit differently, especially if they'd been blind since they were very young as he had been.

'B-but...' Janet was tying herself in knots trying not to be insensitive. 'It's sometimes hard to know, I mean I wear hearing aids, and even with them I get T and D muddled sometimes, and vowel sounds, with all the different dialects, they can be very confusing...'

'Spit it out, Janet.' Viv topped up her glass to give her confidence.

'C-could Isabella have said, "See you soon, *Teddy*?"' Janet looked apologetic. 'Isabella has a boyfriend called Teddy, I think.'

Richard considered this and agreed there was a chance that she could have. 'I'm not infallible, Janet. Never like to say I'm 100 per cent sure of anything, but well I'm pretty darn sure she didn't.'

Over-confident he wasn't, but Zelda wished he'd been a bit more upbeat to boost Janet's mood. Janet seemed to appreciate his honesty, however, and invited him to join them for dinner, but he said he was playing in the Early Evening Concert and needed to get back downstairs.

Zelda saw him feel his Braille watch and read the time.

'It's a quarter to six. We'd better get going, hadn't we, Billie? Zelda, would you mind coming down with us if you've had your fix?' She was fondling Billie's ears. 'I'm not sure I can find the way back as I've only done the route once before. I usually need three or four runs before I'm sure of it.'

As he reached for Billie's lead, the dog left her side and went to his. Zelda got up, loving that he'd asked her for help, loving that he trusted her and wanted her company. But then she thought, as he tucked his arm in hers and she felt the warmth of him, she was starting to love everything about Richard Williams.

40

VIV

Viv had some doubts, but Janet's negativity was annoying. As soon as Richard and Zelda went she'd come up with even more doubts about what he'd heard. 'If he did hear Isabella say "Daddy" it could have been because she was talking to her sugar-daddy.'

'You don't call your sugar-daddy Daddy.'

'How do you know?' Janet sniffed. 'Or she may have said "daddy-o" and he didn't hear the O. It's quite a common expression.'

'Or used to be. It was hip in the 1950s. You don't hear it much now.' Viv reached for the bottle of fizz. 'Cheer up, Janet. Let's finish this and go down to dinner.'

'There are lots of words that sound like daddy.'

'And we may hit an iceberg.' Viv half-filled her glass.

'What do you mean?' Janet spoke sharply. 'Oh. Sorry. I take your point, but I'm being realistic not pessimistic.' She took a sip and rallied a bit. 'Do you think Primrose will join us for dinner?'

'If she does, she won't be alone.' Viv was sure of that. 'If Isabella hasn't locked her up, as she seems to have done for the last day and a half, she'll be glued to her side making sure she doesn't say anything revealing. And we'll have to try again to make sure she does, say something revealing I mean, like telling you her maiden name, because if Zelda can find a marriage certificate showing she was married to someone else that too would clinch it.' Viv got up, her glass empty. 'We ought to be going.'

Janet got up too. 'There's something else I'd like to ascertain, Viv, whether Primrose is in league with her daughter or her innocent victim. I don't think she's dishonest, but I need to know if I am going to continue to be her friend. If, *if* this is a plot to get money from me, and the accusation of bigamy is based on a fabrication then I think it is Isabella's doing, but I want to be sure.'

This was progress, Janet acknowledging those two could be in league.

'So,' said Viv, 'how do we go about getting this assurance? And how do we use the new information we've got, or may have, when we next meet them? Do we confront them? Tell them we know that Isabella is in touch with her father and is going to meet him in New York?' Viv rather relished a showdown.

But Janet predictably wanted to wait. 'We might be able to tell from Primrose's reaction, whether she knew beforehand, but we might not. Also, there is still doubt in my mind – yes, there is, Viv – that Richard heard correctly. He was outside with waves crashing all around. But if we assume that he did hear correctly, we should keep our powder dry – if you'll excuse the cliché.'

'I'm fine with cliché, Janet, you're the one who's not, and I think you're right. Richard's information is a barrel of gunpowder and we need to keep it dry, so we can light the fuse when it suits us, and blow the two of them – or if you're right, just the one – into the blue beyond.'

'I'm not going to reveal that I have heard from Grant either.' Janet picked up her evening bag and checked her appearance in the mirror by the door. 'I don't want her to think that her plan is working in any way.'

Viv thought about this. 'Or perhaps we should let her think her plan *is* working, to give her a false sense of security, and see what she comes up with next? You look great by the way, very Judi Dench.' Janet was wearing an old favourite, a blue and gold brocade tunic over velvet trousers, and could be playing M.

Janet opened the door. 'We're going to have to play this by ear, Viv, but I'll tell you one thing. If Isabella joins us tonight, it will be because she's getting desperate about getting her *little something* before the jewellery shop closes tomorrow, *and* she thinks she's in with a chance. It may be fun to let her think she's right.'

Viv checked her own appearance in the mirror. Would the-borrowed-from-Libby emerald-green jacket draw enough attention, so no one noticed she hadn't had time to change out of her joggers?

She dashed off a text to Zelda:

> Meet you in Britannia at 6. No definite plan if ghastly pair join us, so playing by ear. Janet favours devious over direct. I'm not so sure.

41

VIV

Time was short so they took the lift down to Deck 3 and there was a determined look in Janet's eye as she walked to the restaurant, then stood for a moment in the doorway, surveying the room. 'There they are, in battle position.'

Janet was right, mother and daughter were already at the table. The stage was set for a replay of two nights before when Isabella had played hostess, or tried to. What a bloody cheek! Viv was reminding herself of their aims – one, find out Primrose's maiden name, two, find out how much she knew about Isabella's behind-the-scenes work, three, ascertain her innocence or guilt – when Janet touched her arm. 'Ready? We play along with them, right. Let them think they have the upper hand.'

'Good evening, Janet!' Primrose greeted her effusively. 'Good evening, Viv! Do come and sit down!' Isabella was sitting at on her right-hand side, strategically placed to prevent her saying anything she shouldn't, it seemed to Viv. Did Isabella nudge her mother just then? Viv thought she did. 'Er...' said Primrose as if prompted, 'Janet, would you like to sit by Isabella?'

No, Janet wouldn't. So much for playing along, but a good response. 'How lovely to see you, Primrose!' She sat down on Primrose's left as if she hadn't heard. 'Where have you *been*? I've missed you.'

Primrose didn't answer, Viv noted as she sat down by Isabella, who was looking reptilian again, wearing a jumpsuit in some sort of spotted fabric. Hair! Remembering her failure in the morning, Viv noted Isabella had her hair piled high again, not as easy to get a sample as when it was on her shoulders. On the other hand, Isabella was taking much more notice of her mother than the person beside her, so she might get a chance.

'How *are* you, Primrose?' Janet sounded genuinely concerned, which she probably was. 'Where have you been?' she asked again. 'What have you been up to?'

'Mummy hasn't been well,' Isabella answered for her, 'so she stayed in her room.'

'Oh, no! Poor Primrose! What was the matter?'

'A touch of food poisoning we think,' Isabella answered again.

'Oh dear,' said Janet. 'Did you report it? I think you're supposed to...'

'Or an allergic reaction.' Isabella filled her mother's glass with water. 'To prawns possibly. So she took antihistamines which made her sleepy. Sorry, Janet. Mummy's not up to saying a lot. She has a sore throat.'

She's been gagged.

As Viv wondered how she could help ungag her by distracting Isabella, Zelda arrived in a rush. 'Hello, everyone! Sorry I'm late. I've been seeing a man about a dog. Ha, ha, ha!' She sat down in the empty seat. 'Richard and I have been planning what to do when we get to New York! What have you and your mum got planned, Isabella?'

Excellent question, Zelda!

Isabella looked like a snake in the headlights.

It was bad luck that the steward came for their orders at that point, followed by the wine waiter. Viv planned to repeat the question if Zelda didn't, but once their orders had been taken, Isabella jumped in to change the subject. 'Any family news, anyone?' Clearly she hoped to hear from Janet, if the sideways look she gave her was significant.

'I have,' said Zelda, as Janet searched for something in her evening bag. 'I can't keep up with all the texts and emails I get from mine finalising travel arrangements and so on. I'm going to stay with my father's family for Christmas, when I'll meet the latest member of the clan, my great-niece, little Leanne, for the first time. So after a day's sightseeing in New York I'll be flying to North Carolina where my sister Cynthia will pick me up at

Raleigh airport on Thursday morning. She lives in Raleigh with her husband and kids. Thursday's Christmas Eve if you've forgotten, the day you'll be flying home if you bought the same packages as us. Should say half-sister, but Cynthia and I are so close she feels like a sister. Oh, Isabella,' she said as if it was an afterthought, 'I don't think I've told you my family history, but it's very like yours. My dad disappeared when my mum was pregnant so I grew up without him, and then I started digging into the past, and discovered to my amazement he was still alive...'

Isabella nearly jumped in her seat.

This was close to the bone. Was it wise? Zelda paused as the waiter brought their wine to the table and went round filling their glasses, giving Viv time to watch Isabella register what Zelda had said. She and Janet had heard it before but Isabella was agog, her hands tightly clenched as Zelda carried on. 'I'm so looking forward to seeing my dad – we get on really well too – but it can't compare to the first time I met him, only three years ago, it's hard to believe. I could hardly hold myself together when I saw him walking towards me. I didn't, in fact.' She shook her head slowly as if she were reliving it with tears in her eyes. 'I dissolved, I was a puddle. And so was he.'

'It must have been very emotional,' said Primrose, with tears in her eyes, but not doing that phoney-looking dabbing Viv had noticed before. 'Did you really think he had passed away, Zelda, and then discovered he was alive?'

She looked genuinely moved. Isabella's facial expression was harder to read. She didn't look moved, she looked perplexed and maybe angry. Her hands were still clenched tightly, her knuckles white. Those long red nails must be hurting, digging into her palms. Her brow was furrowed as if she were thinking *what do they know*? Things weren't going her way, that was clear. She wasn't in control any more. This story from Zelda had got to her, but she was fighting to get control back. After a gulp from her glass, she looked across her mother to Janet. 'And have you heard from your family?'

So Viv thought she'd take a turn.

'Patrick, my partner, reports that everything's ready for the big day bar stuffing the turkey and putting the sprouts on to boil. He's cooking for twelve of us with his son Guy acting as sous chef...' She burbled on while keeping an eye on Isabella's hands, clenching and unclenching below the table, and on Janet who closed her bag when the steward arrived with their starters.

'Janet, have you heard from your son in Australia?' Isabella tried again when they were all eating.

Isabella, have you heard from your father in New York? Viv longed to ask.

'New Zealand, not Australia,' said Janet, looking up from her basil and tomato soup, 'and...' But then she noticed Primrose's half-empty glass and paused to top it up. 'I have heard from Grant and he says...' she took a long time putting the empty bottle back in the cooler, 'that they'll be having a barbecue on the beach.' Janet, clearly enjoying herself, went back to her soup. 'It's summer over there at the moment.'

'Like in Australia?' Zelda played along.

'Yes,' said Janet. 'Exactly. Sadly,' she turned to Isabella, 'my son doesn't say a lot, well, not to me.' Picking up her phone, she turned back to Primrose, 'Do give me your number, Primrose, so we can keep in touch.'

'Guy's a surly sod,' Viv added, she hoped helpfully.

Isabella spun the rings on her fingers then blurted out, 'Been to the boutique, lately, Janet?'

'Which boutique would that be, Isabella?' Janet took a sip of Chablis. 'Oh, you mean the *jewellery* boutique. Not yet, no. I thought I'd wait till tomorrow. I gather the thing to do in all the shops selling luxury goods is wait until the last day when they reduce prices to practically nothing. Bargains galore apparently. It's not fair, though, is it, to all those people who bought items at full price. And some people say prices are better in New York.'

Viv saw an opportunity. 'What are your plans for New York, Isabella?'

Isabella, predictably, didn't answer, but Janet turned to Primrose and asked her the same question, which she answered, sounding a bit the worse for wear.

'Shight-seeing in the morning, oh!' She put her hand over her mouth and giggled. 'On one of those buses without a roof, then in the afternoon Ish-abella is meeting a friend she doesn't want me to meet, so I'll be at a bit of a... looshe end.'

Isabella sprang to her feet. 'Mummy, I think you're poorly again. Antihistamines don't mix with alcohol.' With that she near-dragged her out of her seat and out of the room.

* * *

'So, what did we learn?' Viv asked, pen poised, a notebook at the ready.

They were back in Janet's suite, where Janet was making coffee in the Barista machine and Zelda was assisting, putting the filled cups on a tray as Janet handed them to her.

'That Isabella is still hoping I'll buy her something expensive to stop her telling Grant he's illegitimate,' said Janet, expertly filling another cup. 'Though I suppose that's not new.'

Viv jotted it down anyway.

'That Isabella is definitely meeting someone in New York,' said Zelda, 'and she doesn't want Primrose to meet that someone, and she wasn't happy about her telling us.'

'So, can we deduce from that that Primrose doesn't know that Isabella is meeting Daddy – or Teddy, or Sugar-daddy or Daddy-o?' Viv added the last three to appease Janet.

But Janet shook her head dismissively, and possibly apologetically. 'Viv, I am *almost* certain that Isabella is meeting someone she calls Daddy, who may well be her father. I am not completely doubting Richard's word. But I do have another query. How do we know if the man Isabella is meeting is the man whose details we have been searching for? It has occurred to me that if Isabella has lied about Mal and Malcolm being the same person, she could also be lying about this new man on the scene.'

Viv wished she hadn't had so much wine at dinner. 'Are you saying she could have duped another man into believing he's her father?'

'I'm saying we need to know the name of whom she is meeting.'

Of whom! Janet was as precise as only Janet could be.

'And,' said Janet, 'I want to be 100 per cent sure that Malcolm is not Isabella's father, and that he wasn't married to Primrose before he married, or didn't marry, me.'

'You've still got doubts?'

'Yes, one or two, and I will have until…'

'...we've done DNA tests,' said Viv, 'on Grant *and* Isabella. I've thought of that.'

'I was going to say, until I see a marriage certificate proving that Primrose was married to someone else.'

There was work to be done.

42

JANET

Janet wanted action. Now wasn't the time to lounge on the comfortable blue sofas drinking coffee, though she had brought Viv and Janet back to her suite to do precisely that. She felt bad that she hadn't managed to ask Primrose for her maiden name this evening, but she'd been focused on other things like getting her mobile number without giving the game away, and ascertaining if she was colluding with her daughter. Now she had her number she could get in touch with her directly, which she would do in a minute. She put the coffees on the table in front of Viv and Zelda, and sat down opposite them.

'I'm certain now that Primrose is the innocent party.'

'What makes you so sure?' Viv picked up a cup.

'The way she was hauled off by Isabella, who clearly hasn't told her whom she will be meeting. She must be withholding the information from her.'

'But why?' Zelda looked sceptical.

'Your guess is as good as mine, but I think we need to get Primrose on her own, and apprise her of what we know. That Isabella has tracked down a man who may be her father whom she's meeting in New York, secretly. Let us not forget that this man is – or could be – Primrose's beloved husband. Surely she has a right to know?'

Viv saw a drawback. 'Wouldn't she then tell Isabella? Tip her off, I mean.'

Zelda saw another. Was Isabella perhaps wanting to check the man out, to be sure he was her father, before telling Primrose, to spare her disappointment?

'But Zelda, you have been telling us that she addressed the man as *Daddy* twice if I remember rightly. Why would she do that if she had doubts?'

Janet continued. 'What if I invited Primrose here for coffee tomorrow morning? I could say I had something private to discuss with her, which is absolutely true.'

'She'll be locked in her room by now,' said Viv, 'and Isabella will probably keep her there till we dock. She told her she was *poorly*, remember.'

Zelda was more enthusiastic.

'I doubt if Isabella will stay there with her. She'll be off with one of her boyfriends. So, if we kept watch and noted when Isabella left, you could maybe visit her in her room, Janet. Viv, didn't you follow the pair to their room once? So you must know where it is.'

'Deck 6 but I didn't get close enough to see the number. In the 6050s though.'

'No problem,' said Zelda. 'We can find the exact number easily enough. Richard counts as staff so he knows a lot of the stewards, and they know everything. I'll text him now.' She got her mobile out.

'I could even,' Janet thought aloud, 'text Primrose to say I have reason to believe that her husband, her Mal, is alive...'

'And, I repeat, she would tell Isabella,' said Viv, 'if she hadn't already grabbed her phone and read it herself...'

'...and they would ask what that *reason to believe* was,' said Zelda, 'and when you told them they would dismiss it, just like you did, Janet. "A *blind* man heard *a woman* saying Daddy, or something like it!" I can hear their derision. Why have you changed your mind, anyway?'

'I'm sorry, Zelda, mea culpa.' Janet felt a stab of guilt because she hadn't completely.

'It's okay, Janet, you're forgiven. I was the same till I got to know how amazing Richard was, correction, *is*. He is so...' Zelda shook her head and sighed, smitten, absolutely smitten.

'And Janet,' said Viv, after eye-rolling with her at Zelda's dreamy face, 'if Isabella finds out that we know she's going to meet her father, or someone she believes to be her father, that will make it very hard for us to keep tabs on her and follow her to her rendezvous...'

'Follow her to her rendezvous?' Zelda came out of her dream. 'What *are* you talking about?'

'I'm not completely sure,' said Viv. 'But it's just occurred to me that we have got to be there. We've got to *see* this man. We've got to *meet* him. It's the only way to prove to you, Janet, that Mal and Malcolm are two different people, and that Isabella is a liar who has made up this story about bigamy. We really do need to see this man. And, and,' the words were coming so fast she was tripping over them, 'when I say we, that means Primrose as well I think. *Primrose* needs to see if he's the man she married and the father of her child, and the only way that will happen is if we *take* her to see him.'

This was brilliant. Viv was absolutely right.

'Would she recognise him after all these years?' That was Zelda.

'I think she would.' Janet was liking Viv's idea more and more. Primrose had a right to see this man. He might actually be her *husband*, for heaven's sake, her long-lost husband! She pictured the ecstatic reunion, first the hesitant searching of each other's faces, then the slow realisation that the man she thought was dead was *alive* and the collapsing into each other's arms. But she was getting ahead of herself...

'But how, Viv? How do we take Primrose to this rendezvous when we don't know where it is or exactly when? Primrose said that Isabella was meeting her friend in the afternoon and I know you talked about following Isabella but how practical is that? Once we've docked, everyone will go their separate ways. There will be queues for customs and passport control and we might be able to keep them in our sights, even stay close, up to that point, but once we're through we're bound to lose them. We're planning to go to our hotel and leave our luggage there, then do sightseeing, but they'll have their own plans and are almost certainly in a different hotel. I don't think jumping into a yellow cab and telling the driver to follow the one in front is going to work.'

'Idea!' Zelda raised her hand like the eager schoolgirl she had no doubt once been. 'Sorry! I could kick myself. I don't know why I didn't think of this before. Now we suspect this Mal Carmichael is alive, why don't we use Facebook or Twitter to find him? Then, if by some amazing stroke of good fortune he answers in time, we can ask him where he's meeting Isabella. It shouldn't be too difficult to post a "Get in Touch ASAP". We know he was born in the 1950s, that he was a pupil at the Royal High School for Boys, Edinburgh in the early 1960s, and he was a graduate in Economics, from the London School of Economics in the late 1960s.'

Doubt darkened Viv's face as it always did when Facebook was mentioned. 'But how would that work, Zelda?'

'There are groups on Facebook for everything, to draw people with similar interests together, and I'm sure there's one for Finding Lost Friends and Family.'

Viv still looked doubtful. 'How quickly do people respond to these kind of requests? We've got a *day* to find out, Zelda.'

'It depends. Some people are on Facebook all the time, others look in once in a blue moon, but the sooner I get started the better.' She got to her feet.

'Where are you going?' Janet intervened. 'Can't you do it here?'

Zelda was heading for the door. 'Yes, but I said I'd go and listen to the Animus Quartet at nine o'clock, and it's a quarter to now.'

'That's not good enough, Zelda!' Janet nearly screeched, hating herself for being so selfish, for resenting Zelda going to a concert, to listen to Richard Williams, to *drool* over him, when she was needed here. She turned to Viv as Zelda closed the door behind her. Didn't Zelda realise how urgent this was? That she needed to begin her search for Mal Carmichael *now*. That they had *one* day left to find out where he was meeting Isabella. 'Viv, you're absolutely right. *I* need to see this man. *I* need to know if he's Isabella's father, that he's the man she was talking to. It's the only way I can be sure that Mal and Malcolm are two different people, and Malcolm, for all his faults, wasn't a bigamist. I need to clear his name for my son and my grandchildren. But Zelda's got to start now!'

43

ZELDA

Zelda was on the case. She did realise how urgent making contact with Mal Carmichael was, but she had to multi-task. She couldn't let Richard down, giving him the impression that she didn't care. Not again. Now on the front row of the Royal Court Theatre, on the aisle seat, with five minutes to go before the concert began, she got her phone out and logged into Facebook. The quartet were tuning their instruments so she hadn't got much time. She wrote:

> Looking for Malcolm, Malvin or Malachy Carmichael, also known as Mal, born Edinburgh area 1950s, pupil at Royal High School for Boys Edinburgh early 1960s, graduate in Economics from the London School of Economics late 1960s. His long-lost family would like to get in touch.

At the last moment, she added:

> Urgently

and then:

> With a view to meeting in New York. Asking for a friend.

It wasn't as well thought-out as she would have liked but there wasn't time to re-do it, so she pressed post, then sat back to listen. It was Elgar's Cello Concerto in E Minor, one of her absolute favourites, and Richard was the star.

* * *

Viv

Viv was in knots. She was sure Zelda would do what she promised using Facebook but had no faith in the result. Now heading down to Deck 7 for some pampering at the Canyon Ranch spa, she was also losing confidence in her own Meeting Mal in New York plan. Car chases were for films. They weren't Yankee detectives, they were three English women who didn't know New York very well. She felt bad leaving Janet on her own but had failed to persuade her to come to the spa with her. A massage, that's what she needed, she'd decided. Her back was killing her. Janet's anxiety was catching. She wouldn't be happy till she had seen this Mal with her own eyes so they must find a way of attending this meeting. They had brought Janet on this holiday to make her happy, to have a fun day in New York, but she wouldn't be happy till they had proved to her that Malcolm Carmichael wasn't a bigamist and she wasn't about to be denied access to her grandchildren by her nasty son. Viv arrived at the spa.

CLOSED. Opening hours 8 a.m. to 8 p.m.

'F***!'

Thirsty now after the trek from Deck 12 to Deck 7, she hesitated by the door of the bar next to the spa, which was still open. Should she stop for some water – free – and maybe another glass of wine – not free? Primrose had downed most of the bottle at dinner. Deciding against it, thinking about Janet all alone, she was about to set off again when she saw that one of the customers perched on a bar stool was Isabella, talking to yet another old guy with a comb-over. Hair down again today, the short skirt of her silver lamé dress up, she was showing the chap a lot of thigh and possibly her knickers.

Time to collect a DNA sample?

Viv changed her mind again and went in.

The old guy was the one who dressed as if he was on a beach in Hawaii, who Viv was sure she had seen in the jewellery boutique early on in the voyage. Was Isabella still trying to get him to buy her a little something? She could find out perhaps. She found a stool at the bar, close enough she hoped but not so close it looked intrusive, and managed to catch Isabella's eye.

'Hello, Isabella. Hello, er...'

The man had looked up. 'Freddie,' he said, reaching towards her and sticking out his hand. From Yorkshire, she thought from his accent.

'Viv,' she took his hand briefly, 'dining companion of Isabella and her mum. Sorry to interrupt you but I just wanted to tell Isabella how glad I was to hear about her daddy.'

As the words came out of her mouth unplanned, she thought that she probably shouldn't be saying them, but changed her mind when she saw Isabella freeze. You could have heard the proverbial pin drop if the floor hadn't been covered with velvety blue carpet.

Viv wished Janet could see Isabella's face.

She had hit her target. She knew what she'd wanted to know, what Janet wanted to know. Isabella had a daddy, and not a sugar-daddy, though she might have one of those as well. Now what? Would telling Janet convince her? Probably not. *Seeing is believing.*

'A spritzer, please,' Viv asked the hovering barman, and when her drink arrived she went to sit at a table in the corner of the room to wait.

As she hoped, it wasn't long before Isabella joined her, leaving Freddie at the bar. 'Sorry,' she seemed calm and composed as she sat down opposite Viv, 'but I wasn't listening properly and I didn't quite catch what you said just now.'

Viv looked up from her phone where she'd been scrolling. 'Sorry. What did you say?'

Isabella repeated what she'd said, and Viv affected surprise. 'Oh, yes! Isn't it wonderful that your father has turned up? You and your mum must be so happy. I'm surprised you didn't mention it at dinner though?' She made that a question.

Isabella's lip twitched, not so calm now.

'When Zelda mentioned her own reunion with her dad, I mean,' Viv added, sipping her spritzer. 'As she said, you've got so much in common.'

'B-but we haven't,' Isabella was rattled, 'because this isn't true... I w-wish it was but it isn't. And I'd like to know where you got this cock and bull story from?'

'I'm not sure but someone on board must have said.' Viv pretended to think about it then risked, 'Primrose, perhaps?'

'Mummy d...' Isabella bit her lip, stopping herself, Viv thought, from saying, '*Mummy doesn't know.*'

'Must have been someone else then.' Seeing Isabella's shoulder-length hair, Viv remembered her DNA idea, and put out a tentative hand. 'All this artificial snow they sprinkle around. Looks like dandruff, don't you think? May I?' She brushed Isabella's silver-lamé-clad shoulder.

'What the...' Isabella looked at her shoulder, then at Viv, then to the bar when loud laughter drew her attention to Freddie, now talking to a woman with long straight blonde hair and shapely legs. 'I must get back.' She got up and walked away, but then turned round and walked back. '*Don't* tell Mummy about this, right. She would be very upset.'

And so would you.

Viv watched her go back to the bar and reclaim Freddie, then examined her right hand. Yes, there was a hair between her thumb and forefinger. She got a paper napkin from the tub on the table, laid the hair upon it, folded it over and stowed it in her wallet. If they needed to prove who Isabella's father was or wasn't, this was the evidence. Janet would have to get a sample from Grant if she hadn't already got one so they could compare the two, which would take time, but it would be conclusive. She just hoped that peroxide and hair dye and copious amounts of lacquer hadn't destroyed the DNA.

* * *

Meanwhile, at the Royal Court Theatre, the concerto had just come to an end. Zelda, tears running down her face, was clapping so much her hands were stinging. She got to her feet to join others in a standing ovation for Richard. It was a full five minutes later, when the audience started to disperse, and she was about to go and talk to Richard, that she felt the phone in her pocket vibrating. Once she'd pulled it from her pocket, she saw it was a message from Facebook. Someone had responded to her request.

44

ZELDA

'It isn't him.' Zelda got that in first. 'Morris Arthur Lionel Carmichael, also known as Mal or Malc, isn't *the* other Malcolm and he isn't claiming to be him. Sorry.' She felt Janet's disappointment.

'So why have you brought us here?' Janet, hot chocolate in front of her, looked cross too. 'I thought you were going to tell us about a significant breakthrough.' When Zelda's text came in, she was in bed, she said. She'd already taken off her make-up and put on her pyjamas, and she'd taken her hearing aids out, so if she didn't hear properly...

'I hoped to cheer you up,' said Zelda, articulating as clearly as she could. 'This shows people are reading my Lost Persons post and responding...' she tailed off as Janet didn't look impressed.

They were all in the Golden Lion after the show, Viv, Janet, Zelda and Richard and Billie, of course, in the corner booth, Janet with her hot chocolate, Viv beside her with red wine, Richard opposite her with his well-deserved beer, and Zelda beside him with a glass of white. The pub was busy and noisy, full of late-night drinkers, and there was a honky-tonk pianist in the corner belting out Christmas carols, so it wasn't surprising that Janet was finding it hard to hear. *She* was finding it hard to hear with her hearing aids in. The pub had been crowded when she and Richard arrived – they'd got there before the others – but they'd got seats almost immediately because the people in the corner booth saw them standing, with Billie of course, and insisted they have their seats. Zelda had then texted Viv and Janet, inviting them to join them, thinking her news would cheer them up.

Wrong.

Viv was downbeat too, clearly with something on her mind. 'Tell you later,' she'd said, when Zelda asked, which was fine because she still wanted to try and convince Janet that hearing from this new Mal was a cause for optimism.

'Firstly, this Morris Arthur Lionel Carmichael might not be the only one whose initials spell "Mal". This one was known as Mal at school in Berkshire in the 1970s, so obviously isn't the right one. I spoke to him, by the way – and I think it's encouraging.'

'How?' Janet took a sip of her hot chocolate. 'I still don't see.'

'Well,' Zelda tried not to sound exasperated, 'the speed of the response shows the system is working well. And as I said, there are probably other people out there looking, more of them than we realised called Mal Carmichael, I mean. So let's keep our fingers crossed that the one we're looking for gets in touch soon. Very soon.' She willed the phone on the table in front of her to ring, buzz or ping. 'And if they don't, well, I've got more names to look for when I get back online onto the National Register of Births, Marriages and Deaths...' She petered out, confidence draining, as Janet shook her head from side to side.

'So, Zelda,' she sounded sarcastic, 'you'll start looking for the birth and marriage certificates of all the Morrises and Michaels and Martins, not to mention Matthews with one or two Ts and Maxwells and Mileses and Milos, and other names beginning with M, but only those with second names beginning with A and third names beginning with L which would widen the search to how many? Thousands? Hundreds of thousands? More? Is there an algorithm for this? Does the clever man in Connexions know it? And would you do this before or after you've finished trawling through all the Malcolms?' Janet had a Charlie Chaplin-like chocolate moustache on her top lip, which Zelda wished she could see as it might make her laugh, but probably not, as Operation Cheer Up Janet wasn't working.

Viv took a gulp of red wine. 'And, sorry to add to the gloom, Zelda, but genealogical research, helpful in the long term maybe, won't help us find out where this crucial meeting is taking place on Wednesday, the day after tomorrow, if you need reminding.'

No one needed reminding.

'So,' said Viv, 'it's back to hoping the right Mal gets in touch by Facebook, or reverting to my wild plan of somehow following Isabella to her secret rendezvous, which I have to confess I may have recently scuppered.'

'Out with it, Viv.' Janet was sharp. 'What have you done now?'

'I met Isabella earlier this evening, in the bar and mentioned that we'd heard she'd found her daddy...'

'I hope you didn't say where.' Zelda was horrified.

Viv gave them a summary of her blabbing.

'Do I need a bodyguard?' said Richard when she'd finished. 'Should I swap Billie for a rottweiler?' Billie, hearing her name, left Zelda's side where she had her head on her lap, and went over to his.

'I didn't reveal my sources, Richard.' Viv looked shocked at the thought. 'And she said that I was mistaken, but I'm pretty sure I've aroused her suspicions. Or it will do when she thinks about it, and it will make it harder for us to follow her, as she'll be on the look-out and trying to throw us off the scent.'

Zelda didn't say that she'd thought all along that Viv's idea of following Isabella across New York was a non-starter.

'Oh.' Viv looked brighter, remembering something else. 'There was one good result. You'll like this, Janet. I'm now sure that Primrose isn't part of this conspiracy. Primrose doesn't know about the reappearance of the man Isabella calls Daddy, and Isabella warned me off telling her.'

'Presumably,' said Janet slowly, thinking it out, 'because she wants Primrose to carry on believing that she was married to a bigamist called Malcolm, who was legally married to her, not me, and therefore, as his daughter, she's entitled to his money which she could also get her hands on.'

Viv nodded.

'But why?' said Janet. 'Why wouldn't Isabella want her mother to know her husband, *her* daddy, was alive? That would be cruel. Why would she withhold this information?'

'Money,' said Zelda, because it suddenly seemed simple. 'She must think she has more to gain from her daddy if Primrose thinks he's dead.'

'But doesn't *he* know about Primrose?'

Pause for a lot of thinking, sipping and surmising.

Then Richard said, 'Playing devil's advocate here, giving this Isabella the benefit of the doubt, could she be withholding information till she's checked out this man? Could she be protecting her mother from possible heartbreak, by going to meet this man first, and finding out who he is?'

Zelda said she'd thought of that too and still thought there was a slight chance that Isabella was being kind.

'*We* need to check them out.' The Muscateers spoke as one. 'We need to be at that meeting.'

They were back to following Isabella with or without a wild car chase.

* * *

'How about,' Janet, on her second hot chocolate, looked thoughtful, 'we take Primrose into our confidence as I suggested before, so she can come with us? She, after all, is the one most likely to know if the man Isabella is meeting is her Mal or not. How about me inviting Primrose for a tête á tête, tomorrow morning say, and telling her what we know?'

Viv was against it. 'We've discussed this already. She'll tip off Isabella.'

Zelda tried to keep an open mind. 'How might this help, Janet, if we can persuade her not to tell Isabella?'

'I could try to find out which hotel she and Isabella are staying at in New York for a start. Then when they're going on the bus tour Primrose mentioned, because if we knew the time and place we could follow Isabella from that point to the secret rendezvous.'

'But you don't have to tell her that her husband may be alive to find that out, do you?' Viv was back to keeping their powder dry, rather late in the day. 'Couldn't you just chat casually about hotels and shight-seeing as she so memorably called it?'

Zelda tended to agree. Telling Primrose about 'Daddy' could ruin their chances of finding out who he really was.

But Janet seemed attached to her tête á tête idea, though professing an open mind. Yawning, she suggested they all sleep on it and reconvene in the morning to decide. She got to her feet and eased herself out of the booth, Viv close behind.

Zelda picked up her phone, willing the right Mal Carmichael to get in touch.

45

JANET

Tuesday, 22 December

Janet woke up with a bright idea.

But at breakfast in the Britannia restaurant, when she told Viv and Zelda they looked less than enthusiastic. In fact Viv, wind-blown after her walk round the deck, seemed more interested in the kipper she was dissecting.

Janet pressed on because she needed their help.

'Zelda, I haven't got Isabella's mobile number and I want to invite her to meet me in the jewellery boutique. I'm sure she'll come if she thinks I'm going to buy her something. Can Richard get her email or mobile number using his contacts on the staff? Don't look so worried, Viv' – her eyebrows had shot to her hairline – 'I'm not going to buy her anything, or actually meet her. This is my cunning plan to get her away from Primrose, so I can talk to her on her own.'

They looked more interested. Zelda, she was pleased to see, got her phone out straightaway and started texting Richard.

Janet addressed Viv, now eating her kipper.

'I'm going to suggest to Primrose that we have coffee in her room or mine.'

'To tell her what exactly?' Viv looked up.

'As little as I possibly can, Viv, to find out as much as I possibly can. I have taken your advice on board, but...'

Zelda interrupted to say Richard had replied and he thought he could get the info she needed, but needed time.

Janet resisted the urge to say *tell him to hurry up* and got her reward a few minutes later, when she was only halfway through her eggs Florentine.

'Success, Janet.' Zelda looked up from her blueberry yoghurt. 'I'll forward it to you.'

Ping. Janet texted immediately:

> Hi Isabella, let's meet at the jewellery boutique at 10.30 for last day bargains!

The reply with the thumbs-up emoji was instant. Janet now texted Primrose:

> Hi Primrose, let's meet for coffee, your room or mine 10.30.

No reply, but no worries, well, none that were insurmountable. If Primrose didn't reply she would head for her room on Deck 6, as soon as she got word that Isabella was downstairs in the jewellery boutique, where if Viv or Zelda or both cooperated, they would be waiting to tell Isabella that she'd been delayed, and message her that Primrose was on her own.

'Can you do that and keep her out of the way for at least half an hour?' She reckoned she could tell Primrose what she needed to tell her in that time.

Viv said she could. 'I'll throw her overboard if I have to.'

But Zelda said she was sorry but she couldn't, not without letting Richard down, and before Janet could say that was okay, she launched into another paean for the man.

'He's giving a talk to raise money for Guiding Eyes for the Blind which is the US equivalent of UK Guide Dogs for the Blind, and I've said I'd go over it with him this morning. Have you any idea how much it costs to train a guide dog? It's astronomical. Anyway, I'm going to be on standby, so I can prompt if necessary, because he gives the talk from memory, he doesn't read it, though he's given me a transcript, well, a list of points he wants to make, so I know what he wants to say, and I'm sure he won't forget, but if does, well, I'll be there. Of course.'

She paused for breath, at last.

'And so will we, Zelda, if we possibly can. The man's a wonder and deserves our support. Just tell us where and when.'

'Illuminations, Deck 3 at 3 p.m. this afternoon.'

Viv was getting to her feet. 'It's getting on for ten now so we need to move. I need a shower after my run, but I'll be back on the case in twenty minutes. I'll get down to the Grand Lobby ASAP and text you, Janet, as soon as I've seen Isabella waiting for you in the boutique. Then I'll approach and say you sent me to tell her you'll be late while you hotfoot it to their cabin on Deck 6.'

'Number!' Janet realised with a shock that she didn't know Primrose's stateroom number.

'I'll ask Richard to find out.' Zelda texted, but Superman didn't answer this time. He must have taken off his magic cape.

'Don't worry. I'll find him.' Zelda stood up. 'I'll get back to you ASAP.'

But it was another half an hour before Janet got a text. Anxious that time was running out because she hadn't heard, she had already gone up to Deck 6 to be ready, and was standing outside the PlayZone, in the stern of the ship, feeling conspicuous as she hadn't got a child to deliver or collect. But the play centre was the only public place on Deck 6, the rest of which was a very long corridor lined with cabins. She would look even more conspicuous hanging about outside one of the cabin doors. As it was, she felt she had to explain herself to a mother arriving to deliver her toddler. 'I'm meeting my daughter and granddaughter here. They're late. I wonder if I've got the time right.' Quick look at watch. It was 10.30 exactly, when Zelda's text arrived.

> It's 6054. Good luck!

Superman had delivered just in time.

46

JANET

Number 6054 was in the middle of the ship, about halfway down the long corridor. Janet found the room easily and knocked on the metal door tentatively. Then firmly, which was hard on the knuckles, and when there was no response she shouted, 'Primrose!'

'Who is it?' She sounded nervous.

'Me, Janet.'

'I can't come out.'

Janet heard *I can't come out to play* as if they were children, but suppressed a sharp reply.

'Just open the door, Primrose.'

'I'm not supposed to.'

Janet saw a steward at the far end of the corridor, coming her way. When he got nearer, she saw he was bringing a meal for someone, and said, 'Excuse me,' as he was about to pass. 'Could you possibly open the door? My friend isn't feeling well and can't open it herself.' He could and did! All stewards had pass keys, she'd remembered Zelda saying, another fact she'd gleaned from Richard. Within moments she was inside the cabin, small compared to hers, she saw at a glance – but just as attractively furnished in blue and yellow with two single beds side by side. Primrose stood between them, biting a knuckle.

'It's all right, Primrose, Isabella won't be back for a bit.' Janet crossed her fingers. 'She's downstairs having a coffee with someone. I saw her.'

God forgive me for being a liar.

'I'm not well, Janet, that's all.' Primrose drew herself up to her full five feet. 'Isabella said I must stay in bed and rest.' She was still in her night clothes.

Don't criticise Isabella. That is what she must remember.

'You've got a bit of a hangover, that's all, Primrose. You need coffee. Shall I make some?' There was a coffee-maker on the desk. 'And maybe water and carbs. Have you got biscuits?' Janet went into the en suite, which had a shower, loo and basin but no bath, to fill a jug with water and think about how to find out what she wanted to know. 'Don't worry, Primrose, I won't stay long,' she said when she came out, 'but I didn't want to leave without saying goodbye.'

She continued this theme when they were sitting on the chairs, side by side, with coffees in their hands. 'Of course we might see each other in New York, if we're staying in the same hotel?'

Primrose didn't rise to that.

'We're staying at the Millenium Downtown in Church Street.'

Or that.

'It's in Manhattan.'

Primrose's lips stayed pursed, so she tried a direct question. 'Where are you and Isabella staying?'

'I don't know, Janet.' She sipped her coffee.

Janet didn't know whether to believe her or not. This wasn't going well. Clearly Primrose had either not been told where she was staying, or she'd been told to keep her mouth shut. And, Janet reminded herself, Primrose almost certainly still thought that she, Janet, had stolen her late husband from her and deprived her of years of being happily married.

She hates me, understandably, so I must do my utmost to put her right.

'Primrose, we have had good times and bad on this voyage. On that first night when we talked about old times in Edinburgh, I really felt that we were going to be great friends. I wouldn't like this sad and shocking discovery that we *may*' – she had to say *may* – 'have married the same man stop that from happening. If it is proved to be true that Mal and Malcolm were the same person, I am sincerely sorry, for both of us, and as I have said I will recompense you financially to the best of my ability. Sadly, I cannot recompense you for the pain you suffered when you learned your Mal had died all those years ago, leaving you, a young mother, to bring up a child alone. I am truly sorry if I unknowingly played any part in that...'

Primrose's eyes were filling up.

'...but I still don't understand,' Janet went on, 'I don't think you've said – how you learned that Mal had died and you had become a widow?'

'Daddy told me.' Now her tears flowed. 'He came into my bedroom one morning with a cup of tea – he brought me and Mummy tea every morning – and said he had something very upsetting to tell me. I thought Isabella must have hurt herself – she was quite a headstrong child prone to accidents – but he said it was about Mal. Well, I had been worried because I hadn't heard from Mal for several weeks, so I said, "What's the matter, Daddy? Is he ill?" And he said, "No, he has passed away."'

She was reliving it.

'D-did he say how?' Janet asked tentatively.

She wiped her nose on the sleeve of her pink pyjamas and nodded. 'He said Mal had drowned.'

'Drowned?'

She nodded again. 'On a business trip to Australia.'

'But...' Janet had so many questions she didn't know which to ask first but started with, 'Was there a funeral?'

Primrose shook her head. 'Daddy said there couldn't be, not without a b-body.'

'No body?'

She shook her head again.

'*Presumed* drowned then?' Janet had to ask. 'How was this supposed to have happened?'

Primrose shrugged in a hopeless *I don't know* sort of way. 'Man overboard, Daddy said. It happens quite a lot, it seems, more than you'd think, even now, hushed up of course because ship owners don't want people to know. It's why I don't go out on deck and have asked Isabella not to. I didn't really want to come on this voyage but Isabella said I must. Daddy was perfectly lovely and said he would take care of everything, all the legalities, and of course he and Mummy looked after Isabella as I was too distraught to do anything for months.'

'But...' Janet was totally confused, 'he was on a ship, you say?'

She nodded. 'Going to Australia on business. He'd set off from Tilbrook docks in London, Daddy said, but never arrived at Perth where he was due to disembark.'

She *believed* this?

'Didn't you make your own enquiries?' Janet knew the answer before Primrose shook her head and regretted the implied criticism. But there was a bigger hole in this story than the one that had sunk the *Titanic*. Did businessmen sail to Australia in those days, the early 1970s at a guess? Wouldn't that have taken weeks? Surely they went by air to save time even then? What was the name of the ship he was sailing on? Had Primrose seen a passenger list with his name on it? A death certificate? A coroner's report? Why hadn't she asked for evidence? More questions came to mind. Did Primrose get compensation from the bank Mal worked for, insurance money, a widow's pension? People would have required proof to pay these out. A memory surfaced. *I felt like a widow because I didn't have a husband, and I'd been told I was a widow, but I've always clung to the hope that Mal was alive and well. Somewhere. And that he'd come back and find me. Us. Find us.*

'Primrose.' Janet chose her words carefully. 'I remember you saying that you'd always *felt* that Mal was alive and that he'd come back and find you.'

She nodded tearfully.

'So you must have had mixed feelings when you heard that Mal had been living with another woman and had fathered another child.'

'Yes.' It was a little voice.

'Who did you hear that from?'

'Isabella.'

Don't criticise Isabella.

Janet suppressed, 'Could Isabella have been lying?' and re-phrased. 'And what did you say to that, Primrose?'

'That she must be wrong!' It was a cry, the anguish she'd felt still on her face. 'I told her that her daddy wouldn't do a thing like that! I told her it was impossible!'

'So, what made you change your mind?'

'She showed me the photograph of Mal marrying *you*!' She moved back in her seat then, would have moved the chair if there had been room to move it. 'She said we must find you!'

Janet was dumbstruck, overwhelmed by what she'd just heard. Isabella was definitely the source of this story. She must have concocted it from what she found on Facebook, and decided to track her down and extract as much money as she could.

'Primrose,' Janet spoke carefully, 'I agree that back in the 1970s Mal and Malcolm looked very alike, but I am still of the mind, and have reason to believe, that Mal and Malcolm are, or were in Malcolm's case, two different people, and that your Mal is still alive.'

Honesty is the best policy. She had always believed that.

Be as open as you can. She'd learned that.

'I repeat, I have reason to believe that they are two different people, and that your Mal is still alive.' She waited, watching Primrose take in this new information, her mouth slightly open, her hand shaking slightly. 'I should say,' Janet persisted, as Primrose bent over to put the empty cup under her chair, 'that I am 99 per cent certain that your Mal is alive and that Isabella is in touch with him.'

Now she was speaking to the back of Primrose's neck and some tangled blonde curls. She could see white roots. Was she going to stay down there forever? Had she collapsed? Janet was about to put out a helping hand when Primrose straightened up, gripping the arms of the chair, her eyes searching Janet's face. 'W-what are your reasons for saying this?'

Primrose's face was red and it was hard to read her expression, which seemed to change from moment to moment. Her narrowed eyes looked suspicious, then widening to wistful or even wishful.

'Isabella has been overheard speaking to him,' said Janet.

Primrose's eyes near-bulged. She couldn't have opened them wider. 'You're sure?'

'Ninety-nine per cent. I wish I could say it was 100 per cent but the person who overheard the conversation, who heard Isabella talking to someone she called Daddy, didn't actually see who she was talking to, so we can't be certain till...' But before she could say *till we've followed Isabella to her secret rendezvous and met this man*, the door opened.

'I thought I'd find you here,' said Isabella.

47

JANET

'I couldn't keep her talking any longer.' Viv was cross with herself.

'It's all right, Viv, you did your best.' Janet was keen to get on with the next step.

They were sitting on high stools at the bar in the Golden Lion where they'd repaired for a post-mortem, after meeting in the lift. Janet had been on the way down to find Viv after being near-pushed out of the door by Isabella and Viv was coming up to Deck 6 to find Janet and rescue her if necessary. The pub was crowded with people coming in for elevenses, early aperitifs or late breakfasts so they kept their voices down, not wanting to be overheard. The uncomfortable stools were the only seats they could get. They were drinking coffee, though Janet, still shaken from Isabella's onslaught – she'd sworn a lot – wondered if a cognac would be justified.

But she must keep a clear head. All was not lost, though Viv seemed convinced it was. They'd blown it, she said. 'Between us, I mean. I'm not blaming you, Janet. I blabbed to the daughter first, you merely repeated it all to the mother. There is no way we're going to be able to follow Isabella to her secret rendezvous, if she actually goes there now. She'll be doing everything she can to outwit us.'

She went over what had happened in the jewellery boutique. Isabella had seemed suspicious from the start, or if not the start, from when Janet hadn't turned up after five minutes. 'Where is she then?' she'd said several times. Viv explained that she wouldn't have been able to detain her as long as she had if Carlos hadn't helped out with conversation – she thought he might have been tipped off by Richard – bringing out one item of jewellery after another that she might be interested in. And then luckily one of Isabella's sugar-daddies had turned up, to buy her a little thank you, he said, and she'd let him buy her a pair of earrings at a bargain end-of-voyage price. When she couldn't persuade him to buy her anything else, she'd said she'd see him later and rushed off. 'I rushed after her of course, fearing for your life, after texting you saying she was on her way.'

Janet had only just got the text.

'Viv, let's move on. I need to get Primrose on her own again, out of Isabella's hearing. So how are we going to bring that about? You just said Isabella said she'd see her friend later...'

'It was a casual remark, Janet, no time or place was mentioned, and from what you've told me, Isabella will know by now that she's been overheard talking to her daddy. I stupidly told her that I'd heard her father was alive, and Primrose will have told her that you'd heard too, so she'll be on full alert wondering how much more we know.'

'I'm not sure that Primrose will have told her.' Janet remembered the hopeful look in Primrose's eye. 'I definitely sparked her interest and may even have gained some trust. I'm actually feeling a bit hopeful, Viv.'

'About what exactly?'

'That this could end happily.'

'Happily? For *whom*, as you would say?'

'For me and Primrose, especially Primrose, who may have started to see that she's been lied to.' She told Viv about the 'drowned at sea' story that Primrose had been told all those years ago. 'So I think there's a strong possibility that there is a Mal who isn't Malcolm. Or at least a man Isabella calls Daddy who wasn't Malcolm. Honestly, Viv, Primrose has been lied to all her life, by her father first and then Isabella.'

'Let me get this clear, Janet. You're certain now that Malcolm wasn't a bigamist.' Viv visibly brightened.

'Almost, but – don't open the fizz yet – I still need to go to that meeting, Viv, to remove the smidgen of doubt that remains. I need to see this other man for myself, in the presence of Primrose. I need to know that he is Mal and she was married to him, not Malcolm. I want it for myself and my grandchildren and I want it for Primrose. I want her to be reunited with her long-lost husband, Viv. She deserves it after being treated so cruelly.'

'To the barricades then. All for one and all that. I just wish we knew where the bloody barricades were.' Viv felt in her pocket and pulled out her phone. 'I'm texting Zelda to see how the Facebook search for Mal is going. Seems to me he's our only hope of finding out where the meeting is.'

It seemed so to Janet too, but then her phone pinged:

> I would like to resume our conversation. Going to Guide Dog talk this afternoon. Primrose

Jane texted back:

> I'll be there.

Primrose texted again:

> Isabella too so discretion required.

Janet texted back with a thumbs-up emoji, then showed Viv the exchange. 'What do you make of that?'

'Promising. If she tells you where they're meeting.'

'I fear not. I really don't think she knows. What I told her was a complete surprise. Now she wants to know more.'

'Is it wise to tell her though?' Viv obviously still thought Primrose would blab to Isabella.

'I think I must, to get her on our side – unless Zelda has come up with the goods?'

Viv glanced at her phone. 'Not yet.'

'If Primrose trusts me and wants to see this man for herself, she might let us know which hotel she and Isabella are staying at. If I can persuade her to let us know, we can try to follow Isabella from that point on.'

Viv slid down from the bar stool. 'There are a lot of ifs, but it's good that she wants to meet you. We'll all be at Richard's talk but I'll keep my distance so you two can have a heart to heart.'

They were getting closer. Janet sent up a prayer.

48

ZELDA

Zelda was waiting in the wings, watching the crowds pouring in. The cinema was already packed but they kept coming. It seemed as if everyone on board wanted to hear Richard speak.

'We'll have to stop them soon,' a steward waiting with them said. 'No more room. Fire regulations.'

'Billie's a very popular lady.' Richard stroked her ears.

'And you, popular man, I mean. Are you nervous?' Zelda had butterflies just imagining herself in the same situation.

'Only nervous enough to get the adrenaline going. I need a few nerves to give my best. I've done this before, by the way.'

Joke. He'd done it lots of times, he'd said.

'The lights in the auditorium have gone down,' she told him. 'Ready?' He nodded, put Billie's harness on as deftly as always and took hold of her handle. He'd turned down Zelda's offer to walk on with him, because he wanted to begin with Billie in work-mode, he'd said, demonstrating the independence she gave him. They'd practised the walk to the podium several times that morning. 'Okay,' she said, 'break a leg, you're on.'

'Forward, Billie.'

Zelda hung back slightly, as they made their way to the centre of the platform, stopping at the spotlit podium, where Richard took Billie's harness off. Then he checked that the water he'd requested was on the table beside him and tested the microphone. As Billie settled at his feet, off duty but still his devoted friend, Zelda sat down a little way behind them, ready to prompt if necessary, but from the moment he began she knew he didn't need her.

'I was born a few years ago on a homestead farm, outside Orlando, Florida. My dad grew peanuts there, and watermelons, okra and a host of other crops that meant we were self-sufficient in fruit and veg, and made some cash from selling the surplus. My mom, an amazing woman, taught school. When I was three, my parents noticed that I was extremely sensitive to light, not a good thing in the Sunshine State, not a good thing anywhere, in fact, as it's a sign of glaucoma. Glaucoma is the result of damage to the optic nerve which connects the eye to the brain and it can cause blindness. Don't be alarmed if you have it, a lot of older folk do, and in most cases it's treatable and doesn't lead to loss of sight, but in my case it did. It was most likely caused by pressure on the nerve way before I was born. Anyway, my parents took me to the docs and that was the diagnosis so I was stuck with it.

'I was fast going blind. My parents gave me as normal a life as they could – so I did most things my brother and sister did, including picking crops – but at the age of seven, with mixed feelings, they enrolled me at the Florida School for the Deaf and the Blind in St Augustine, because they thought I needed more help to fulfil my potential. I had to go as a boarder because it was far from home, about a hundred miles away. Incidentally, that's where Ray Charles had been a few years before, so I was in good company so to speak. That man has been an inspiration. Like him, I got a good all-round education there, and I learned how to read and write Braille. I also studied classical music – the cello in my case, the piano in his – and learned how to read Braille musical notation, which involves reading Braille with one hand and playing with the other. There will be time for questions. Any so far?' Richard paused and drank from the bottle of water.

No hands went up, no one called out, because everyone was gobsmacked, Zelda thought, looking out at the audience, who sat in silent awe. She did too, though she knew this story, but reading it was one thing, hearing it was another, though his delivery was matter of fact and unemotional and a bit too fast if she had to be critical. A steward took the empty water bottle from Richard's hand and he continued.

'Now I'll come to what you've all been waiting for, the star of the show.' He looked down at Billie. 'Meet my best friend, if you haven't already. Meet Billie.'

This got a round of applause.

'Ray Charles, The Genius, is, as you'll have gathered, a hero of mine and a role model, but – now fast-forwarding to when I was living in New York – there's one decision I made that he didn't. Can't think why. Unlike him, I chose to have a guide dog. Billie is my seventh, by the way. A lovely lady called Alma was my first. Till Alma came along I used a white stick and that in New York was hair-raising, especially on the subway. Once I stepped between two carriages of an underground train, thinking the gap was a doorway, and ended up on the tracks. A stick didn't know the difference. I was down to zero seeing by then, because I'd walked into a shelf in the new apartment I'd just moved into with my partner, and working in New York became even more perilous. So, encouraged by friends, I made the best decision I've ever made in my life. I put in an application for a guide dog and a year later I went to St James's in New York to train with Alma.'

My partner. The apartment I moved into with *my partner*.

'When I say "I went to train",' he went on blithely, 'I mean I went to *be trained. I* went to be trained. Alma was already trained. She had been training for years.'

My partner...

* * *

Janet

Janet, sitting at the back of the auditorium with her hearing aids turned up to maximum volume, noted that too, but moved as she was by Richard's inspiring talk – how could anyone not be? – she was also wondering where

Primrose was. Meeting her was, if not the main reason she'd come, an important one. She checked her phone again.

> Going to Guide Dog talk this afternoon.

She had read that correctly. So where was she? Where were *they*? Janet turned to her right to see if they were on the other side of the aisle, but the only face she recognised was Viv's at the far end of the back row. She straightened up to scan the rows in front of her, the hundreds of back-of-heads, looking for Primrose's blonde curls and Isabella's mound of pink-blonde hair, as she had been doing since she came in, but she still couldn't see them. Not that she could see everyone in the room even from this seat on the back row by the centre aisle. Primrose was short and always wore black, which made her hard to see in a darkened room, and that shade of blonde hair, though visible, was not uncommon. She checked her message from Primrose again.

> Isabella too so discretion required.

Had Isabella locked her in the cabin?

Richard's talk was coming to an end. He finished with a quip which brought forth laughter, and the audience applauded, at least half of them rising to their feet. When the applause died down and everyone was seated, he asked for questions. There were a few, all of which he answered, but then, after a word from a steward, he said their time was up as the room was needed for another event. Thanking them for coming, he reminded them that the real stars deserving their praise were Billie and the dogs before her and the people who had trained them. He couldn't have done it without them, he said, and he hoped people would give generously so others like him could benefit and be independent too. Independence, Janet remembered Zelda saying how important that was to him.

There was Zelda now, stepping forward to help – if he needed her help, but he didn't. He needed Billie's, that was all. Zelda stood back as he reached for the dog's harness which he'd put on the table beside him and was now putting onto the standing dog. The dog was on her feet in working mode in seconds. Then she was leading Richard off the stage, Zelda following, looking glamorous in a rainbow-patterned caftan, her head high, but how was she feeling? How was the Richard and Zelda story going to pan out? Janet wondered. Was it a shipboard romance or something more? The auditorium was nearly empty so she got to her feet, preparing to leave. Reaching for her phone to text Viv and ask her where she was, she felt someone tap her arm.

'Janet.' Primrose was by her side. 'We've only got a few minutes. Isabella has gone to the loo.'

49

JANET

They stayed in the auditorium, at the back, near the door because Primrose was sure Isabella would come back to find her. As they sat down side by side, Primrose seemed nervous but pleased with herself. 'Isabella was annoyed when I said that I wouldn't go to the bathroom with her. I didn't need to go, but she couldn't stay to argue because she did.'

Too much information, Primrose, and not enough.

The lights were all up now and there were only a few passengers hanging around and several stewards rearranging the room for the next event.

'T-tell me, quickly, what you know.' Primrose kept looking from one side to another as if Isabella might appear at any moment. 'Tell me why you think my daughter is deceiving me.'

Did I say she was deceiving you? Janet was wary despite Primrose's new defiant attitude and the impression she gave that she thought Isabella might not be completely open and honest. It still felt like a good idea not to criticise Isabella, to keep Primrose listening so that she reached the obvious conclusion for herself. She would therefore play the devil's advocate again.

'Primrose, I don't think you should think badly of Isabella. Her motivation may be a good one. I mean that she may be withholding the fact that she's in touch with the man she called Daddy for a good reason. This might be a kindness on her part, to spare your feelings, to protect you, in case this man isn't who he says he is. She may be wanting to check him out first, hence the, er... secret meeting.' This, she still thought as she spoke, might in fact be possible.

'Secret meeting?' Primrose's eyes opened wide.

Janet told her what Richard had said without saying it was Richard and as she finished, her phone pinged. 'Excuse me.' It was a text from Viv.

> Have Isabella on my radar. In loos. Long queue. Think you have 10 minutes. Vx

Viv was on the case! Feeling buoyed, Janet pressed on. 'So I think you and I, Primrose, should go to this meeting, but first we need to find out...'

Primrose nodded but then said, 'You didn't say who said they overheard Isabella talking to someone about a meeting...' and Janet took a chance.

'The wonderful man we've just listened to.'

'The blind man?' Primrose frowned. 'The cellist, Richard Williams?'

Janet nodded.

'So he didn't actually *see* Isabella?'

'No, but he recognised her voice.'

'But he didn't *see* her or the person she was talking to?'

'No,' Janet had to admit. 'She was on the phone.'

'I thought perhaps it was Skype or FaceTime and they were *seen*. But, let me be clear, you think Isabella was talking to her father because a blind man told you so?'

'He heard her say "Daddy". "See you soon, Daddy." And they talked about a meeting in New York.'

'But she could have said Freddie. Or Teddy. Or Paddy. She has a friend called Freddie, Janet. Where did this overhearing take place?'

'But Primrose, why would Isabella want to have a secret meeting with Freddie?'

Primrose came straight back. 'You say secret, Janet, I say private. She doesn't want me to be there, because as I've said before I cramp her style. Where was this overhearing supposed to have taken place?'

Janet noted the *supposed* and her own doubts resurfaced. *Seeing is believing.*

'On Deck 3 where people walk their dogs, though there was no one else about. Richard had just finished walking Billie round the deck and was sitting down to make a phone call because reception is good there, when Isabella walked past him and sat down in a deck chair further along and started a phone call.'

Primrose was shaking her head, incredulous.

'I don't go out on deck, Janet, for reasons I've explained, but there are windows. I've seen the waves crashing against the side and I've *heard* them when people have opened doors, I've heard the wind whistling and the waves crashing, sometimes onto the deck. It's noisy out there, Janet. I'm sure people can hardly hear themselves speak, let alone overhear other people's conversations. I don't want to be unkind about the marvellous man, a brilliant musician, but he must have been mistaken. Isabella and I have our difficulties, but she tells me everything, well, almost everything, including things I'd rather not hear about... but, well, we're very close and I'm sure she would tell me about something as momentous as finding her father.'

Another text came in from Viv.

> Isabella gone to her room to change. Soaked!
> Have gained you extra 20 mins.

What was Viv up to? Janet wanted to text her back but also wanted to know more about the things Primrose would rather not hear about that Isabella told her.

'It's difficult when children tell you things you don't like, isn't it? I can't bear it when Grant tells me the children are ill.'

Primrose nodded.

'You want to know their worries,' Janet went on, 'but at the same time you don't, because you don't want them to have worries, especially ones you can't help with.'

Primrose agreed. 'I wish Isabella didn't tell me about her money problems, because I can't help her any more.'

Janet waited.

'I've paid off several credit card bills over the years, for considerable amounts, but clearly it hasn't been enough. Isabella tends to be extravagant. And now she's saying she is behind with her mortgage payments and is in danger of losing her house unless I sell my home, which was my parents' until they passed away six years ago, so she can pay off her mortgage.'

'She wants you to sell your house and give her the proceeds?'

'Most of them,' said Primrose.

'But where would that leave you?' said Janet.

'On the street,' said Primrose, 'well, in a less-nice street, if I kept a bit back to buy another house. So I have declined, while telling her that she would be very welcome to come and live with me.'

'And what did she say to that?'

'She said that wouldn't work out,' Primrose looked sad, 'but I don't see why not.'

Primrose is lonely and completely deluded about her daughter, who will stop at nothing to get what she wants. How wonderful it would be to reunite her with her long-lost husband. Primrose's dismissal of Richard's evidence had reignited Janet's own doubts, but also her determination to prove things one way or another. She must persuade Primrose to do everything she could to find out the name of the hotel she and Isabella were staying at, so they could be followed from there.

'Excuse me, ladies.' A steward stood in front of them. 'I'm sorry, but I must ask you to leave the auditorium, as it is about to be rearranged for another Sky at Night talk. There are seats in the lobby outside, and afternoon tea is being served in the Champagne Bar and the Commodore Club and the Golden Lion.'

'Primrose.' Janet linked arms as they headed for the door. 'We have reached an impasse. We don't know who is right and the only way we're going to know is to go to that meeting and see whom Isabella meets there. I am afraid we, I mean you, must use subterfuge. You need to search Isabella's things and find out...' But before she could say *where you're booked in*, Isabella was upon them.

'Mummy,' she grasped Primrose's other arm none too gently, 'it's time for your tablets.'

50

VIV

'What the hell!' Viv swore as Isabella hauled Primrose past her, just as she was coming in. 'That bloody woman nearly knocked me over!'

'And for nothing.' Janet looked distraught.

'Didn't you get my text warning she was on the way?'

Janet shook her head.

'Ladies, if you please.' The steward held open the door.

'Okay, we're going.' Viv took Janet's arm. 'Reviving cuppa in the Golden Lion? With cake? Bit too early for anything else.'

Viv's warning text pinged into Janet's phone as they settled in a booth. As she poured tea, builder's for herself, well, Morning Breakfast, the nearest to it, and Earl Grey for Janet, Viv tried to be positive. 'Lesson learned. In future we must ring if it's urgent.'

Janet looked as if the future had been cancelled. 'I feel worse than I did before meeting Primrose. All I learned was that Isabella is in dire financial straits.'

'...which shows she has a motive...'

'...which we already knew, and then Primrose near-convinced me that Richard was mistaken. It *is* hearsay, Viv. We only have his word...'

'...which we can rely on totally according to Zelda. She says his hearing is amazing. Where is she by the way?'

'With her paramour, of course. Honestly, Viv, if we can't prove this other Mal exists we're back to Malcolm being a bigamist and me losing everything...'

'...and the ship may hit an iceberg, as I may have said before.'

Keeping Janet afloat was hard work. But a lifeboat was on its way – maybe.

Viv was feeling optimistic. She was getting better at sleuthing. Her latest attempt had gone well. Isabella wasn't that bright, she'd discovered, and she had a weak bladder. With a bit of ingenuity, she could be outwitted as she had been today without too much trouble. Once Viv had got Isabella in her sights early on in Richard's talk – she wasn't hard to spot with all that hair – it had been quite easy to follow her when she got up. At the end of the talk, she'd been quick to her feet, obviously keen to get out, pushing past people to get to the aisle. Then, realising that Primrose hadn't followed her, she'd stopped and started calling her, beckoning frantically, but Primrose had stayed in her place looking at the stage. Then, clearly desperate to get wherever she was going, Isabella headed for the exit at the back of the auditorium, rushing past Viv on the back row.

She'd set off after her as quickly as she could, and soon spotted her heading for the loos, which were midway down the deck. It was a bit of a trek and when she got there, a few seconds after her prey, she'd been pleased to see there was a long queue, moving slowly. Isabella was now clearly desperate for a pee, standing first on one stilettoed foot and then another, even clutching her crotch, not a good look in a catsuit, the pink one that made her look like Lady Godiva. It was a good five minutes before she'd reached a free cubicle and when she came out she looked very relieved but, clearly in a hurry to get back, she made no more than a token show of washing her hands – turning the tap on and wriggling her fingers – but not putting them under the water. That's when Viv had her brainwave, if that's what an action quicker than thought was called. Instinctively, she'd stepped forward and put her finger over the outlet of the tap, spraying water all over Isabella, most of it landing between her legs. Then Viv had beaten a hasty retreat, fortunately not needing the loo herself.

Janet was gratifyingly open-mouthed, as Viv regaled her with this.

'I left her desperately trying to cover herself with one hand while reaching for paper towels with the other. Once outside, I took a sneaky look back in and saw her standing in front of the dryer to no avail – the current didn't reach her crotch – before heading for the exit herself, covering the wet area as best she could with her handbag. At that point I flattened myself against the wall as she passed, then watched as she headed for the lifts. I guessed she was going back to her room to change, so I followed at a discreet distance, using the stairs to go up to Deck 6, where I texted you again as I waited for her to come out of her room. When she came out in dry clothes, I texted again to say she was on her way back. That's the text you've only just got, but I think it proves she can be followed. So, my idea of following them tomorrow, from the ship if we have to, isn't as crazy as you seem to think. Hear me out, Janet.' She was shaking her head.

'We'll have to get up early, so one of us is down on Deck 6 watching their cabin, but we'll be up early anyway as arrival time at the Brooklyn Terminal is 6.30. Whoever that is keeps close, but not too close obviously, through all the disembarkation procedure, and keeps in touch with the rest of us by phone...'

'No, Viv.' Janet held up her hand. 'No more, please. You've been watching too many films and you're crazy if you think Isabella won't have guessed it was you spraying her with water. She'll be even more vigilant now Viv, and out for revenge. *And*,' she was scrolling on her phone, 'you obviously haven't read the disembarkation advice on the ship's website.'

Viv had to admit she hadn't.

'Read this then.'

Viv read.

Disembarkation takes place between 08:00 & 11:00. The upper decks disembark first (decks 9, 10, 11, 12), the remaining decks at the later time.

'In other words,' said Janet, 'we will disembark before them. They will be following us.'

Viv conceded defeat. 'Have you got a better idea?'

'No, as I have said, I am bereft of ideas. I am totally bereft.'
So much for buoying Janet up. Viv texted Zelda.

> Janet sinking fast. Heading for bottom. My plan kiboshed so need to find Mal fast. Any more replies?

51

ZELDA

Zelda heard a text pinging in but left the phone in her pocket.

'Aren't you going to answer that?' Richard had heard it too.

She shook her head, still moved beyond words by his talk.

'What's the matter, Zelda?'

You, she didn't say. *You don't need me.* They were in the Godiva Chocolate Café where they'd come to celebrate his success with coffee and posh chocolates. Richard was in a celebratory mood because his talk had gone well and he'd raised an incredible sum for Guide Dogs for the Blind, more than he'd ever raised before with a single talk. She was still reeling from what she'd learnt about him and about Billie and the dogs he'd had before her. His words were in her head but it wasn't just what he said but the way that he said it, so matter of fact, so devoid of self-pity. Independence defined him, or had done ever since he'd got his seeing-eyes. Billie now lay between them – actually and symbolically, she couldn't help thinking – stretched out half under the table between their cream leather armchairs, off duty now but ready to spring into action at a word from him. *He needs you but he doesn't need me.*

'Don't be mawkish, Zelda.'

Mawkish!

He nodded at her pocket. 'Could be an important message.'

'It's from Viv,' she said, reading it, still wondering what he meant by mawkish. 'She says Janet's depressed and I need to find Mal fast. She wants to know if I've had any more replies, but I haven't, not since this morning. That was from a Mark Alwyn Liam Carmichael, also saying his initials spelt Mal. This one was fifty-five so wrong age and he came from Cardiff, so wrong place too. I told Val this morning before breakfast – but not Janet as there didn't seem to be any point.'

'So, what's the plan now?' He murmured something she didn't catch to Billie, who got up and came over to her.

'Wait till we get home, I guess, and hope the lawyers can sort it out.'

'Which will put a bit of a damper on your day in New York.'

'Exactly.' She stroked Billie's head, warm on her lap.

'Zelda, I'm sorry I can't stay and help out by showing you all a few of my favourite spots, but I'm flying on to Raleigh as soon as we've disembarked.'

'And you're playing tonight?'

He nodded. 'First with Animus then later with the Steve Goffe Trio. No time for dinner, I'm afraid.'

So this is the last time we'll meet!

Where do we go from here? she wanted to ask but a steward arrived to take their orders. Richard said he was having coffee, chocolate *and* ice cream and he hoped she would too. She said she would because she couldn't focus on the menu in front of her, so thought she might as well. I think you're *extraordinary*, she wanted to say, *I've never met anyone like you, and...*

But he was touching her hand. 'Here are the chocolates I ordered for starters and the coffees. I need your help now.'

The steward put a silver dish containing six heart-shaped chocolates between them. Three were milk chocolate, three dark.

'There's Coeur Lait,' he read from the menu on his phone, using his Braille device, 'which is filled with "our signature hazelnut praline", and Coeur Noir, a dark heart "filled with an intense ganache", which I gather is even more chocolate made with even more cream, so I'm having one of those at least, but you'll have to tell me which is which, because my Colorino isn't up to the task.'

'Colorino?' She found her voice.

'My colour detector. I use it to make sure that I put on matching socks in the morning and my shirt doesn't clash with my tie. It's good, but no,' he was pointing a small device at the chocolates, 'it isn't telling me which is milk and which is dark. It only registers brown, which doesn't do them justice.'

She was stupidly speechless.

'Zelda, I'm asking for your help.' He held out his hand. 'I *need* a chocolate, dark, please. Now.' He sounded amused, but she couldn't tell if he was laughing at himself or her. If only she could see his eyes, but the rock-star dark glasses kept their expression hidden.

'There.' She put a dark chocolate in his hand, her fingers touching the smooth sensitive tips of his.

'Thank you. Your turn now, though, I apologise, you should have had first choice, so take two.'

She chose one of each, biting into the milk chocolate first, and fortunately it melted in her mouth, filling it with deliciousness and sliding down her dry, tight throat.

'Good, eh?'

She nodded, then remembered and said, 'Very.'

'So, what is the matter?'

It came out in a rush. 'Apart from chocolate choosing, you don't seem to need me, not like you need Billie.' She sounded pathetic – mawkish? – even to herself and she hadn't even mentioned *my partner*.

'I sure need Billie,' he said after a pause. 'I couldn't live the life I want to live without her, and you're right, Zelda, I don't need you...' He stopped as her phone pinged. 'I think you'd better get that. We can sort the other stuff later. I've got a hunch this might be good.'

I don't need you...

As she picked up her phone, she had a hunch that it was Viv saying, *Where the hell are you? Come and help me stop Janet throwing herself overboard*, but as that was preferable to hearing Richard expound on why he didn't need her in his life she logged into Facebook Messenger and read something that made her gasp.

> I think I'm the Mal Carmichael you're looking for. I was at Royal High School for Boys Edinburgh early 1960s, graduated in Economics though from LBS, London Business School, not LSE late 1960s. I'm pleased to tell you I'm already in touch with another member of my long-lost family who I'll be meeting in New York. Would you like to talk?

52

ZELDA

'Zelda, I gather you're still there.' As Richard's fingers touched the back of her hand, she heard his voice as if from a long way off.

'Y-yes,' she nodded, staring at what she'd just read.

'What does it say?'

She read it out, which made it feel more real, and it brought a smile to his face. 'This calls for more chocolates – or a bottle of something?' His hand went up, without waiting for an answer, summoning the steward to their table. 'Forward the message to Janet, Zelda. Now. Put her out of her misery. Text her and Viv. Get them here. A bottle of Veuve Clicquot with four glasses, please,' he said to the waitress who'd come instantly when he'd raised his hand.

'B-but shouldn't I check him out first?' Zelda still couldn't believe that her quest had come up with the result she wanted.

'Yes, he'll need checking out as he could be the biggest conman ever, but you can't do that till you meet him and maybe follow up with DNA tests like Viv says. But the omens are good, the *evidence* is good. He says he's meeting another long-lost relative in New York. That's got to be Isabella. So you need to ring this man and find out where he's meeting her. Zelda, I don't want to tell you what to do. I know you're shocked, but please, start thinking. You're very good at that.'

'Okay.' She picked up her phone. 'So what do I say?' She put it down again. 'Should it even be me?'

'Good questions. Maybe wait till the others get here? Here's the fizz. Tell them to hurry.'

* * *

It didn't take Viv and Janet long to join them, once Zelda had texted and forwarded the message. 'Wow!' was the first response from Viv when she'd read it.

'Phew!' the second from Janet, tearful with relief.

Viv's eyes lit up at the sight of the fizz in the ice bucket, but Janet insisted they wait till Zelda had made the call before opening it. They all agreed that it must be Zelda, as she was the one who'd contacted the man on Facebook. Viv said, 'Just ask him where he's meeting the other long-lost member of his family.'

But Janet's natural scepticism had returned. 'Maybe put a few questions to him first, to verify who he is?'

'Like?' Zelda paused, wanting all the help she could get, but when no answers came from Viv or Janet, she picked up the phone again, anxious to get going before she lost her nerve. 'I'm putting it on speaker phone so you can all hear.' They all leaned in over the table. 'I'm going to have to play this by ear, so if you think of something to ask when he's speaking scribble a note, okay?' Viv got a notebook and pen and she keyed in the man's number. 'Ready?' They all nodded and she pressed green for go.

There was a very long pause. Then, 'Hello, Mal Carmichael speaking.' He sounded Australian.

'Hello, this is Zelda Fielding, responding to the direct message you sent me on Facebook.'

Another pause. There must be a time lag.

'Thanks for getting in touch, Zelda. Can I ask the name of the person on whose behalf you made that enquiry?'

'Primrose Carmichael.' She didn't know why she'd said that as it was Janet she'd done it for, but well, she shrugged, done now.

Pause. Again. She waited. It made for stilted conversation.

Then, 'Primrose?' He sounded surprised. 'You're an old friend of hers?'

'No, I'm, er... more of a new friend, actually.'

Long pause.

'New friend?' He sounded puzzled.

'Yes.'

Longer pause.

'How new? I mean how far back do you go?'

'A week.'

Very long pause. This was more than a time lag.

'Come again,' he said at last. 'Sorry, my hearing isn't too good.' He gave an apologetic sort-of-laugh. 'I thought you said a *week*.'

'I did. Primrose and I have only just met – on the *Queen Mary*, the *QM2*, on the way to New York. It's a ship,' she added because she got the impression he had no idea what she was talking about.

'I know it's a ship, Zelda,' he came back quickly. 'The other person I mentioned, the other long-lost relation is on there too. But...' He went silent again as the four listeners gasped in unison. The tension round the table was palpable. They were all holding their breath, till Viv let hers out in a gasp and started scribbling. Then she held up what she'd written.

ASK IF IT IS ISABELLA?

The others all nodded.

Zelda asked.

Silence. The seconds ticked by. No reply.

Zelda checked her phone. They were still connected. 'Are you still there, Mal? We, er... I would like to know if the person you're in touch with is Isabella.'

'Yes, it is. I'll call you back later.' He disconnected.

* * *

They all eyed the bottle, still in the cooler.

'Not yet,' said Janet. 'Give him time.'

'How long?' said Viv.

'We could perhaps have a chocolate or two while we're waiting?' Richard called for more. Zelda handed them round. She was on her third Coeur Lait when Australian Mal called back.

'Apologies for the delay, but I've been trying to contact Isabella, sadly to no avail, so I need to ask you a few questions about Primrose. Firstly, how old is she now?'

Janet mouthed sixty-nine.

'Sixty-nine,' said Zelda.

'And what school did she go to?'

Janet scribbled 'St Margaret's' on a page of Viv's notebook.

'St Margaret's,' said Zelda.

Janet scribbled again.

'You met playing table tennis at St Andrew's youth club,' said Zelda – and the gasp on the end of the phone was audible. They'd won, game set and match.

Mal didn't say Isabella was a liar. He didn't mention her name at all, not at first. He said he'd been *led to believe* that Primrose had died of cancer many years ago. It took some very careful questioning on Zelda's part to tease out of him that he'd been contacted by his long-lost daughter only two years previously. That she had found letters from him to her mother, and to her grandparents, when she had cleared the attic after both grandparents died. That the letters had shown her that he cared about her – that he'd wanted Primrose and Isabella to come with him to Australia, that he'd sent money for her support.

'So she set about finding out more and discovered I was alive, though she'd been told that I'd passed away when she was a little girl, on a trip to Australia.'

'That you'd fallen overboard?' Zelda asked tentatively.

'That was what she was told. That I'd never arrived in Australia.'

'That's what Primrose was told too.'

'Yeah, so putting two and two together, I think Granny and Grandad are the villains of the piece. I reckon they didn't want Primrose to take their little granddaughter to Australia so they intercepted my letters and made up this story, not before cashing a lot of my cheques, I should add.'

'Does Isabella know about this?'

'Too right she does, she got there first. Bright girl, woman, I should say. The letters she found referred to the cheques I'd sent. Some of them still had the torn-off corner of the cheque stapled to the letter. She reckoned her grandad cashed them. In those days if you got the recipient to sign the back, another person could legally cash them. She said her grandad handled her mother's financial affairs and she would have signed anything he told her to.'

There was a lot to take in.

Janet scribbled something else and pushed the note across. Zelda read it and asked, 'Did she tell her mother about this?'

'No, she said her mum had already...' He hesitated, maybe gulped. 'She said she was glad in a way that she wasn't alive because knowing that her mum and dad had deceived her would have broken her heart.'

Zelda didn't know what to say next. Viv got the notebook back and started scribbling. Zelda thought of something else. 'When did you stop sending money to Primrose?'

'When her father told me to stop. He said Primrose didn't want to have anything to do with me. He said she regarded my going to Australia as desertion and she never wanted to hear from me again.'

'And you believed him?'

'Yes, eventually. I believed him because I didn't hear another word from Primrose. She hadn't been answering my letters for a while, or answering the phone when I rang but it never occurred to me that she hadn't even seen my letters because he was getting to them first...'

Viv pushed her note across.

WHEN AND WHERE ARE THEY MEETING?

But Mal was still talking. 'Of course I could kick myself now for not trying harder to get in touch, but well, I guess my feelings were hurt, masculine pride and all that, and I was a young man trying to make my way in the world. I'd accepted this challenging job with the bank and gone over as a Ten Pound Pom as they used to be called and... well.' He sighed audibly.

Poor man. Zelda didn't want to probe the wound, but still had questions. 'Did you just leave it there? Didn't you...'

'...try and get in touch later on? Yes, I did, and my letters were returned NOT KNOWN AT THIS ADDRESS so I gave up except for setting up a trust fund for them both in the hope that one day they would turn up.'

'And Isabella did turn up?'

'Yes!' There was no mistaking the joy in his voice. 'It seemed like a miracle.'

'And now so has Primrose,' Zelda said gently.

'Yeah, well, so you say, which is an even bigger miracle. I have to say it's hard to believe after such a long time. Over forty years. How is she, by the way? I should have asked earlier. Is she in good health?'

Zelda noted the *so you say*, but answered his question, though Viv was waving the notebook in front of her face.

ASK WHEN AND WHERE ARE THEY MEETING!

'She seems to be well, but,' Zelda dived in, 'why not see for yourself, Mal? Primrose could meet you tomorrow. Just say where and when and I'll let her know.'

Viv gave a thumbs up, but there was no answer.

Zelda prompted, 'Mal, I'm sure Primrose would love to meet you.'

Viv pushed across another note.

NOT JUMPING AT THE CHANCE IS HE? WHY'S THAT?

Then they all heard the sound of a throat being cleared, or possibly a crackle on the line, but nothing else.

Zelda said, 'Mal, are you still there?'

Pause. Then, 'It's complicated, Zelda. I need to think about this.'

Janet was scribbling.

OMG IS HE MARRIED? ASK!

Zelda said, 'What's the problem, Mal?'

'Isabella,' was his reply. 'Either she's lying or you are. Or more likely she's been given wrong information. There has after all been a lot of lying in that family. Whatever, this is going to take a bit of sorting out. Either way, she's got a big shock coming. I think she genuinely believes her mum has passed away.'

No, she doesn't. They're sharing a cabin!

But before Zelda could say this, he said that he was signing off, as he needed to speak to his daughter.

Janet burst out, 'Ask him if he's married!'

'Mal!' Zelda rushed in. 'Before you go, just tell me one thing. Are you married now?'

Pause, while they held their collective breath.

'Yes,' said Mal, after a bit, 'I am.'

'Oh, no!' Janet covered her face with her hands.

'To Primrose,' he said firmly, 'the love of my life.'

53

ZELDA

Janet was teary with relief.

Grant wasn't illegitimate, she wasn't about to lose her fortune and Primrose was on the brink of being reunited with her long-lost husband, who still *loved* her. It was so romantic and *right*.

'Let's celebrate! Open that bottle, please, someone, and Richard, it can go on my bill.'

'No, Janet.' He shook his head at her offer to pay. 'It's my pleasure.' He summoned the steward who came straight over, opened the bottle and filled their sparkling flutes.

Janet raised her glass. 'To success! Thank you all for your endeavours on my behalf.'

Zelda raised her glass, not wanting to be a wet blanket, but she couldn't help feeling that celebrations were a bit premature. Yes, it looked likely that this Australian Mal was Primrose's long-lost husband, but surely they should meet him first and see if Primrose recognised him. Viv's idea of DNA testing to see if he really was Isabella's father, and Malcolm wasn't, was a good one too. She had that hair of Isabella's, so all she needed was one of his. There had been so much lying in that family – as there had been in hers – so facts must be checked. Half an hour later, when he hadn't got back to them, her doubts increased. As time passed, she started to think that he was probably a chancer, answering her lost person request on a whim. Surely, if he was who he said he was, he'd have jumped at the chance to meet Primrose and told them where he was meeting Isabella. The others still looked very celebratory.

Zelda felt a bit out of it, though Billie's head was on her knee, sensing her need for support. This might be the last time this happened, she couldn't help thinking, as she stroked her ears. Tomorrow they would be going their separate ways and Richard had said nothing about meeting tonight or ever again.

Mal hadn't rung back by the time they'd finished the bottle, at which point Richard felt his watch and said he must be off to get ready for the evening's performances. Billie moved to his side and he clipped on her harness and wished them all goodbye, wished them *all* goodbye with a communal wave of his hand.

Was that *it*? she wondered as she watched him walk out of the door.

'Any messages, Zelda?' Viv drained her glass.

'No.' She didn't need to look as she'd been constantly checking her phone.

Janet was getting to her feet, saying she'd like to go and change for dinner and maybe close her eyes for twenty minutes beforehand.

'Hold on a sec,' said Viv. 'Before you go, what's the strategy for tonight?'

'Strategy?' Janet frowned.

'Plan,' said Viv, 'or plans, depending on who joins us for dinner, Isabella and/or Primrose. What are we going to tell them?'

Janet was brisk. 'If Primrose comes on her own, we tell her we've found her long-lost Mal. That will make her so happy.'

Viv put out a restraining hand. 'Is that, er... fair? To raise Primrose's hopes, I mean, and dash them, if he isn't who he says he is.'

Was Viv having doubts too?

Janet looked exasperated. 'Viv, we've *found* him. And, as to what we do if Isabella comes too, I'm rather relishing confronting her with the truth and seeing her flush busted. She'll crumple.'

Zelda intervened. 'I'm not sure she'll crumple that easily, Janet. She could fight back, so I think we should proceed cautiously too, whoever turns up. If it's Primrose on her own, and we tell her what we know, she will tell Isabella and we don't know how she's going to react. My bet is she'll do whatever she can to stop Mal and Primrose meeting. By the way, did anyone else clock Mal's mention of a trust fund?'

They all had, and that he'd said it was for *them*.

'Isabella *and* Primrose in other words,' said Viv, as if they couldn't work that out for themselves. 'So, we have a clear motive for Isabella's lying about Primrose. If her mother is dead, she's the sole beneficiary and stands to gain a small fortune. There must be quite a lot in the pot if Mal has been paying into it for over forty years.'

'Money is what motivates her,' Janet agreed, 'and Primrose said she is in debt.'

'And lying is her modus operandi,' Zelda added her bit. 'She lied to her father about her mother, saying she was dead, and she lied to her mother about finding her father.'

'So, we can be pretty sure she'll lie again,' said Viv, 'if she doesn't resort to anything worse.'

'What do you mean by that?' Janet raised her eyebrows.

'I mean,' said Viv, 'that she needs her mother out of the way so that she inherits all the money.'

'You don't mean...' Janet half-laughed. 'Yes, you do! You're talking *Midwinter Murders!*'

Viv didn't deny it.

54

VIV

The weather had taken a turn for the worse. It was snowing and the doors to the ~~outside decks~~ were locked so they couldn't go outside. If you managed to peer through a window all you saw was a blanket of snow and thick ice. As Viv went down for dinner at six o'clock with Janet and Zelda, it was all anyone was talking about. What would it be like in New York? What would they wear? They were now only twelve and a half hours away from land and the captain's latest weather report had warned of freezing temperatures. Snow was piling up in the streets of the city, but it would look very Christmassy.

As they sat down at their table in the Britannia restaurant, Viv was feeling a bit got at, by Janet if not Zelda. She had been a bit OTT hinting that Isabella would stop at nothing to ensure she got all the cash from her father's trust fund, and truth to tell it was only when Janet mocked her that the wider implications of *she needs her mother out of the way* had occurred to her. She hadn't thought of murder up to that point, but the more she thought about Isabella, the more ruthless and determined she seemed. Lust for money drove her. What wouldn't she do to stop Primrose having her share of the money in the trust fund?

Viv was pleased to see that neither Primrose nor Isabella was at the table when they sat down, but it wasn't long before Viv, facing the room, saw Primrose approaching, wearing a knee-length black dress and black strappy sandals. Tonight there was a black fringed shawl round her shoulders, completing the widow's-weeds look. Isabella wasn't joining them, she said, as she sat down. Relief was Viv's first reaction, quickly followed by concern. Where was Isabella? What was she up to? Primrose soon enlightened them.

'Isabella is dining with *Freddie*,' she said, pointedly Viv thought. It was as if she'd said *not Daddy*. She burbled on about a possible engagement. 'They are dining privately, in the Queen's Grill, and I'm wondering if he's popping the question.'

'How would you feel about that?' Janet asked diplomatically, not saying what she was probably thinking. *Don't you think she's after his money?*

'If Freddie makes Isabella happy then I would be delighted for her.' Primrose seemed excited at the prospect. 'He is a few years older than her, but she has always gone for older men. I've often thought she was searching for a father figure.'

Or a father? But Viv kept her mouth shut as agreed. Zelda too. She was keeping an eye on her phone, but what was she most hoping to see, Viv wondered, a message from Mal or from Richard? While they'd been upstairs getting ready for dinner Zelda had confided, ruefully, that she didn't know where her relationship with Richard was going, but he'd made it clear that he didn't need her in his life. Theirs had been a shipboard romance, a fling – that was all it was to him – so once they'd stepped off the boat it was over.

Viv ached for her.

Janet seemed to be sticking to their mouth-shut strategy as she chatted away to Primrose about the weather and the wine, but approached the forbidden subject once the waiter had brought their starters, by which time they'd all had a glass of the delicious Cloudy Bay Sauvignon Blanc. Janet talked about first drinking the wine in New Zealand when she'd visited her son there and mentioned the difficulties of staying with Grant and his family, giving Primrose an opening to talk more about Isabella. But she hadn't. The bottle was empty when Janet asked Primrose, as if it had just occurred to her, if she still thought that Isabella could be meeting Freddie in New York. When Primrose didn't answer, she added helpfully as if to remind her, 'I mean that private meeting, the one she doesn't want you to go to. Might they be going to buy a ring in the famous Diamond District on 47th Street? Or is Freddie going to pop the question in an iconic location, Top of the Rock for instance, with a big sparkly rock? If he isn't popping it right now.' She laughed and so did Primrose, a bit flushed now, as was Janet.

The two of them had drunk most of the wine. Viv was going steady deliberately and Zelda hadn't had much. She was busy regularly checking her phone. 'Any word?' Viv managed to murmur without the other two hearing and Zelda shook her head. Viv tuned back into Primrose and Janet, who was saying, 'Primrose, you are very welcome to join the three of us tomorrow when Isabella goes to her meeting.'

Primrose said thank you, she'd love to. 'Just let us know where you'll be and we'll pick you up.' Janet took a sip.

Primrose said she was sorry – she looked sorry – but she still didn't know the name of the hotel they were staying at.

'Why do you think Isabella hasn't told you?' Janet asked tentatively, with a little smile, clearly trying not to sound critical or suspicious.

'She says she wants it to be a lovely surprise.'

'You have asked her then?'

'Oh, yes.' Primrose nodded.

'And have you asked her where her rendezvous is?' Janet was nothing if not persistent.

Primrose nodded again. 'She said *she* didn't know. It's exciting, really. I suppose the person she's meeting wants to give her a lovely surprise.'

Was Primrose as naïve as she sounded?

Janet seemed to think so. 'Primrose, we, Viv, Zelda and I, The Muscateers, we have a policy of always telling each other where we're going, when we're meeting someone new, for safety reasons. Secret liaisons seem romantic but there are dodgy people out there, not to say dangerous. Are you happy about Isabella meeting someone – who may or may not be Freddie who, incidentally, you don't know very well – and not telling you where she's going?'

Primrose blinked.

Zelda looked up from her phone, which was on her knee. 'Janet's right,

Primrose. I was in a spot of bother once with a too-persistent male, but thankfully I'd told Janet and Viv where I was going and they rushed to the rescue.'

Primrose looked from one to the other. Clearly, amazingly, she hadn't thought of this before.

'We've done the same for Libby, another friend,' said Zelda.

Viv added her penny's worth – or should that be cent's? 'How would you feel, Primrose, if Isabella didn't return from this rendezvous? It has happened.'

It was clear to all of them except Primrose that she was being kept in the dark so she couldn't tell them anything. More to the point, so that she couldn't go to that meeting herself, which would detonate Isabella's plan to do Primrose out of half the trust fund. Primrose had accepted Isabella's reasons for not telling her but now seemed to be having second thoughts. 'I must ask Isabella again. I must tell her what you've told me. She is being too trusting.'

'But will she take any notice?' said Janet. 'You know what children are like.'

The steward came to clear their dishes. Zelda looked down at her phone again, hoping, Viv knew, to hear from the Australian Mal, but also Richard. Janet poured herself some water. The atmosphere at tables nearby was festive and jolly. It was their last night aboard after all. A few party poppers were going off but it was subdued, even tense at theirs. Viv could see that Janet was thinking. She wasn't squiffy, not at all, but Primrose might be. Janet hadn't ordered a bottle to go with their main courses, Viv noted with mixed feelings as their mains arrived. They had all gone for the lemon sole meunière with new potatoes in parsley butter and roasted fennel. A glass or two of Pinot Grigio would have gone down well, Viv thought, as she started on hers. They were about halfway through their meals, when Janet looked up from her plate and said, 'Any news, Zelda?'

Zelda stopped eating, checked her phone and shook her head. Janet turned to Primrose and Viv wondered what was coming next, as she took a deep breath. 'Primrose, there's something I need to share with you...'

What the hell was she going to say?

55

VIV

Janet told Primrose absolutely bloody everything!

'It is in your own interests to hear me out,' she said as Primrose looked catatonic, 'though you may hear things you do not want to hear. About your daughter, I mean. I know how painful that will feel as I have been in that situation with my son. But you have to know that we are 99 per cent certain that Isabella is meeting her father, your husband Mal, somewhere in New York, tomorrow.'

Primrose's eyes opened wide. Like a rabbit in the headlights did not describe her frozen features. A rabbit was hop, skip and jumping by comparison. She gripped the edge of the table with white-knuckled fingers as Janet went on.

'As I've said, we are only 99 per cent certain, but we need to find a way of going to that meeting to be 100 per cent. To see if the man Isabella is meeting is Mal, your not-late husband. You need to see him, Primrose. He needs to see you. Viv, Zelda and I need to observe and assess from his reactions whether he is genuine or not. If necessary, we will get biological material from him so a DNA test can be carried out. This may be a case of stolen identity, but we hope not. The happy outcome would be that you are reunited with Mal, your Mal, who has never married again, and is in fact still married to you and still loves you.'

Was Primrose taking this in? She still looked catatonic.

'Zelda has talked to him on the phone,' Janet continued, 'and we are waiting for him to get back to us – to Zelda – to tell us where they are meeting.'

Absolutely bloody everything!

In her own defence, Janet said afterwards, when they were back in her suite – without Primrose, who had declined Janet's invitation to have coffee – that she hadn't been able to wait any longer. 'This Mal hasn't got back to you, Zelda. What if he doesn't? What if Isabella has convinced him we're the bad guys trying to get money out of him? What if he isn't who he says he is?'

Viv was finding it hard to keep up with Janet's rapid changes of mind and she wasn't the only one. Zelda said, 'This afternoon you were convinced we'd found our man. Now you're having doubts.'

'Because he hasn't got back to you,' Janet didn't quite snap back. 'He said he would and he hasn't. This afternoon I thought he sounded plausible, but now I've started to think he might be a very clever conman in cahoots with Isabella.'

'How would that work?' Viv tried to follow her reasoning.

'I don't know,' Janet had the grace to admit, 'but unlike you, Viv, I think Isabella is clever as well as devious. I think we should try and imagine ourselves into her shoes, work out what her options are and which of them she's likely to choose.'

They surmised a bit about what *Might Be Mal*, as Janet now called him, might have said to Isabella and she to him. Zelda said, 'If he has told her about me saying Primrose is alive and aboard the QM2, she could say I'm lying, or she could deny that she'd said that her mother was dead.'

'Either way,' she continued, 'we've got to turn up with Primrose, so he can see her for himself. Agreed?'

'Agreed.' They raised their coffee cups, soberly, and moved on to the harder question – how?

They formed a new plan, very tentative because there were so many variables. It was based on Viv's original, so she should have been pleased, and she was, but with one big reservation. Success depended on Primrose's cooperation and Viv wasn't sure they would get that. At dinner Janet had sworn her to secrecy. *Do not tell Isabella what we know*. Primrose had said she wouldn't but after dinner she'd declined Janet's invitation to come back to her suite and scurried off on her strappy little sandals. She'd said she was going to the finals of some quiz or other but Viv could find no mention of any quizzes in the Daily Programme. More likely she'd gone to seek out Isabella and blab.

'When are we going to tell Primrose what we need her to do?' Viv asked the others. 'If she hasn't already scuppered our chances of making it work.'

'Not sure,' said Zelda, 'but you two will have to decide. I'm off to hear Richard play.' She left soon afterwards, looking gorgeous as usual in a silk caftan with broad rainbow stripes, her beaded hair swinging jauntily, but with an anxious look on her face.

Janet said she'd take responsibility for giving Primrose all their mobile numbers, and instructing her to keep in close touch next day. The plan's success was entirely dependent on Primrose informing them of Isabella's exact whereabouts at every point, so they could keep track of her, and then follow her to her meeting with Might Be Mal.

'When are you going to give Primrose this information?' Viv thought relying on Primrose was risky to say the least.

'Why not now?' Janet picked up her phone. 'I'm also giving her the name of our hotel so she could get a cab and come to it if need be.'

'Is she capable of getting a cab?'

Janet frowned. 'Primrose isn't stupid, Viv, and nor is Isabella, as I've already said. Underestimating people is not a good policy.'

Viv wasn't hopeful.

56

ZELDA

Zelda's phone was switched to silent so a call wouldn't disturb the recital. Her hi-tech hearing aids were connected to an app on her phone, which wouldn't work if she disconnected completely and she wanted to hear every note of the piece the musicians were playing, Quartet by Beethoven, No. 12, Opus 127 if she wasn't mistaken. Arriving late, but not so late that she missed the beginning, she hadn't picked up a programme, so couldn't be sure. The first movement, the Allegro, was well under way; light and skipping, it brought a smile to her lips, not unconnected with the thoughts coming into her head as she watched Richard embracing his cello. Embrace was the word. Arms round its curved body, holding it close, then further away, then close again, his fingers caressing the strings, firmly then lightly, moving so fast she could hardly see them like... she had to stop herself laughing aloud. Oh my God! The green-eyed monster was back! Yesterday it was Billie, today it was his cello. *She* wanted to be in Richard's arms, hugged close, his fingers on...

Listen to the music.

She tuned in again, but then, distracted by someone coming and standing behind her chair, she felt for the players, performing in this difficult venue. The Grand Lobby was a thoroughfare. There were dedicated listeners but also passengers coming and going all the time. It must be hard to concentrate. The stage, not much more than a slightly raised platform, was in the corner, not far from the Christmas tree and the *Wind in the Willows* tableau, which were always surrounded by admiring onlookers. And people were climbing up or coming down the grand staircase leading up to the balcony on Deck 3. There was always someone on the move, occasionally wandering over to the stage to listen for a few moments then walking away, as the man behind her did now. The group, though, were totally absorbed by their music-making and didn't seem to notice. Zelda, deep in a comfortable armchair, felt the music throbbing through her. She was on the end of the row, if you could call the curved line of chairs a row. Focusing again, she warmed even more to the lively piece which the group were obviously enjoying playing, exchanging smiles from time to time. Richard's playing thrilled her as it always did. *He* thrilled her. She couldn't deny it. He excited her. That had been a surprise. She'd thought she was done with men, and had told her friends so, so they wouldn't keep trying to match-make. She was happy that they'd found lovely men they could love, she'd said, but she didn't want or need one herself. For seven years this had been true. She had her studies, her business, her lovely stepfamily including grandson Albert, her friends and of course her darling Westies, Mack and Morag, to fulfil her. She'd got all the love and affection she needed from friends and family and dogs, and she gave them all the love and affection she had to give. That was enough. Until now. Until Richard.

I don't need you, Zelda.

As the second movement began, her feelings like the music became slower and sadder. Richard didn't feel the same as she did, that was clear. He didn't need her in his life. He'd said so. It had been a pleasant interlude for him, that was all. Tomorrow, if not tonight, he would say goodbye, if he hadn't already said it, and she'd never see him again. He'd go back to 'his partner' with whom he'd probably got an 'agreement'. Next voyage he'd hook up with someone else. Now the low vibrating notes of the cello reached depths of sadness only they could reach and she felt tears welling up.

'Sorry. Excuse me.' The woman in the seat next to her, a large lady, was getting up and needed Zelda to move back so she could leave.

Zelda almost thanked her for interrupting. The third movement was livelier, dance-like again, and the violinists and viola player exchanged delighted glances as they had done in the Allegro, and bows in hand, seemed to dance with their instruments and each other. Richard and his cello now looked like a cheery old couple who'd been in love with each other for a long time, she thought, the long, lean man and the plump curvy wife, completely in step, enjoying each other's company. A glance at the programme left on the seat beside her confirmed that this was the piece she thought it was, and that this third movement was the Scherzando Vivace. Vivace! It made her think of Viv, and as if she'd been summoned by the word she appeared, rushing in, squeezing by to the vacant seat where she picked up the programme and sat down. *Please, Viv, keep quiet till the piece is finished.* Amazingly, she did, even through the short pause before the fourth movement, and she waited for the applause to die down at the end before asking, 'Anything from Might Be Mal?'

Zelda checked her phone. 'No.'

* * *

Viv

Viv felt she had barged in on a love fest. She'd only come to remind Zelda to have her phone switched on, while Janet went in search of Primrose, and it was already on, on silent. Looking at it hadn't been a priority though, and it still wasn't. Now Zelda was with a cluster of admirers talking to Richard and getting her fix of dog-patting with Billie. Clearly the dog was as delighted to see Zelda as she was to see her, but Richard's body language was harder to read. No wonder Zelda didn't know where this was going.

When she returned to her seat, she said that Richard had to hurry to the Chart Room on Deck 3 for Jazz Club with the Steve Goffe Trio – he was standing in again – but he'd like to meet up for a nightcap later that night, when the session ended. Later that night? Viv checked her Daily Programme. The session began at 9.30 and finished at half past twelve. Well, Zelda might still be awake by then, but she would be in bed fast asleep, with luck. She'd already set her alarm for five, so she could be out on deck next morning to catch her first glimpse of the Statue of Liberty as they sailed into Brooklyn harbour.

As they climbed the grand staircase to Deck 3, to listen to the Steve Goffe Trio, Viv mentioned to Zelda that Janet had gone in search of Primrose to finalise arrangements for tomorrow, but got no reaction from Zelda, clearly lost in her own thoughts.

'Zelda, are you sure you want me to come with you to this?' she said when they reached the top and paused for a breather, looking over the balcony onto or more accurately *into* the towering Christmas tree standing in the Grand Lobby. They were still a few feet from its summit and the huge golden star which crowned it.

'Oh, yes, Viv.' Zelda assured her she wouldn't be intruding on anything. 'There'll be nothing to intrude on, I can assure you.' She said she probably wouldn't stay till the end herself. 'I'll catch Richard in one of the breaks. It won't take long, Viv. I'm sure he just wants to say goodbye tonight, because he's shooting off to the airport as soon as we've disembarked tomorrow. And that will be it, I'm sure. End of. If you think he's going to schmooze me to his room for a night of unbridled passion you're very much mistaken.'

'I never...'

'You didn't need to, Viv, I know the way your mind works, and he'll be shattered anyway. He'll have been making love to that cello for the last four hours.'

'You're not...' Viv felt her eyebrows rising.

'Yes, Viv, I am. It's pathetic, isn't it. I'm jealous of a bloody cello and a dog.' Tears of sad laughter were running down her face.

57

JANET

Janet found Primrose in the Golden Lion.

She was in a booth with the other members of the team celebrating winning the final of the Evening Trivia Quiz. She had once again done exactly what she'd said she would do. She'd kept her word, proving she could be trusted. She'd promised not to tell Isabella they were going to follow her to her rendezvous and she wouldn't. Well – Janet noted the fizz bottle upside down in the cooler beside the table – if she remembered she'd made a promise. She had had rather a lot to drink, fizz and the Cloudy Bay at dinner.

Primrose seemed pleased to see her and introduced her to her friends.

Janet said she hoped she wasn't intruding and Primrose assured her she wasn't. 'We're about to disperse anyway because most of the team are late diners.' She stood up to let two of them out of her side of the booth. 'I hoped I'd see you, in fact, because I wanted to see you to discuss a dilemma.'

'Dilemma?' Janet sat down and a steward arrived to see what they wanted to drink. Primrose, she was pleased to hear, asked for water, and she did too.

'Dilemma?' she prompted when the steward had gone. 'You were saying...'

Primrose leaned forward and lowered her voice. 'I am aware that I promised not to tell Isabella that we are planning to follow her to ascertain if the man she is meeting is Mal, the man I married. But that was before I'd thought deeply about your Muscateer rule.'

The steward arrived with glasses of water.

'I now think,' she continued when he'd gone, 'that I must insist she tells me where she is going for her own safety. Of course I want the man she is meeting to be my husband Mal, or even Freddie, as I have said before, but I am aware that she may have met this other person on the internet – she does meet people on the internet – and I feel I should warn her.'

'But Primrose...' Janet wasn't sure what to say.

'I do so want this man to be her father.' Primrose gulped water. 'But...' she gulped again, 'I know that in this day and age it's all too easy for a man to say he is someone he isn't.'

These were Janet's thoughts exactly, the source of her own doubts. Her friend was learning by the minute, but she must stop her revealing their plan to Isabella. 'Primrose, it would be really helpful if you could find out where Isabella is meeting this man.' It would, it really would. 'She would be safer for a start, because we would definitely be there too to keep an eye on her. But...' – how did she put this? – 'could you do it without telling her that we're going to be there too?' Oh dear, she must make it clearer. 'I mean, if she thinks that *you're* going to be there too, she will make sure you can't be.'

Janet was trying not to hurt Primrose more than she needed to. She didn't want to tell her that Isabella was stealing money from her, and, even worse, preventing her from meeting the man she loved. Sharper than a serpent's tooth it is to have a heartless, money-grabbing child...

'Janet, your phone is ringing.' Primrose touched her arm.

It was Zelda saying that she'd forwarded a message from Might Be Mal. Janet thanked her and went to messages.

> Haven't managed to contact Isabella yet but still trying and thinking about things a lot. Mal

Mmm. What could she draw from that? He didn't seem keen to tell them where he was. Was he going to disappear into thin air? 'Thank you, Primrose.' Janet put her phone down and fibbed. 'That was Zelda asking where Isabella is?'

'She's still with Freddie in the Queen's Grill. As I said, I hope he's popping the question.'

Janet decided to pop one of her own, if *pop* was the right word for a tentative suggestion. 'What if you don't bother Isabella with our questions tonight, Primrose? You know what children are like. They don't always cooperate and it would be a shame to spoil her evening. In fact, Primrose, I think it would be best if we went back to Plan A.'

'Plan A?' Primrose yawned and looked a bit glazed over.

Now, she spoke as clearly as she could, hoping Primrose was taking it in. 'Plan A was that one, we don't tell Isabella anything about our plan, and two, you stick close to her tomorrow, and keep us informed of her whereabouts. May I have your phone, Primrose, so I can give you our contact details?'

Primrose handed it over and Janet keyed in Viv and Zelda's numbers after checking hers was there. It was all she could do, unless... As she handed back the phone, she thought of something else she could do. 'Shall I help you to your room, Primrose?'

Primrose was a bit tottery as they made their way to the lift, and more tottery when they got out of it on Deck 6. She linked arms and leaned against Janet as they walked down the long corridor to her room. 'I think I can manage now,' she said when they reached the door.

'Where's your keycard, Primrose?'

It took her a while for her to find it in her bag and Janet had to open the door.

'Thank you sho much, Janet.'

Janet guided her to her bed, no mean feat as the space between the twin beds was narrow, and Primrose was wobbly. She helped her out of her clothes and into her nightie. Primrose's eyes closed as soon as her head hit the pillow. Excellent. Janet pulled the duvet over. 'Good night, Primrose. Sleep well. See you in the morning.'

But Janet didn't leave.

Not usually a snooper, Janet had a bit of a snoop, starting with the drawer in the cabinet between the two beds and moving on to the wardrobe.

58

ZELDA

Why am I still here?

Viv had just gone to bed, saying she couldn't keep her eyes open any longer, so there was an empty space on the sofa where Zelda was still sitting in the Chart Room, listening to the Steve Goffe Trio. Steve himself was on the shiny white grand piano, Marguerite on violin and Richard on cello. There were others still drinking in the elegant lounge where dark wood panels and glowing golden table lamps created a relaxed romantic mood, for the white-haired couple holding hands next to her anyway. Sigh. Time to go to bed herself, perhaps. Around her the ever-helpful staff were taking away empties and bringing more drinks for passengers reluctant to believe this was the last night of their marvellous holiday.

'Every time we say goodbye I cry a little...' Cole Porter's words came inaccurately into her head as the group began another soulful melody. 'Every time we say goodbye I *die* a little...' she corrected herself because die was right. She had come alive on this voyage in a way she hadn't been for years, but when he left, a bit of her would die.

Don't be mawkish, Zelda.

Reaching in her pocket for a tissue, she found one under her phone, reminding her she hadn't checked for messages from Might Be Mal or anyone else. And, oh no, her phone had run out of battery so she couldn't check now. What sort of friend was she for heaven's sake? Wrapped up in her own misery, she'd forgotten she was supposed to be helping Janet recover her joie de vivre. And that meant sorting this Might Be Mal business once and for all. On her feet now, she glanced at her watch. Half past eleven. Time to go back to her room, put her phone on charge and go to bed. There was no point in waiting here for Richard. There had been several breaks already between numbers and he hadn't come over once to have a word, or even looked in her direction.

Because he doesn't know you're here. He doesn't know you're in the room, idiot, let alone where you're sitting. She sat down with a thump. *Did you tell him you were coming?* No. When he'd said he'd like to see her at the end of the evening she hadn't answered because she was feeling so sorry for herself. She had in fact forgotten he couldn't see, because when she was with him she just saw a talented, funny, loveable, very fanciable man, unusually intuitive. She might, though, have overestimated his amazing intuitive powers, and his heightened sense of smell. He'd once said he knew she was in the room because he'd recognised her perfume but that was a smaller room and she'd been standing closer. She sniffed her wrist. *She* couldn't smell her own perfume, Eau de Jardin, sprayed on liberally earlier in the evening, so how could he now, in a crowded bar? How could he know she was there?

Ev'ry time we say goodbye...

As the piece came to an end, Zelda got to her feet again, resolved to have one last go. Others got to their feet too, applauding the players now standing and bowing, throwing kisses in Marguerite's case, acknowledging the applause. Then Steve and Marguerite sat down, but Richard stayed standing as he picked up Billie's harness from the chair beside him, and put it on her. Then, after a word with the violinist, he walked away from the group – towards her, *towards her*, with Billie leading the way.

'I asked Marguerite if you were in the room,' he said when he at last stood in front of her, and Billie's cold nose was in the palm of her sweating left hand. 'And she said there was a beautiful black woman wearing a caftan in rainbow colours three sofas back, in the middle of the bar.' He'd been wondering all night if she was there, he said, but stupidly it had only just occurred to him to ask someone. 'Zelda, are you really there?' He reached out.

'Yes.' She managed to speak as their fingertips touched.

'Good, because I'm free now for the rest of what's left of the night. Marguerite and Steve have some numbers they do as a duo, which will take them through to midnight, so they're happy if I leave them to it now. I'm knackered though,' he added, 'and dying for a beer.'

* * *

They went to Sir Samuel's Lounge which he thought would be quieter than the rest of the Chart Room and it was. The music was only a background hum as they sat down at a table in the corner, and there weren't many other people around. A waiter soon served them.

'We need to talk, don't we?' he said, wiping beer froth from his lip.

Zelda nodded, sipping water.

'You're worried about something.'

She nodded again, forgetting he couldn't see.

'Can you tell me?' He answered as if he could.

'Yes, but...' She hesitated. 'Sorry, this is awful, gives completely the wrong impression, but I need to charge my phone first.'

He laughed. 'Sleuthing again?'

'Sort of.' She explained about the call she was waiting for, apologising because it was so embarrassingly like the first time they'd had a drink together, but he seemed amused and even wanted to know more about Might Be Mal.

'Zelda, I don't mind playing second fiddle to your friends sometimes, as long as you don't mind playing second fiddle to my music and even Billie. Now.' He put his hand in his pocket and pulled out yet another device. 'A charger. If it fits your phone, we can talk *and* charge your phone at the same time. It works fast. Try it.'

Miraculously it fitted, and they began to talk.

He didn't *need* her, he agreed, when she reminded him what he'd said earlier, but that didn't mean he didn't *want* her. He didn't need her like he needed Billie, and he didn't want her at his beck and call as Billie was twenty-four hours a day. 'You're a woman, Zelda, not a dog, an independent woman with a life of your own, with dogs of your own, and a family and friends and a business to keep an eye on and studies you want to pursue. From what you've told me, you haven't got time to be my devoted helper and I don't want you to be. But,' he took her hand in both of his, sending shivers up her arms, 'I do want you in my life, Zelda, if you want me to be in yours, and we need to talk and work out how, living as we do on opposite sides of the Atlantic, both with busy lives, we're going to make this happen.'

They talked till the barman lowered the lights, by which time they'd exchanged addresses and discovered that when they arrived in North Carolina they wouldn't be living too far away from each other. Richard had a flat in Cameron Village which wasn't far from the Brier Creek area where Cynthia lived and both places were quite near to the airport. He suggested they meet at Charlie Goodnight's, his local in the village. 'Come for the day so I can show you round, or I can come to Brier Creek if you prefer. I like the Olive Garden there...'

'When?' She had to be brief, the barman was hovering. Everyone else had left.

'As soon as you can make it, though I'm spending Christmas Day with my family.'

'And me with mine, but...' Talk of family reminded her of something. She got to her feet. 'Richard, you mentioned a partner, are you married?'

'No.' He stood up and so did Billie. 'I was once but it didn't work out. Don't think marriage and me mix. How about you?'

'Long story, but no,' she added quickly. 'And I'm not, er... attached to anyone.'

'Good, because,' Richard picked up Billie's harness but didn't put it on, 'I'd like you to attach yourself to me, if that's okay with you.' He held out his arm. 'Billie's had a long demanding day.'

If that's okay with me! She linked arms with him and the three of them set off to find his room, the closeness of his long, lean body making hers sing with gladness.

She'd think about 'I'd like you to attach yourself to me' later.

59

VIV

Wednesday, 23 December

Viv woke early, well before the alarm set for 5 a.m.

No need to ask where Zelda was, though her bed was empty and obviously unslept in. The heart-shaped chocolate was on the pillow where the steward had put it. Viv texted Janet:

> Awake.

Janet texted back:

> Me too.

Viv replied:

> See you on Deck 13 in 30 mins.

Janet replied with a thumbs up. They had arranged this early-morning meeting late last night when Janet had phoned with her momentous finding. 'The rendezvous is at Grand Central Station, 3 p.m. Under the clock.'

She hadn't said how she'd found out.

'Isn't that where someone sat down and wept?' Viv had said, wittily she thought, but Janet wasn't appreciative.

'Don't be flippant, Viv. This vital piece of information is our only chance of a happy ending, or a not-unhappy one. We've got to be there, at Grand Central, all of us, but especially Primrose. This could make or break her.'

Or you, dear Janet, Viv thought, *this could make or break you.*

In Viv's mind, the Grand Central meeting with Might Be Mal was entirely for Janet, so with luck she could put aside any remaining doubts that the bastard she'd first married wasn't a complete and utter bastard, and she could go home a bit happier than when she'd left instead of totally devastated after discovering something even worse about him. The on-deck meeting they'd planned for this morning was to make final arrangements as well as to catch their first glimpse of Lady Liberty as they sailed into the Brooklyn Terminal.

But Zelda wasn't here. She hadn't even packed her bags yet. While Janet had been discovering Isabella's plans in the pocket of a coat in the wardrobe, Zelda had been... well, she hadn't been checking her phone. So she didn't know about Janet's brilliant discovery, or the meeting this morning – or maybe she did, now? Viv's phone was ringing. Yes, it was a breathless Zelda.

'Brill news! Sorry, only just read your message. On my way. With you in five.'

She came through the door four minutes later. 'Sorry, I...'

'No need to explain and no time. Let's get moving. I've made a start on your packing.'

They threw the rest of her things into a couple of bags and put her biggest case outside the door for collection, hoping it wasn't too late to be picked up by a steward and taken to the baggage hall at the terminal on arrival. Viv's, put out the night before, had already gone. After one last check, she said, 'Bye bye, room, thanks for having us,' and closed the door, though Zelda was still wondering if she should bring her case with her. 'No! Come on!' Viv headed for the stairs. 'And look where you're going,' she shouted as Zelda looked back at her luggage. 'That's all we need now, you falling over!'

Zelda seemed more focused when they reached Deck 13. Clearly she had been thinking. 'Viv, has Janet told Primrose she's found out where Isabella is meeting Might Be Mal?'

'No,' Viv paused for a moment for a breather, 'Primrose was asleep when Janet left her room, which is good in my opinion. I still think she could blab to her daughter and scupper everything. Janet will have to let her know later, obviously, and tell her how to get there, unless she arranges for her to meet us first and we all go together. Janet says she's given Primrose all our mobile numbers. She keyed them in for her, and she's sent us Primrose's in case we get split up, though the idea is we stick together.'

'All for one?' Zelda had a smile in her voice.

'And one for all.' Viv would have crossed her fingers if she'd had any that weren't tightly gripping her hand luggage.

Janet was waiting for them outside on the portside of Deck 13, like a general about to cheer his troops on before a dawn raid. It was only just getting light, stars were fading, and Janet looked militant, dressed for the worst of winter weather in boots, a long coat with padded shoulders and a faux-fur hat that wouldn't have looked out of place in the Kremlin.

'We await orders,' Viv saluted, and Janet sighed.

'Eyes right for a start, comrades. Any minute now you should see the Statue of Liberty, especially if you can elbow your way to the front.' She pointed to where people were jostling for position, trying to reach the railing to get a better view. 'Now.' She started to fill them in on the day's programme, reading from the phone in her hand. 'One, we get a cab to our hotel to stow our luggage. Two, we find a café and go out for breakfast. Three, we do our top of the bus tour. Four...'

But a cry of 'There she is!' cut her off and they all turned to see the iconic statue, Lady Liberty herself, emerging from the mist, glowing dimly at first, but more brightly minute by minute the closer they got. Wow! Viv was surprised to find herself welling up. Was it relief at finally seeing land after a week at sea, or thoughts of the millions of travellers who'd done this journey before in much less luxurious circumstances? Refugees from poverty and persecution would surely have sobbed with relief at the sight of this symbol of freedom and hope, as they neared land after gruelling weeks at sea. How would she feel tomorrow, she wondered, when they went to Ellis Island to see where all these people with their bundles of belongings had been vetted and processed? Her stomach lurched as the ship swung round into the terminal and she felt the swell.

Then they were there, actually there, in reach of land with ropes being thrown and tied around bollards as they must have been for thousands of years, but it felt slightly odd seeing them thrown from this very modern highly computerised vessel. A cheer went up as the sun broke through the clouds as if to welcome them, and Viv unzipped her fleece. It was in fact quite warm, very warm for a December day, and it wasn't long before there was talk of unseasonal weather and records being broken.

It had been snowing heavily in New York for days. Piles of snow banked at the sides of throughfares showed that snow ploughs had been busy but it wasn't snowing now. They first realised they were wrongly dressed for the weather while queuing for customs and passport control. They'd just collected their cases from the baggage hall, and were still outside though under cover, when Janet took off her fur hat. By the time they reached passport control, Janet had taken off her coat and put it round her shoulders amid mutterings about the heat from other passengers, also divesting themselves. Viv unzipped her fleece. Zelda unbuttoned her stylish jacket. As they queued for a yellow cab, they all agreed that the sooner they got to their hotel and changed into something cooler the better.

The weather was their first surprise but not their last. As the cab drew up by the Millenium Hilton in Manhattan, Zelda's phone rang.

60

ZELDA

It was Might Be Mal.

Zelda put her phone on loudspeaker so Viv and Janet, sitting either side of her in the back of the cab, could hear. Might Be Mal said he was sorry he hadn't got back to her earlier but he had been thinking.

'And...' Zelda prompted.

'I've, er... decided not to tell Isabella what you told me,' he said, 'well, not yet.'

'So,' she prompted again as Viv and Janet held their breath.

'I would like to meet Primrose first, see her for myself.'

Well, that was decisive enough, but this Mal didn't sound like the Mal she'd spoken to yesterday – if it was only yesterday – it seemed much longer. That guy had been talkative and enthusiastic, this one was hesitant, wary, as if he didn't believe what she'd told him. Understandably maybe – she tried to be fair – she, *they*, weren't sure about him either. That's why they wanted to meet him.

'Where would you like to meet, Mal?' *Might Be Mal. He's only Might Be Mal.*

'Could you bring her to my hotel?'

Could we? She turned to the others, but Janet was paying the cab driver and Viv was getting out.

Zelda, still sitting, shuffled sideways towards the door and Viv, now on the pavement – should that be sidewalk? – waiting beside their luggage. 'Where's your hotel, Mal, and when were you thinking of doing this?'

'This morning?' he said, as Viv took her arm to help her out. 'I'm at The Tempo, 1568 Broadway, near Times Square. As early as you like. Could you come for coffee? Say eleven o'clock?'

Zelda was out now, phone against her ear. The cab drove away.

'The Tempo did you say?' She had to remember that.

'Yeah, on Broadway. A cabbie will know.'

'Mal, I'll do my best, but I'm not sure if I can get hold of Primrose...'

'Get hold? What d'ya mean? I thought she was with you.'

What was going on in the man's head? Did he still think that Isabella didn't know that Primrose was alive and had been aboard the *QM2*?

'Mal, Primrose isn't with me, she's with Isabella. They're travelling together. I did say, yesterday.'

'But...' He didn't finish, couldn't, she guessed because he was confused, and now Viv was tugging her arm and jerking her head at the hotel door where Janet was going in.

Zelda picked up her case with her free hand, and let Viv guide her to the hotel door, and through it, still speaking to Mal, she hoped, as she couldn't hear anything from the other end of the phone. 'I'll explain when I, er... *we* see you, Mal. There will be more than one of us, including Primrose, with luck. We'll do our best to be on time, but don't go, whatever you do. Stay put. We *will* come. The Tempo, you said, right? In Broadway?' There was no answer. 'We'll meet you in the foyer. Bye for now.'

'What was all that about?' said Viv as they reached Reception where Janet was pleading with a young man to let them into their rooms early.

* * *

Zelda allowed herself a few minutes to zonk out in the room she was sharing with Viv. There was no time to inspect it but it seemed well-appointed and plush. She lay flat on her back on the bed, eyes closed, trying to take in what had happened. Viv lay on the other bed. After five minutes' shut-eye came the questions. Can we contact Primrose without alerting Isabella? Can we get Primrose to The Tempo this morning? *This morning!* What time was it now? Nine-thirty already by the clock on the table between their beds, but they hadn't showered, or changed into cooler clothes or had anything to eat or drink, since getting up at an unearthly hour.

Zelda thought fleetingly of Richard and Billie, who she'd left sleeping.

A message came in from Janet. She'd ordered breakfast in her room next door to theirs for 10 a.m. They had half an hour to shower, dress, eat and get in the cab she'd ordered for 10.30 to take them to The Tempo. The only thing she hadn't managed to do was get hold of Primrose.

'I think her phone's turned off,' she said as they downed bagels and coffee half an hour later, 'or Isabella has taken control of it. Have you looked out of the window by the way?'

Neither of them had but when they turned their heads to look they saw high towers behind a boarded barrier. 'The One World Trade Center,' said Janet. 'It was Ground Zero but not any more.'

'Oh my God. Was this where it happened, Twin Towers and all that?' Viv looked awed and they all fell into a shocked silence.

Janet brisked them out of it. 'It's nearly ten-thirty. We should be downstairs.'

As they waited for their cab in Reception, a maroon-and-cream open-topped bus went by and they said as one, 'Primrose!' Not that they saw her, though the bus stopped a bit further up for passengers to peer out and see the boards round the site covered with the names of all those who'd died on that tragic day. But they all remembered that Primrose had said that she and Isabella were going on a tour of the city in an open-topped bus in the morning. *This* morning. They had planned to do the same till Might Be Mal's phone call had made them reschedule. 'Our tickets are valid all day,' said Janet, who had booked online. 'Maybe we can do it later? Who knows what the day will bring.'

Who knows what the day will bring?

It was the thought in all their minds as they got into the cab and Janet messaged Primrose yet again. Zelda read as Janet wrote.

> If you are on hop-on hop-off bus, hop off at Times Square and find The Tempo hotel. To meet the man of your dreams?

She finished with a crossed finger emoji and a heart.
They all crossed their fingers as the cab drew up at The Tempo.

61

ZELDA

Janet looked as if she'd seen a ghost when a stocky, suntanned man, about the same age as them, stepped forward to say hi as they stood in Reception at The Tempo. 'Mal Carmichael, pleased to meet you.' He stuck out a tanned hand and shook first Zelda's own hand, then Viv and Janet's, by which time she'd recovered and gone into her default polite mode. Primrose had been contacted, she said, and told where they were, so she could join them. 'But if she doesn't, we will try to bring her to your meeting with Isabella at Grand Central Station this afternoon.'

'You know about that?' He seemed surprised.

'Yes,' said Janet without saying how she knew.

'Coffee?'

As they followed him to a coffee lounge off Reception, Zelda noted he carried a briefcase which didn't quite go with his casual slacks and blue linen shirt, and Viv murmured that her chances of getting a DNA sample were zero as he was as bald as an egg, a brown egg. This man clearly loved the sun and maybe sport. He seemed fit from the way he walked, though he dragged his left leg slightly as if a hip joint might be troubling him.

'Thought I should show you a few credentials, for the removal of doubt and all that,' he said while they were waiting for their coffees, leaning over and opening the briefcase. 'I don't expect you to believe I am who I say I am without a bit of proof. Brought this stuff to show Isabella as well, by the way, though we have done DNA testing, well, I did when she first got in touch with me. Got her to send me a couple of hairs from her head so I could get them analysed and compared with this.'

This, they could see when he took it out of the tissue paper it was wrapped in, was a baby tooth. 'Isabella's,' he said, 'her first one. Primrose sent it to me when it fell out, after the tooth fairy had delivered her silver sixpence obviously.' He smiled ruefully and wrapped it up again carefully. 'That was the last time I heard from her.'

Who knows what the day will bring? Zelda wondered how much more was coming.

The other 'stuff' he mentioned were documents of various kinds, including his passport, his birth certificate and paperwork relating to his adoption.

'You're adopted?' Janet asked, unnecessarily Zelda couldn't help thinking.

'Yes,' he nodded. 'I was born Malcolm Carmichael and I stayed Malcolm Carmichael, called Mal, because my adoptive parents were Carmichaels too. Happened a lot in those days, I gather, family members helping each other out of embarrassing situations.'

'Those days?' said Janet frowning. 'What year were you born?'

'In 1943,' he said, 'during the war. That was part of the problem, the war, I mean. My birth mum was lonely...' He paused. 'How much of this do you need to know?'

'Everything,' said Janet, who had been hanging on his every word. 'May I just check that all of this was happening in Edinburgh, where I come from, incidentally, yes?'

And so does my late husband Malcolm, she might have added, who looks very like you.

'Yes,' he said.

'And your birth mum was lonely... do go on.' Janet was like a dog with a very juicy bone. She wasn't letting go till she'd scraped off every morsel.

'To cut a long story short,' Mal sped up a bit, 'my birth mum had an affair while her husband was away at war, and that was even more scandalous than the usual out-of-wedlock fling, because he was a German, a

German prisoner of war in fact – there was a POW camp near Edinburgh – and even worse she became pregnant, with me. It was hushed up as far as it could be – but she couldn't pass it off as her husband's because he'd been away too long – so she went away "to stay with an auntie" as they used to say, and in this case it was true. Well, it was an auntie by marriage, a relative of her husband. His parents helped her hush it up, to save the marriage, and spare their son a lot of heartache. This Auntie Hattie wanted a child very much, so she kept the baby and became my mum.'

'And your birth mother,' said Janet, 'what was her name?' But a waiter arrived with the coffees before he could answer.

Where was this going? Zelda wondered. Janet surely had enough evidence to prove that Mal and Malcolm were two different people, albeit with the same name. She could be sure now that the one she'd married wasn't a bigamist, so why didn't she look happy and relieved?

'Mal, what was your birth mother's name?' Janet asked again.

'Lottie, I think I called her Auntie Lottie. I can't be sure because there was a falling-out and the two families stopped seeing each other when I was very young.' He looked round the table. 'Can we talk about Primrose and Isabella now?'

Viv, who'd been unusually quiet for the last quarter of an hour said, 'You need to know that Primrose and Isabella have been sharing a cabin on the *Queen Mary* for the last week, and they are very definitely mother and daughter unless someone else is hiding a story of secret love and changeling babies.' She spelled it out in case he hadn't caught on. 'Isabella knows her mother is alive and she has never been in any doubt about it.'

After a long pause, head in hands, he looked up. 'So Isabella's been lying to me.'

Viv nodded. 'You and a lot of other people, us included.'

He looked troubled as well he might. Coffee untouched, he blew his nose into a handkerchief and Janet clearly felt for him. 'Primrose will be delighted to see you, Mal, and so am I, for reasons of my own.' She looked teary but managed a smile. 'The question is, how are we going to ensure that you meet her before she flies back to Edinburgh?' She checked her phone. 'Unfortunately I haven't heard from Primrose since last night, though she has my number, and that of my friends. I'll try her again now.' She rang but Primrose's phone was dead.

Zelda and Viv checked their phones. Zilch.

'But,' Janet touched Mal's hand, 'all is not lost, you are meeting Isabella this afternoon at Grand Central Station, yes?'

He nodded.

'Mind if we come along too, with Primrose if we can?'

He nodded again. 'And if you can't find Primrose, I'll...' He didn't finish his sentence.

'You will?' Janet prompted.

'Get the truth out of my daughter somehow.' He was wringing his hands or, possibly his lying money-grabbing daughter's neck, Zelda couldn't help thinking. Then, more positively, she found a recent photo and sent it to him, copying in Janet.

'Mal.' Janet obviously got hers instantly. 'Zelda's sent you a photograph of Primrose as she is now. That photo was taken at our table on the *Queen Mary*, three nights ago I think, or four. It also shows Isabella.'

If he had any doubts that Viv and Janet had been speaking the truth, they evaporated. His eyes filled up. 'Primrose, I'd recognise her anywhere. Primrose, my beautiful wife.' He raised the phone to his lips.

It was time to leave. Zelda got up. 'Hold on a minute.' Mal reached into his briefcase again and brought out a picture postcard, which he wrote on the back of. 'If you see Primrose first, give her this, will ya?' He handed it to Zelda, not in an envelope, so she couldn't resist reading his message.

Loved you then, love you now. Can't stop. Don't know how. Mal

Sweet!

62

JANET

Janet knew she should be rejoicing and deep down she was, for Primrose and for herself. An undercurrent of happiness and relief was beginning to flow through her veins. She felt a bit lighter, and seeing the twinkling Christmas lights in Times Square, the throngs of happy shoppers and sightseers, and the buskers playing merry tunes made her feel lighter still. So did the closeness of Viv and Zelda, their arms tucked into hers, as the three of them made their way to a pick-up point for the hop-on, hop-off bus, directed by Zelda, guided by some device on her phone. They buoyed her up, which she needed, because there were still some nagging doubts about Malcolm. They had begun as soon as she saw Might Be Mal, because for about three seconds she'd thought she was looking at Malcolm. It was the eyes that riveted her, the deep blue eyes topped by heavy brows, white now, which she'd always thought were Malcolm's most attractive feature. She'd had to stop for a moment and tell herself that *her* Malcolm Carmichael, the one she'd been married to, was very definitely dead. She'd been with him when he died. She'd seen him buried. There wasn't a shred of doubt in her mind, but it had been disconcerting.

'A penny for them, Janet?' Viv untucked her arm as they reached the bus stop.

'I wouldn't know where to begin.' Janet shook her head.

'Shouldn't we be looking at this?' Zelda held out a map of the bus route, a paper version she'd picked up somewhere. 'And deciding what we want to do for the rest of the day, well, till we all meet at Grand Central. It's a quarter past twelve already by the way, so we've got less than three hours to do what we can. We need to decide what we want to have a closer look at, so we get off at the right places.'

Viv said she'd like to go to Central Park if possible, taking in Top of the Rock on the way, or on the way back, and maybe eating at the Rockefeller Centre if they could find somewhere where they could sit and watch the ice-skaters on the rink under the famous Christmas tree. 'Or even stand and watch with a hotdog in our hands as we'll be eating again tonight and it's not long since breakfast.' Both places were on the bus route, she said, pointing them out, and so was Grand Central, so that could be their final getting-off place. Zelda said that all looked good to her. 'But what about you, Janet? We want to know what you want to do.'

I don't care. She couldn't say that. They'd think she was depressed, which she wasn't, but...

'Janet.' Zelda nudged her. 'We're in New York, remember, having the holiday of a lifetime. We're here to make you happy. What's on your wish-list?'

'I'd like to know the name of Malcolm's mother, please. I mean, sorry,' she nearly laughed at their open mouths, 'what I'd really like is that you, Zelda, get online and use all your genealogical know-how to find the name of Malcolm Carmichael's mother, the one I married, I mean.'

'Now?' said Zelda.

'As soon as possible. By three o'clock if you can.'

A flicker of understanding crossed Zelda's face. 'Is this to do with Mal being adopted?'

'Yes, it is,' she said as the bus arrived and they shuffled forward in the queue and got on.

'I'll do my best,' said Zelda, climbing the stairs to the top deck as the bus started to move, 'but you may have to wait till I'm on stabler ground.'

Once on top, they had to clutch the seats to stop themselves lurching from side to side as they headed for the front of the bus.

'And,' Janet pressed on when they were sitting down, 'I want to find Primrose.'

'That might be harder,' said Viv. 'Let's hope she's getting your messages even if she isn't replying to them.'

Janet remembered Viv's OTT thoughts about Isabella stopping at nothing to prevent her mother getting her hands on the money her father had put away for her. Suddenly they didn't seem so OTT. As they passed one iconic landmark after another, the Empire State Building, Trump Tower, Fifth Avenue and Brooklyn Bridge, Janet's thoughts strayed to Malcolm's upright, not to say uptight, strict Presbyterian family, especially his mother. She'd only met Mrs Carmichael a few times, and never called her by her Christian name, only Mum, rather awkwardly. She was a lady, very tidy, who gave the impression that she didn't exist below the waist, and the television was turned off if a couple looked as if they might approach a bedroom. It hadn't seemed odd at the time, her family were like that too, and – oh dear – so was she and so was Malcolm. Malcolm's mother had been pleasant enough, always polite. But had she been hiding a guilty secret?

'Charlotte Wallace,' said Zelda, looking up from her phone, as they approached the gates of Central Park from Fifth Avenue. 'That's Malcolm's mother's maiden name. I've just found Malcolm's parents' marriage certificate. It's on there. Look.'

'Lottie is short for Charlotte. Must be.' Janet felt as if she'd found the last piece of a jigsaw. Those deep blue eyes and heavy eyebrows completed the picture. 'This proves it. My Malcolm – she felt unusually warm towards him – *my* Malcolm has, I should say *had*, an older brother, also called Malcolm, who was given away by his mother. I have a brother-in-law. Grant has an Uncle Mal. Primrose and I are sisters-in-law.'

Where is Primrose?

They almost forgot to get off the bus as they took in this new development. Viv was the first to come to her senses and chivvy them down the stairs and off the bus and through the park gates. Janet was still in a daze as they toured the park in a picturesque, old-fashioned open-topped carriage. Wedged between Viv and Zelda, sitting behind the top-hatted driver, the unseasonal sun warm on their bare heads, the white horse's hooves clip-clopping rhythmically on the hard paths, they passed through places she'd only read about or seen in films. Now under the avenue of arching elms like the nave of a cathedral called The Mall, now past the beautiful statue of the Angel of the Water rising from the lake, now past the Bethesda Fountain and the terrace with its carved panoply of fruit and flowers, her thoughts raced ahead. *Imagine*, she read as they stopped in Strawberry Fields to gaze at the mosaic floor dedicated to the Beatles singer, and as the words of his song came into her head, she was filled with hope for the future.

Imagine! Imagine if just *some* things got a *bit* better.

63

VIV

They arrived early at Grand Central.

Good, thought Viv as they got off the bus on 42nd Steet, trying not to lose sight of Janet and Zelda among all the other people getting off. This gives us time to book dinner tonight at Cipriani's, if we can get in. The famous restaurant was high on her wish-list and Janet and Zelda's too. Soon, arm in arm, they were inside the station, crossing the magnificent concourse, with its vaulted starry ceiling, pausing for a moment at the famous four-sided clock, where in half an hour's time, Mal would meet Isabella for the first time in forty-odd years. How would that go? she wondered, as they headed for the double staircase leading up to the restaurant at the far end. More mundanely, how would coming here to book a table go? Viv crossed her fingers that personal contact would be more successful than the online booking system which had said no tables were free till February.

'How many for?' asked the friendly waitress at the desk by the door, after saying they'd just had a cancellation for seven o'clock.

'Three at least but possibly more.' Janet was back in organiser-mode. 'Most likely five.'

Viv uncrossed her fingers; the gods above were on their side.

'Er... could you add one more?' said Zelda, looking up from her phone, which she'd just answered with a gasp when it rang.

No prizes for guessing who she'd been talking to. Had the man really changed his plans to be with her tonight?

'Would you like to see where you'll be sitting?' said the obliging waitress, confirming the booking. 'It's a great table and the lunchtime clients have just left.'

It was possibly the best in the house, right at the front of the balcony-restaurant, with a great view of the concourse below, where people looked, not like ants – it wasn't that high – but maybe like a herd of colourful migratory animals seen from a safari-goer's hide. They also got a closer look at the gods and goddesses on the iconic turquoise and gold ceiling just above them and the Arrivals and Departures boards and the people looking up at them, heads bent back.

'Where exactly is the famous clock?' Janet asked the waitress.

'We've just walked past it, Janet!'

'We've just walked past *one* clock, Viv, but I'm checking it's the right one. We don't want any mistakes. I believe there are two.'

'Your friend is right,' said the waitress. 'People miss each other because there's another clock over the entrance, and they see that first and stop there. But the famous meeting place is down there above the information booth.'

It was the one they'd paused to look at when they were downstairs.

Viv checked the time on the clock's shining opal face. A quarter to three. Who would arrive first, she wondered, Mal or Isabella? Would they both go to the same clock? How would Mal handle this difficult encounter? She heard the waitress offering Janet coffee, saying there was half an hour before the next diners arrived, but Janet declined. Wonderful as the view was, it wasn't close enough to the action, she said as she led the way downstairs again.

Back in the concourse, they found a spot at the side, in the doorway of a shop, where they could see the information desk without being seen. A carousel of postcards helped. Not that they were intending to deceive. Zelda had messaged Mal to say they would be there, but keeping out of the way till he'd talked to Isabella. He was hoping they would bring Primrose with them. Where was Primrose? What had Isabella done with her? Would Mal manage to find out from Isabella?

'Viv.' Janet clutched her arm. 'There she is.'

Isabella, not Primrose. There was no mistaking the piled-up hair and signature catsuit, part-covered today by a poncho-like cape. She looked anxious or maybe impatient, pacing up and down in front of the information desk, checking her phone. Viv reminded herself that this was a woman about to meet her father for the first time since she was a little girl. She didn't like Isabella but couldn't help feeling for her. This was a big emotional moment and time to be generous.

Janet broke into her thoughts. 'Viv, Mal's arrived too.'

There he was a few yards away from Isabella, who hadn't seen him yet. But he'd seen her. He stood watching, looking down at his phone a couple of times, maybe comparing a photo with the woman he was looking at. Or just wondering if he really wanted to meet this person. Then, mind made up, he stepped forward and she saw him and stopped pacing. He stopped. Then, after a cry of, 'Oh, my daddy!' – reprising *The Railway Children*? – she teetered forward on her high heels and threw herself into his arms. He did hold her for a while, but then disengaged and held her at arm's length as if he didn't know what to do with her. It wasn't what you'd call an ecstatic reunion.

Viv didn't realise she'd been holding her breath until she could hold it no longer and let it out with a gasp. Janet too and Zelda. She heard them, and then the three of them turned as someone said, 'Janet, it's me.'

'Primrose!' Janet saw her first, probably because she was clutching her arm. It took Viv a few moments to be sure it was Primrose as she looked so different, almost girlish, in a short-skirted bluebell-blue suit with scalloped edges and shoes the same colour and a blue bow in her fluffed-up hair. Not a thread of black in sight.

She didn't seem to have seen Mal and Isabella.

'Primrose.' Janet tried to point him out. 'Look.'

'Here, Primrose.' Zelda found something in her bag and handed it to her. 'Mal asked me to give you this.' It was the postcard which she started to read out loud, 'Loved you then, loved you now...'

Viv focused on Mal and Isabella still talking to each other. Mal seemed to be doing most of the talking, sternly or more in sadness than anger, it was hard to tell from where she was standing. Then, after a bit, Isabella handed over a phone, and as Mal pocketed it he turned, looked around, wondering where they were hiding perhaps, and saw Primrose. Viv would never forget the moment. At first he peered, frowning as if he couldn't believe it was her, then he smiled, he *beamed*, radiating happiness. It was as if a switch had been turned on inside him, flooding him with light.

'Primrose,' Janet tried again to tell her he was there but, wiping her eyes, she was talking away, clearly pleased with herself about something else. 'I followed her, Janet, I followed Isabella. She told me to stay in my room, but I made up my own mind as I've learned from you and followed her.'

'Primrose,' Janet tried yet again, but Primrose carried on, 'she took my phone, Janet, so I couldn't get in touch.'

'Primrose.' Janet gently took hold of her shoulders and turned her round to face the man walking towards her. 'Here's someone I know you're longing to meet.'

Now it was Primrose's turn to look as if a light had come on inside her. For a single moment, she stood stock-still staring, then with a joyful cry of 'Mal!' she fell into his outstretched arms. Janet started to say something about leaving them together for now and meeting later, but gave up when she saw she was wasting her breath. Primrose wasn't listening to her or anyone else and nor was Mal. Primrose's face was buried in the crisp blue shirt covering Mal's manly chest – blue was obviously their favourite colour – and his arms were wrapped round her, his face buried in her gold and silver curls.

It was time for friends to retire, and definitely the enemy.

Isabella was still standing under the clock, rigid with fury, looking as if she might rush forward and try to tear the pair apart. But as Mal and Primrose came up for air, shaking their heads with wonder as they gazed into each other's eyes, Isabella covered her face with her hands. Then she turned and headed for the exit, pushing people aside in her rage.

'Good riddance,' said Zelda, watching till she was lost in the crowds. 'Let's hope that's the last we see of her.'

'Don't count on it.' Viv feared the worst when she heard Janet tell Mal and Primrose that their daughter would be welcome to join them at Cipriani's for dinner.

* * *

But Isabella had the sense to decline the invitation. Phew!

When Viv arrived with Janet at just before seven o'clock, Janet told the waiter on reception that there would be six of them. 'This is a celebration and we will require a lot of your prosecco.'

'Fizz on me,' said Mal, arriving with a beaming Primrose, but Janet waved his offer aside.

'My treat. This is a happy day for all of us, not least for me, with discoveries made and mysteries solved, thanks to my friends' forensic skills.'

'Forensic?' Mal raised one of the white eyebrows that Janet had found so indicative.

'Not an entirely accurate use of the term,' said Janet. 'Zelda's research was more digital than scientific, but Viv did obtain DNA evidence to be used if necessary, which I believe it isn't?'

He nodded. 'Isabella is indubitably my,' he corrected himself, '*our* daughter. She didn't lie about that.'

Just a lot of other things, he didn't say.

'Mal,' said Primrose, 'Isabella has said sorry for all the trouble she's caused.' She spoke as if Isabella was a seven-year-old who had told a few fibs to get herself out of stealing a packet of sweets.

But she wasn't here. That was a plus, and here was another, Zelda with Richard and Billie all looking very happy! Billie was off duty, she saw. Richard held her lead in his left hand and his right arm was tucked into Zelda's elbow. Those two couldn't have got much closer. Viv hadn't seen Zelda since she'd rushed from Grand Central that afternoon, saying that Richard's flight had been cancelled and she was going back to the hotel to meet him. There had only been time to yell 'Rules, Zelda, rules! Text me which hotel!' before she'd shot off.

'Sorry we're late, yet another change of plan.' Zelda was a bit breathless, but beautiful as usual in black pants, shiny black knee-length boots and a white thigh-length jacket. 'We had to go to left-luggage first, at Penn

Station, not far from here.' They were leaving for North Carolina that night by train, a twelve-hour journey, she said, 'But with a sleeper, so don't worry,' she added, seeing Viv's worried face. 'Richard needs a good night's sleep because he has a can't-be-missed gig in the afternoon, which he'd like me to go to. And so do I, need a good night's sleep, I mean. You too, Billie,' she said, reaching out with her hand to touch her. 'Your bed will be there.'

'Right,' said Janet, back in charge. 'As we're all present and correct, let's go to our table.'

The waiter led them to their table overlooking the balcony.

'It's fate,' Zelda said dreamily, a glass of fizz later, looking up at the golden stars and the muscular Greek gods in the turquoise sky-roof above their heads. 'That we all met on the ship, I mean, well, five of us, no six. And that we all came to Grand Central this afternoon and Richard's flight was cancelled at the last minute so he could join us tonight and I could cancel my flight and get a train ticket so I could travel with him. It's as if the gods above have brought us all here together, don't you think?'

'Definitely,' said Richard, clearly loving Zelda's company. 'And may they go on with their complex logistics.' He raised his glass. 'To the gods of togetherness!'

Viv raised her glass along with the others, enjoying the stunning ambience and the palpable happiness of friends delighting in each other's company. Zelda and Richard would work something out she felt sure, with or without the gods. It would take more than an ocean to stop those two getting together. She wished Patrick were here, but knew they were spending Christmas together and with luck, many more. Not so Janet. She would spend her first Christmas Day without Alan, with Viv and Patrick, but then it would be back to her Alan-less house to get used to living on her own again. Would she be okay? Janet looked fine now, enjoying the happiness of her friends, but had this holiday really lifted her spirits enough for her to start living life to the full again?

* * *

'Yes, Viv, and my spirits are still rising,' Janet assured Viv the next day when she asked her tentatively, 'and before you say something not-witty about them rising because we're in a lift, it's not. It's because you and Zelda have dragged me to the other side of grief by being there for me through everything.'

They were in yet another glass elevator, this time in the seventy-storey Rockefeller Center, going to the top of the tower surrounded by the low- and high-rise wonders of New York.

Seventy storeys.

'F-lip!' As they reached the famous Top of the Rock and stepped onto the viewing platform to see New York stretched out below, Viv stifled a word that might have offended Janet.

Odd. It felt oddly quiet and cold and clammy. Head literally in the clouds, Viv hoped she was imagining the slight swaying from side to side as she peered through the mist and made out Central Park, where they had been yesterday, and the Empire State Building, which they'd passed by in the tour bus, and the Statue of Liberty, which they would look at later when they went to Ellis Island. But Janet, after a few oohs and aahs, said, 'Enough, Viv, I feel a bit queasy. Let's get down to earth and talk.'

The sadness would always be there, she said, as they sipped spicy mulled red wine, beneath the celebrated Christmas tree, watching skaters skimming by on the iconic ice-rink. She would always miss Alan and always wish he was with her, but she was very thankful for the four loving years they'd had together. 'And,' she said defiantly, jutting out her chin, 'as he said infuriatingly often, "life goes on", and it does, Viv, it does, with surprising bursts of happiness.'

It began to snow as they sat beside each other with their thoughts – the temperature had dropped again to something more seasonal – and they didn't need to say a word as they watched the flakes floating past.

ACKNOWLEDGEMENTS

Writing is paradoxically a lonely occupation and an act of teamwork. This book wouldn't be in your hands without the help of all the people mentioned below.

Firstly, thank you to my travelling friend, Liz Wilson, who came with me on that 'bargain holiday', back in 2013, sailing from Southampton to New York in the luxurious *Queen Mary* 2, and for lending me her diary. The novel is set in 2015 so I have taken poetic licence with some facts including the weather and the entertainment on board, but I hope I've given an honest picture of life aboard that amazing vessel.

The story and characters, all except one, the astronaut Dr Jeffrey A. Hoffman, are the product of my imagination, harder to explain. I can tell enquirers quite a lot about 'where I get my ideas from' but I can't say why Richard, a blind cellist, came into my head, and wouldn't go away, giving me two problems. I knew very little about the cello and even less about what it is like to be blind. Help was at hand. Kind neighbours, Pam and John Blackmore, puppy trainers for assistance dogs, put me in touch with the inspirational Martine Clarke and her guide dog, Willow, who were exactly what I needed. Martine, blind from an early age, grew up in Bordeaux, where her parents were wine makers. How perfect was that! It gets better: she is also an accomplished musician who trained as a concert pianist and, most importantly, she is a very articulate, determined, well-connected woman. Martine introduced me to her cellist friend, Kevin, so that I could hear him play and examine his fingers. I am in awe of Martine's many talents and cannot thank her enough for all the help she and her husband Steve have given me. Martine and Willow and I have walked and talked a lot. Martine has also proof-listened to the script of

Widows Waive the Rules several times, pointing out errors, so that I could correct them. If any still remain they are my fault entirely.

I must also thank Liz's friend, Susan Woods, a puppy trainer in the USA, who has given me useful information about the guide dog scene on the other side of the Atlantic. Richard and his dog were trained in the USA, so I had to explore possible differences.

Friends Trevor Arrowsmith and Linda Newbery did the *QM2* crossing too, and they both read my script, at various stages, and gave me valuable feedback. Trevor made useful musical contributions too. Cindy Jefferies read the script and made useful suggestions, as did Sue Davies, meticulous as ever, and Liz Wilson. Jeni Patel, a school friend of my brother, now living in Raleigh, North Carolina, has answered my questions about life in that town almost instantaneously, despite the time difference. I hope I didn't wake you up too often! Writing buddies Georgia Bowers and Celia Rees have given constant encouragement as have all the above, and yet more below. Thank you, lovely editor, Sarah Ritherdon, and everyone at Boldwood Books for bringing the book to you. Thanks to Rachel Sargeant, proof-reader and more. Thank you, supportive agent, Caroline Walsh at DHA, for thinking up the title, as soon as I said I was sending my widows on a cruise. Thank you, Tom Ianiri of Power Computers, Kempston, for saving my widows yet again when I inadvertently pressed delete on the whole thing! Thank you all!

ABOUT THE AUTHOR

Julia Jarman has written over a hundred books for children, and is now turning her hand to uplifting, golden years women's fiction. Julia draws on her own experience of bereavement, female friendship and late-life dating.

Read an exclusive bonus chapter A Day in the Life of Libby Allgood for FREE by signing up to Julia Jarman's newsletter here. Follow author Libby as she takes on a day of writing her next work with her cat Cornflake.

Visit Julia's website: https://juliajarman.com/

Follow Julia on social media:

facebook.com/juliajarman
x.com/JuliaJarman

ALSO BY JULIA JARMAN

The Widows' Wine Club
Widows on the Wine Path
Widows Waive the Rules

BECOME A MEMBER OF

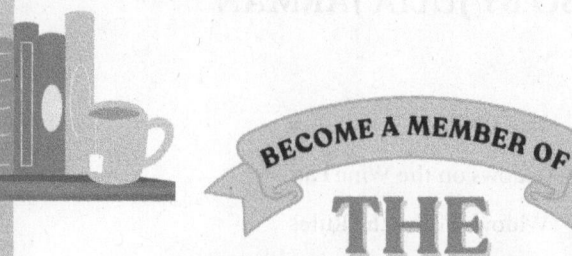

THE SHELF CARE CLUB

The home of Boldwood's book club reads.

Find uplifting reads, sunny escapes, cosy romances, family dramas and more!

Sign up to the newsletter
https://bit.ly/theshelfcareclub

Boldwood

Boldwood Books is an award-winning fiction publishing company seeking out the best stories from around the world.

Find out more at www.boldwoodbooks.com

Join our reader community for brilliant books, competitions and offers!

Follow us
@BoldwoodBooks
@TheBoldBookClub

Sign up to our weekly deals newsletter

https://bit.ly/BoldwoodBNewsletter